Who Dung It?

Robert Archibald

Cactus Mystery Press
an imprint of Blue Fortune Enterprises LLC

WHO DUNG IT?
Copyright © 2021 by Robert Archibald.

All rights reserved. Printed in the United States of America. No part of this book may be used or reproduced in any manner whatsoever without written permission except in the case of brief quotations embodied in critical articles or reviews.

This book is a work of fiction. Names, characters, businesses, organizations, places, events and incidents either are the product of the author's imagination or are used fictitiously. Any resemblance to actual persons, living or dead, events, or locales is entirely coincidental.

For information contact :
Blue Fortune Enterprises, LLC
Cactus Mystery Press
P.O. Box 554
Yorktown, VA 23690
http://blue-fortune.com

Book and Cover design by Wesley Miller, WAMCreate

ISBN: 978-1-948979-66-5
First Edition: July 2021

Dedication

This book is dedicated to my friends Rich and Sudie Watkins. When COVID-19 hit, the Archibalds and Watkins decided to form a bubble. We went to each other's house for dinner two times a week and took several out-of-town trips. Together we were able to weather the epidemic in fine spirits.

Fiction by Robert Archibald:
Roundabout Revenge
Guilty Until Proven Innocent
Crime Might Pay

Reviews for *Roundabout Revenge*

Fascinating plot, thoughtfully developed. Looking forward to what story twists his next book will bring.
Fred Cason, Amazon review

I loved Roundabout Revenge. Author Robert Archibald is a retired college professor whose writing demonstrates that he is a scholar not only in his professional field of study, but also in his observations on society. In this engrossing novel, he sheds light on why law and justice are sometimes at odds with each other. There also are wonderful discussions among the characters about sports, diversity in schools and society, and about how conservatives and liberals have come to hold their beliefs. I look forward to the sequel.
CW Stacks, Amazon review

Reviews for *Guilty Until Proven Innocent*

Another Archibald masterpiece... This quality page-turner encompasses a number of adventures that sometimes end not as anticipated. The expected becomes the unexpected...
If you enjoyed "Revenge," you'll enjoy this too. If you missed "Revenge" pick it up with the knowledge that you'll have two enjoyable books to occupy your time.
Wilford Kale, Virginia Gazette review

Acknowledgments

Who Dung It? is a work of fiction. Any resemblance between the characters in this book and anyone I have known or met is a complete coincidence.

This book benefited greatly from the efforts of Kirk Lovenbury who read the complete draft twice and made several important corrections. Kirk is also responsible for suggesting the title. I am greatly indebted to my writer's group: Tim Holland, Elizabeth Lee, Caterina Novelliere, Peter Stipe, and Susan Williamson. They read and commented on the vast majority of the manuscript. Their comments were a great help. They should not be blamed for any remaining errors or awkwardness.

I would like to especially thank Narielle Living for an extensive edit that improved the manuscript immensely.

Finally, everything I do benefits from the help of my wife, Nancy.

Chapter One

THE BELL FOR DINNER CLANGED throughout the tented camp. Judy Clayton saved her work and put down her laptop. The safari in the Okavango Delta in Botswana was fascinating. Unfortunately for a writer, it was too fast-paced. She didn't have enough time to work on her story. All she'd been able to do was compile some random notes. She planned to put them into a reasonable form on the plane ride home. She checked herself in the small mirror. She wasn't sure she liked the results, but there was little she could do about it.

George Wilcox rolled his misshapen ball of elephant dung toward the safari camp. It was hard work. Maybe it would be easier if he'd been better at getting a perfect sphere. Somehow, he was never able to get it right. He saw the good looking, young, red-headed chick leave her tent, and he made it through her open tent flap with no difficulty. His luck held. She'd left her computer on the ground beside the bed. He set his dung ball aside and hopped on the keyboard. To make space between what the girl had been typing and his message, he jumped on the Enter key. Nothing happened. A few more attempts revealed he was just too light.

George climbed down from the keyboard and retrieved his dung ball. Pushing the ball onto the keyboard wasn't easy. Finally, he managed it. Lifting the ball and letting it drop on the Enter key worked. Within a few seconds, he'd created enough space to start his message. Looking down, he realized he was making quite a mess on the laptop. When he finished, he rolled the ball off the keys and waited.

As she walked back to her tent, Judy was mad at herself. She knew the safari fed them too much. Still, it was her fault. If she really was concerned about her weight, she didn't have to finish everything. She'd thought this trip would give her a chance to take off a few pounds. It hadn't worked. There was too much good food and not enough exercise.

When she entered her tent, she noticed a bug of some kind on her computer. She wasn't afraid of bugs, so she bent down and asked, "What are you doing, little fella?"

Almost as if the bug was responding to her, it rushed to the screen, flew upward, and hovered next to it. Judy's eyes were drawn to the screen. She shrieked, "What the hell?" Her screen read:

`please don't squash me`

The bug ran down and picked up a big ball and dumped it on two keys.

`hi`

Judy was freaked out. She rubbed her eyes and looked at her computer again. She started to leave to get one of the guides. For some reason she paused when she could tell the bug, she thought it was a dung beetle, started dumping the ball on the keys again. Judy stepped back to look.

`don't go`

Judy didn't know what to do. Dung beetles can't type. *Who's playing a trick on me, and how the heck are they doing it?* She rushed outside and ran around her tent. She found no one. At her tent flap she did a quick count, and all ten of her fellow travelers were milling around getting ready for wine time. One of them, Jim, yelled at her, "Coming Judy?"

"No," she responded. "I'm beat."

Entering her tent, she approached the beetle. "Okay. I'll play your game. What's your name?"

The beetle retrieved his ball and started dumping it on keys.

george

Judy was astounded. She paced frantically, not knowing what to do. *This has to be some kind of prank, but I have no idea how it's being done.* Finally, she asked, "How did you get in my tent, and what are you doing here?"

The beetle went into action.

reincarnated

"You're telling me you're someone named George who's been reincarnated as a dung beetle."

scarab please

"So, you don't like being called a dung beetle," Judy whispered. *They have to be picking up my voice somehow.* She continued whispering, "You have a last name?"

wilcox

Judy nervously paced around her tent. *This is crazy—an incredible prank.* Another tactic came to her. She went to the computer and the dung beetle. "Can you come on my hand?" The dung beetle flew up and landed on her hand. She inspected it carefully. As far as she saw, it was just a bug. There was no evidence of any miniature radio or anything out of the ordinary. She realized she didn't really know what an ordinary dung beetle looked like. Still, this one didn't look unnatural. With it close to her face, she smelled an unpleasant odor. *I wonder what my computer smells like.*

Judy told the dung beetle he could go back to the computer, and it flew there. *Was it true? Could a person be reincarnated as a dung beetle?* She racked her brain. *What do I know about reincarnation? Do reincarnated people remember their previous lives?* She recalled reading stories about people claiming to have had previous lives. Frankly, she hadn't believed them, and they were all human lives. Now she didn't know. She certainly didn't have any memory of previous lives, human or otherwise. After considerable thought, she asked, "How can you understand English, and how do you know how to type?"

`don't know`

"Tell me more about George Wilcox."

`google george wilcox cleveland`

I've got her hooked, George thought. He was tired from lifting the ball for all the typing. He looked up, and the woman was reaching for the computer, so he rolled his dung ball back to the ground. He'd thought she was good looking when he saw her walking out of the tent, and up close he was sure. She had red freckles to go with the red hair and large, bright green eyes. She was petite and probably in her mid-twenties. While he wouldn't have called her a knockout, she was clearly attractive.

Judy was astounded. *I am actually going to do what the dung beetle suggested.* She reached for the computer and realized it was a mess. It stank and the keys were dirty—*actually shitty*, she thought. "These keys are a mess!" she remarked to the dung beetle. She went outside to borrow a wet rag from the dining tent.

This whole thing is ludicrous. Is it real? Is this dung beetle actually the reincarnation of someone named George Wilcox? Judy couldn't think of any way around Googling George Wilcox. Maybe the prank would be revealed when she did.

She returned to her tent with the rag and cleaned off the keys. The result was a bunch of gibberish on her screen, which she erased. She then searched online for George Wilcox, Cleveland. Several entries popped up. Now she was stymied. *Which one does the bug want me to select?*

"Which one?"

Judy saw the bug getting ready to roll the dung ball on to her computer. "Wait, wait. I don't want the dung on my keyboard again. There has to be a better way." The bug stopped. Judy continued, "In the future, if you want to type, why don't you stand by the key, and I'll press it? And before you get anywhere near the keyboard, let's get you cleaned up a bit."

The bug flew onto the rag Judy had put down on the edge of the bed and scuffed its feet. Judy was fascinated. *This can't be part of a prank.*

The bug positioned himself near the down arrow key and sort of bowed. Judy pressed the arrow key. The bug repeated his gesture, and Judy pressed again. On the fourth entry, the bug flew off the keyboard and positioned himself so he could see the screen better.

Judy pressed Enter and an obituary from the *Cleveland Plain Dealer* appeared on the screen. The obituary was for George Wilcox, a twenty-four-year-old. Judy looked at the date. The death occurred a year and a half ago. The obit said he was a private detective. No cause of death was listed. Most of the rest of the information was the kind of thing one would expect. He was survived by his parents, Harold and Maud, and a sister, Meredith, who had a different last name. *She must be married*, Judy thought. George had attended Shaker Heights High School and Oberlin College. It was a bare-bones obituary. He was young and hadn't had many life accomplishments.

Judy looked up when she'd finished. "This is about you?"

The bug flew up on the keyboard and positioned himself on the Y key.

"I'll take that as a Yes."

The bug scurried to the Backspace key and made his little bow. Judy realized he wanted to return to the Google results. When she got there, the bug went to the down arrow key again. Judy pressed the key each time the bug bowed. He finally stopped on another *Plain Dealer* entry. The headline stated, "Young Detective Murdered."

Judy read the short story. It told of the murder of George Wilcox, twenty-four, of Shaker Heights who worked for the Acton Detective agency. One evening while working, he was shot in the back of the head. The police told the reporter they had no suspects. The investigation was just starting. The remainder of the article repeated information contained in the obituary.

The bug flew onto the Backspace key. Returning to the Google results, they repeated using the down arrow. After thirty or so repeats, the bug flew next to the little square with the W on the bottom of the screen, so Judy opened Word again. The bug directed Judy to type.

`not much of a life`

"What do you want from me?"

`I want to know who killed that george`

"You're the detective. I don't have the faintest idea how to help you."

Just then they heard someone say, "Knock, knock." Judy opened the tent flap and saw Jolene.

"Oh, Jolene. I wasn't up for wine tonight. As you know I'm supposed to be writing a magazine story about this trip, and I haven't had time to do much writing."

"I'm glad you're okay. Some of the others were worried."

"No, I'm fine. No problems. See you at six-thirty for breakfast, right?"

"Right."

Judy returned to the computer and the dung beetle. "As I was saying,

I don't see how I can help."

`trust me you can help`

Judy realized she was extremely tired. The whole business seemed to have taken a great deal out of her. "Look, George the scarab, I'm not sure this is going to work. It's just so weird, and I'm really tired. If you're still here tomorrow, maybe we can talk more."

George knew when he shouldn't push, so he rolled his dung ball out of Judy's tent. Truth be told, he was thrilled. When he'd seen her luggage tag and the Cleveland address the day before, he hatched this plot. It was working better than he'd ever expected. He thought he'd been murdered but seeing the online article proved it. *Now I know for sure. I'll be back in the morning.*

Chapter Two

THE NEXT MORNING, JUDY REACHED to turn off the alarm on her phone. She jumped when she saw a bug sitting beside it. Then she remembered; it was the dung beetle. She'd hoped it had all been a strange dream. No such luck. The beetle flew down and landed on her keyboard. Judy struggled up and went to her computer. The beetle bowed on the keys, and she followed his directions.

`good morning`

Judy wasn't pleased. "Up yours, Mr. Scarab. I'm not a morning person, so you're going to have to cool your heels until I've had my shower, actually maybe until I've come back from breakfast. They have coffee there."

Judy stripped off her pajamas and went into the shower. She was not normally an early riser, and the mornings weren't her favorite part of the safari. When she walked out of the little addition to the tent housing the toilet and shower, she saw the beetle jumping up and down on the keyboard. She figured she had time to give him a minute. She pushed the keys he indicated.

`yowzah`

"What?" Then she realized her small towel didn't cover very much.

"You cad! Turn your back and let a lady get dressed." Judy didn't know whether she was blushing, but she thought she might be. And at the same time, she was amazed. She was bantering with a dung beetle.

After she returned from breakfast, she told George she had an hour before the Land Rovers would be there to pick them up for their morning game viewing. This would be their last day at this campsite. The beetle jumped up and down on the keyboard, so Judy went to type for him.

`take me with you`

"You want to go on the game viewing today?"

`tomorrow`

"We'll see. Right now, I have a question for you. Suppose I take you to Cleveland with me. What do you want me to do?"

`catch person who killed me`

"How can I help? I'm no detective. Do you want me to introduce you to the police? I might be able to. Is that what you want?"

`police at end`

"I get it. You want me to find the person who killed you and then tell the police."

`give evidence too`

Judy stood up. She figured if she wasn't at the keyboard, the dung beetle wouldn't be able to talk to her. She liked it. She could shut him up any time she wanted. When she needed time to think, she'd have it. She looked at her watch. Right now, she had to get ready for the day's activities. She used the toilet, put on her safari jacket, and grabbed her camera. When she was ready to leave, she finally spoke to George. "I'll consider it. Okay? That's all I'll promise."

George waited until the Land Rovers took the tourists away. *Things could be going better.* Judy wasn't sure she wanted to help him. Still, she hadn't turned him down flat. He decided his best bet was to be prepared for her to take him when the safari moved tomorrow. He had to get a stash of food. He peeked out of the tent and saw some of the camp personnel moving about. He avoided them easily.

George worked hard all day. By the time Judy and the others arrived in the late afternoon, he'd rolled four balls of elephant dung into the corner of her tent. He was very proud of himself.

Judy came into the tent. "What's the smell?"

George jumped up and down on the keyboard, so Judy went to see what he had to say.

`dinner`

"Oh, your dinner—elephant poop."

The bug hopped by the Y key.

"Look, I was planning on humoring you. You can come with me tomorrow morning. We only have two more days on this safari, and then I'm heading home. Smelling your dinner brings up a problem, a big problem. There's no way I can carry any food for you. It stinks to high heaven. The other people on the safari wouldn't put up with it. Is there anything else you eat?"

George indicated he wanted to type.

`DUNG beetle`

"That's it, just dung. How long can you go without a meal?"

`3 or 4 hours`

"We're stuck. There's no way I can carry your shit, no pun intended. It really stinks."

He thought, *No, it smells really sweet. It's fresh stuff.* He had a great sense of smell, and he was proud of the four balls he'd been able to roll into the tent. *I have to figure out what to do.* He started to jump up and down.

`air tight container`

Judy looked at him. "Bright boy. It might work. Some people take stuff away from dinner. You know, like desserts they don't want to eat right then. The waiters have little boxes for them. The box lids might fit tight enough. I'll see what I can do at dinner. Right now, I'm going to get a rag from the cook tent. Wait, maybe I'll get two—one to cover your food and one to wipe off my computer and your feet. You've been pushing balls of poop all day."

Judy returned with the rags and covered George's food. The maneuver didn't cut the smell much, only a little. Next, she wet the rag in the bathroom and wiped the computer and had him remove the dung from his feet.

"Look, I'm going to dinner. You can stay here and do whatever dung beetles do.

He jumped up and down.

`scarab please`

"Okay. Do whatever scarabs do. I'll try to get one of those boxes at dinner."

Judy returned from dinner a little over an hour later. She waved a plastic box with something in it. "I conned an extra serving of the peach cobbler from one of the waiters. The lid on this box is very tight. It might just work."

Judy sat on her bed and opened the box. Using a plastic fork, she attacked the cobbler. *I shouldn't be doing this*, she thought. *No self-control.* At dinner she'd told herself she'd trash the extra cobbler and then wash the container, but it hadn't turned out as planned.

When she finished the cobbler, she went into the bathroom and rinsed the box. Using a towel, she dried it thoroughly and then returned to the main tent. "I'm going to load your shit in this box."

George jumped up and down.

`leave out one a guy has to eat`

"Okay. I understand." Judy used the cloth covering the balls to place three of them in the plastic box. The balls were big, and the lid squished them a little before it was tight. Judy put the box up to her nose. It still smelled fairly strong. Then Judy thought, *This tent probably smells like elephant dung. George still has a ball and the rags have some on them too.*

"I'm going to wash my hands and then take this box outside. Everything smells like this stuff in here."

She felt ridiculous going outside to see if her plastic box of elephant dung had an odor. She did it anyway. When she was about fifteen feet away from her tent, she put the box up to her nose and didn't smell a thing.

She ran to the tent. "We're golden, George. The odor doesn't penetrate the plastic."

`hooray`

Judy rousted around in her suitcase and came up with a small cloth bag. She turned it upside down on the bed and two sets of earrings tumbled out. "I can put these earrings in something else, and you can ride in this."

Chapter Three

IN THE MORNING, JUDY MADE sure to take underwear with her on her way to the shower. When she emerged, the dung beetle wasn't anywhere to be seen. *Maybe he's thought better about going with me.* Somehow Judy was a little disappointed. She finished dressing and went to breakfast.

When Judy returned from breakfast, the dung beetle was poised by her computer. "No you don't, mister. I'm getting a washcloth. You've been rolling dung all night." He flew up to the wet washcloth. After he scuffed his feet, he flew down to the laptop.

`aren't we fastidious`

"Look, I suspect you spent most of the morning chowing down on elephant dung. You sure smelled like it."

`a man has to eat`

"Whatever; I have an hour to get my suitcase packed. I have to put it outside the tent then. Fifteen minutes later, we load up. I take my backpack on the Land Rover. I'll keep you and your food, using the term loosely, in there. Somehow, I'll figure out how you can eat when we take our lunch stop. There's always a john. I might have to have you eat there."

```
wow the ladies room
```

"You're awful. Yes, the lady's room. Excuse me while I get my packing done." Judy finished packing her suitcase and put it outside the tent ten minutes early. She'd had to rearrange things to have enough room for George's food, which had to go in the backpack. When she loaded the plastic box of dung, she was extra careful to be sure the lid stayed on tight. She was sure he had been paying attention to her packing, so she asked, "I leave anything out?"

```
me and the computer
```

"Good, I know about those two." She slid the computer into the special sleeve in the backpack and motioned for him to crawl into the little cloth bag she'd shown him the night before. Judy put the bag in the top of the open backpack and didn't zip it shut.

Judy felt a like she was getting away with something as she joined the rest of her group to load into their Land Rover. It was the sixth day of the safari, and the guides were struggling to show them animals they hadn't already seen. The big deal in the morning was a bluff overlooking a river where they were able to take pictures of hippos swimming. At noon they stopped at a wide place in the road where the crew had set up the dining tent and the toilets.

George smelled baby elephant dung a few minutes before the Land Rover stopped. When he was sure the vehicle was no longer moving, he struggled and managed to loosen the tie holding his little bag shut. When Judy hefted the backpack as she exited the Land Rover, he extracted himself and flew in search of the baby elephant dung.

After lunch, Judy excused herself and took her backpack to the lady's room. She was sure George must be starving. He told her he had to eat very frequently. The room wasn't large. It was a bit of a struggle to position the backpack so it would sit upright. When she looked inside, the little bag had been opened somehow. No dung beetle. *Why had he gotten out of the bag? Where did he go?*

Judy returned to the lunch table wondering what happened. It would be absurd for her to ask, "Has anyone seen my dung beetle?" *No, if he escaped, it was a problem of his own making.* Judy worried, but there was nothing she could do.

On the off chance he'd flown off in search of fresh dung, Judy took a wet napkin with her as she went to the Land Rover. Sure enough, she saw George crawling along the top of the back seat as she entered. Judy put the backpack on the floor and motioned for him to wait. She showed him the wet napkin, and he flew down on it. As she was dealing with the dung beetle, she had her back to Jill, the girl who occupied the seat with her.

When Judy didn't sit right away, Jill waited a bit and then yelled, "Move it, Judy. What's the hang up?"

George had finished washing his feet and was headed toward the cloth bag, so Judy sat down. "Sorry."

As they were driving away, the crew was pulling down the dining tent. They would have it up at the evening campsite. *The company running the safari certainly has its act together.* Judy was sure tonight's tents would be as nice as those at the other locations. She wondered what the people who'd cleaned her old tent thought. There had to be lots of evidence of elephant poop in the tent.

In the evening, Jill put her backpack on the shelf in the new tent and took out the bag. George was in there this time and flew out. "What was that stunt at lunch?"

Judy realized he couldn't answer without the computer. *What a ninny,* she thought as she retrieved the computer, opened it, and fired it up.

`baby elephant dung`

"I went to all that trouble. Packing your elephant shit in the little box and lugging it into the john all for nothing, just to have you skip off for baby dung. I decided you'd split. You didn't want to go to the states after all."

delicacy

"I don't care if baby elephant dung is a delicacy. I can't have you flying off without telling me. This isn't going to work if I can't count on you."

not my mom

"Sure, I'm not your mother. Still, we need to work together. I was worried at the lunch stop. If you split again, I'm calling it off. Understand? You have to promise you won't do it again."

promise

Judy opened her suitcase and unpacked. She only had two nights in this tent, so she only unpacked what she thought she'd need. As she was coming back from taking her cosmetics bag to the bathroom, she saw George jumping up and down by the computer.

scouting trip

Judy was puzzled. *What did he mean?* Eventually, she understood. "You're asking permission to go out on a scouting trip."

George went to the Y key.

Judy paused, then responded, "Actually, it's a good idea. If you find some food, eat it outside. I don't want you rolling any balls of shit into this tent. If you don't find anything, I can let you eat some of what we have stored."

goodbye

Judy watched as he crawled to the tent opening and flew off. She laid down on the bed to rest. She felt good about the recent interaction. She'd established some ground rules. Their method of communication was awkward. On the one hand, she liked being able to shut him up any time she wanted. On the other hand, there were drawbacks. If they'd had another way of communicating, a mix up like the one at lunch wouldn't have happened.

After dinner, Judy returned to her tent. The dung beetle wasn't there. She decided she'd join the others for wine. She was finding it difficult to be a full participant in the group. She had this incredible secret—a person reincarnated as a dung beetle—yet she didn't want to tell anyone. It was too weird.

Judy only had one glass of wine before excusing herself. When she entered the tent, her nose told her George had returned. "Time to wash," Judy said holding up a wet rag she'd prepared before going off to join the wine group. When he was thoroughly clean, he flew onto the keyboard.

`found good meal`

"I'm happy for you. Our food was good as well. I went to the wine gathering too, and it made me a little tired. I'm not up for much of a chat tonight.

`long hike for me`

"Oh, so maybe you're tired too. Good night." Judy still felt a little creepy getting undressed in front of George, so she took her pajamas into the bathroom. When she finished, she didn't see him. He wasn't by the computer where she'd left him. She finally found him. He was in a corner and appeared to be sleeping. *Good*, she thought. *He's being very agreeable.*

Chapter Four

THE FINAL DAY OF THE safari went smoothly. George chose to forage instead of eating his lunch with Judy. It was fine with her. Judy suspected several of her fellow travelers were of two minds about the safari ending. While they were ready to go home, they weren't looking forward to the arduous flights. Neither was she. Her booking to Cleveland was going to take her three long days. She had almost turned down the assignment for the safari story when she looked at the information on the flights. At this point, she figured she made it to Africa, so she'd be able to make it back.

For their final night in a tent, they arrived at camp late in the afternoon. Judy put down her backpack and dumped George out on the bed. He flew to where he expected the computer to be. Judy extracted her computer from the backpack and positioned it to comply with his wish. He clearly wanted to type.

`let's not do that again`

"Did you have a bad lunch?"

`ostrich ugh`

"I see. You had ostrich dung and didn't like it. This morning you turned down your chance at the elephant in our stash. It serves you right."

`ostriches should chew more too crunchy`

Judy laughed. "I don't know what you know about tomorrow. It will be the start of a grueling trip. We go on a little plane to Maun, the only real airport in Botswana, and then to Johannesburg. It will take most of the day. We overnight in a Joburg hotel. Then the following day, we start some real flying—Joburg to London to Atlanta to Cleveland. With layovers, it will take two days."

`better get more food`

"I hope you can find something other than ostrich. Anyway, I'll get one of those plastic boxes again. There's not going to be any chance for you to forage on our way to Cleveland. You'd better have some good luck tonight."

The next morning when she woke up, Judy smelled the result of the dung beetle's night-time work. She put the new dung balls in the plastic box she'd snagged at dinner. After she'd washed herself and George, she went to the computer to see what George had to say for himself.

`pooped`

"Pun intended?" Judy said, laughing.

He jumped to the N key.

"So, you're tired. That's all right. You won't have to do too much today. First, we'll be in a little plane. We won't have security to worry about then. At the bigger airport there will be security. If they see the dung, I'll tell them I plan to use it as fertilizer. What do you think you should do? They'd see you on the x-ray if we leave you in my backpack."

`fly around near ceiling`

"I can see how it will work. Being able to fly is a considerable advantage. Is it as much fun as it looks?"

hard work

"I can imagine. Here, get in the bag and catch up on your sleep. I'm going to breakfast. I expect they'll give us the schedule for the short flights there. I hope we'll be on one of the first planes out. I'm ready to leave." Judy looked at George. He appeared to be sound asleep. She wondered if he'd even heard her last remarks.

At the entrance to the Maun airport, Judy roused George, and he flew out of her backpack right after they entered the building. She didn't see him again until she'd cleared security. Figuring he'd try to fly near the wall, she positioned herself on the outside edge of the gate for the Johannesburg flight, and the beetle dropped gently into her open backpack.

"Very well done, George," she whispered.

Judy hustled into the restroom and managed to give him a chance to eat. She wasn't able to stay long, because there were only two stalls.

The flight to Johannesburg was only about three hours. They stayed at a hotel near the airport. At the airport the next morning, Judy purchased one of those cloth bags used to organize clothes in a suitcase. In the restroom, she put the two plastic boxes of dung in the newly acquired cloth bag. When she repacked, she put the new bag toward the top of the backpack. Judy figured it wouldn't look too weird if, during the flight, she took the bag with her to the restroom. George would have to eat at least a couple of times on the way to London.

During the flight to London, Judy did a lot of work. She turned her notes into a story about the safari. Since she'd run into George, she realized she'd slacked off on the notes, but she was able to remember the safari's last few days. When she reviewed what she'd written, she was pleased. While she never managed to sleep on airlines, she could work.

The time passed quickly.

In London, Judy camped out in a restroom stall and gave George a big meal. The elephant dung had a very strong odor. Her current location was probably the only place she'd be able to get away with feeding him. While he was eating, she took out her computer to check something in the story. Immediately, George wanted to type. She used some toilet paper to clean his feet.

`how much longer`

"We have another two-and-a-half hours here, about six or so hours to Atlanta, another three-hour layover there, and then a little more than two hours to Cleveland."

`need fresh air`

"Sorry pal, if I go outside, I'll have to clear security again, and I'm not doing it. It was your idea to get to the States, so you'll have to bear up."

The dung beetle went back to his meal.

When they finally arrived in Cleveland, Judy went to another restroom. George was overdue for a meal. He was so hungry, he almost dived on the dung when she opened the box. "It's okay. Chow down. We're on the last leg. When you're finished, I'll find the shuttle bus to the long-term parking. I'm awake enough to drive home."

Judy opened the cloth bag for him to load up for the last part of their journey, and he went in obediently. After Judy hefted her backpack onto her back, George pushed his way out of the bag and crawled so he was riding on the top of the backpack. He'd been inside, either in airline terminals, or worse yet on airplanes, for way too long. He was really looking forward to outside air, even the polluted air of Cleveland.

It was dusk, about seven-thirty, and the airport was bustling. Judy found the place to wait for the long-term parking shuttle and took last place in a fair-sized line. As Judy finally hustled on the crowded shuttle bus, she was surprised when the guy behind her seemed to be reaching into her backpack. She swirled around with a quizzical look on her face.

"There was a bug on your backpack. Don't worry, I grabbed it and threw it off the bus."

"You did what?" Judy yelled as the bus started.

"It was a fair-sized bug, so I threw it out of the bus."

Judy was panicked. She realized there was nothing she could do, so she just turned around. Finally, the bus had dropped off a few people, and she had a chance to sit. Quickly she took off the backpack and extracted George's bag.

It was empty.

Chapter Five

GEORGE DIDN'T SEE THE GUY'S hand coming, so he was completely surprised to be hurtling through the air. All sensation ceased when he went headfirst into a concrete column beside the shuttle stop. When he came to, he had a difficult time remembering where he was. He finally realized he was lying on the side of a busy street. *Where did Judy go? Why am I in the street?* He tried to clear his head with little success.

A few panicked minutes later, George started thinking more clearly. He was on a street in front of the Cleveland airport. Somehow, he'd been thrown out of the bus as Judy was entering. Now the bus was gone. *Maybe it had been gone for a long time.* He looked around. *I'm not safe. If I go into the street, I'll be run over by one of the vehicles whizzing by, and if I climb the curb to get on the sidewalk, I'll have a good chance of being stepped on. I'd better stay put for a while until I'm completely recovered. Then I can fly somewhere safe and figure out what to do.*

A few minutes later, he felt up to flying, so he flew to one of the crosspieces on the awning above the exit from the airport. He looked around and decided he might be able to get to town by hitching a ride on a taxi. The taxi stand was about a hundred yards away, so he flew over to see what his options were.

Just as George was flying toward the taxi stand, Judy exited the shuttle bus from long-term parking. She explained the round trip by telling the driver she'd left something at the terminal. Exiting where she'd gotten on before, she found no sign of George. She felt extremely silly calling his name. People looked at her funny. A woman came up and asked if she'd lost a child. Judy told her no and turned away. She didn't want to tell the woman what she was looking for. She searched the ground near where the shuttle bus loaded but didn't see anything. *If he was here, he would see me*, she thought. *Either he's been run over, or stepped on, or he's flown away somewhere.*

George looked down on the taxi stand from the perch he'd found. Unfortunately, the background noise made it difficult to hear what people were telling the taxi drivers. When the next taxi drove up, he took a chance and hovered over it. He heard the passenger saying to the driver, "Hilton Cleveland Downtown." He didn't know where the hotel was. Given its name, it must be downtown, the right direction. When he saw the driver slam the trunk, he flew down and settled into the crack between the trunk lid and the rear window. He wedged three legs into the crack, so he felt secure.

Judy finally gave up searching for George. He was nowhere to be seen. She felt incredibly frustrated. All of those trips to bathrooms on the planes and in the terminals had completely gone to waste. And, truth be told, she was looking forward to trying to help him. *There was no way to do it now.* She felt like she'd lost a friend, an incredibly interesting friend. Despondent, Judy hopped on the next shuttle bus that came by.

George had an idea how the cabbie would try to go downtown. When the taxi turned onto interstate seventy-one east, he knew he was right. At the sign for the exit to Fulton Road, he flew off and headed south. As he flew along Fulton, he saw the signs for the Cleveland Metroparks Zoo. Working in the detective agency came in handy. He'd had jobs in many parts of Cleveland, so he knew the metro area very well. Growing up in Shaker Heights, he'd only known the east side.

When he arrived at the zoo, he let his nose guide him. It didn't take him long to find the elephant enclosure. He wasn't really hungry yet. Judy had fed him right before they'd headed out to get her car. He landed and settled on a nice pile of elephant dung. It was warm and smelled very good. He was pleased with himself. At the same time, he realized how stupid he'd been not to memorize Judy's address. He'd been so elated to find her luggage tag with Cleveland on it, he hadn't paid any attention to the address. *Now it would have been really handy. Maybe she'll realize my limited diet would make the zoo the only sensible place for me to go. If she doesn't show, I'll have to try the whole thing again. It's really too bad. I was getting her well trained.*

Judy was exhausted when she finally made it to her apartment at nine-thirty. She tiptoed into the apartment so as not to wake her roommate, Clarice Washington. Clarice was a television reporter who worked the morning show and was usually in bed by nine. *Clarice has to get up at some ungodly hour.* When Judy was two steps inside the door, Jangles, Clarice's Siamese cat, rubbed against her leg. *That's odd, Clarice always shuts Jangles in with her when she goes to bed.* Judy turned on a light and saw Clarice's door was wide open. It was unusual for her to be out this late.

Judy was unpacked and had a load of clothes in the washer when Clarice came in. "Judy, it's great to see you!" Clarice exclaimed, giving her a big hug.

"Great to see you, too. I thought I'd have to be real quiet doing my unpacking. Don't you have to get up early tomorrow?"

"No. I guess you have no way of knowing. I got promoted to the evening news. Starting tomorrow, my world shifts. Most days I work from ten in the morning until the eleven o'clock news finishes. No more early mornings."

Now it was Judy's turn to hug Clarice. "Congratulations, I know it's what you wanted all these years. How did it happen? Tell me all about it."

"Sure thing. What about you? What time is it where you woke up?"

"God only knows. I don't understand what time my body thinks it is. Right now, I'm really tired. Planes do that to me. Nevertheless, I'm not sleepy for some reason."

The two roommates sat down at the kitchen table and swapped stories for a couple of hours. Judy was so tired she didn't think she'd remember Clarice's stories about the TV station's politics. Also, she was sure she hadn't given a very coherent explanation of her safari experience. She didn't mention the business about the dung beetle; it was way too weird.

George woke up the next morning with a funny feeling. It was like he and his pile of dung were floating. When he was fully aware of his surroundings, he realized he and his dung were being carried in a shovel. One of the cleanup crew at the zoo was taking him somewhere. Just when he was about to escape, he and the dung went flying through the air. He landed on a big dung pile, and the dung he'd been on came down on top of him.

While he was a little woozy, he wasn't worried. He'd eat his way to the surface of the dung pile. As he was finishing breakfast, he was near the surface. He didn't need more food, so he wriggled his way to get some fresh air. A few seconds after he'd pushed his way to the dung pile's surface, a glass jar came down over him, capturing him.

"Look at what I caught, Luke. I don't know how those dung beetles get out of their cages. This is the third one this year."

George saw a big, distorted eye looking at him.

"Yep, it's one of them, José. Better take it to the insect room and tell them to check for escape routes."

"Right, it won't take me long."

Holy shit, George thought. *I can't catch a break. Some bozo threw me out of the bus last night, and I lost Judy. Now look what's happened.*

He wasn't able to see anything clearly through the glass jar. Finally, he sensed José had carried him into a building. "Look what I found in the dung pile, Sarah."

"Let me see."

"It's one of yours. You've managed to get a hole or a crack this guy must have found."

"I don't think so, José. Let me count. I'm pretty sure we have all our dung beetles. We found the crack they were using to escape, and we had it repaired. It's been about three months since you caught one, right?"

"I guess so."

"No, we have our six. Let's put the one you found in a separate cage. If it has a disease, I don't want it exposing the others."

George and his little bit of dung were dumped in some kind of glass cage. After he tumbled about a foot, he stood up and looked around. He saw a bunch of dung beetles in the next cage. When he looked up, he saw a woman staring at him. She had thick glasses, which made her eyes look really big.

He heard the woman talking. "Yeah, José, it's a dung beetle, no question about it. I wonder how the heck he found his way into your dung pile."

"Beats me. Luke and I thought it was one of yours. Anyway, I'm sure you'll know what to do with it. Goodbye."

George started to explore his cage. He couldn't stand the idea of winding up in a cage in a zoo. *I'll never be able to track down the person who killed me from here.*

Chapter Six

JUDY WAS STILL GROGGY WHEN she wandered out of her bedroom at nine the next morning. She was surprised to see Clarice at the kitchen table, reading something on her phone. Then she remembered the job change.

"How ya doing, Champ?"

"Coffee."

"Sit down. I'll go get you some."

With a few sips of the coffee in her, Judy started to become more fully awake. "Not so good is the answer to your first question. I guess I didn't tell you last night. I started to get along with a guy on the trip. Unfortunately, we never exchanged information. Now I realize it was a huge mistake."

"Can't you get on the internet and find him?"

"I tried, and I came up empty."

"What kind of weirdo doesn't leave footprints on the internet?"

"Yeah, good question. I mean, I've Googled myself, and I show up lots of places. And I've Googled every guy I've ever dated. I always found something. This guy is definitely weird."

"I'd forget him. If he didn't have the good sense to get your number, he's a loser."

Although Judy felt like telling Clarice the truth, she decided against it. The more she thought about it, the more she was sure continuing the conversation wouldn't make her look good. She decided to stop talking and prepare some breakfast. She missed the big breakfasts the safari staff had prepared.

At noon, Judy went three blocks away to her favorite sandwich shop. She'd spent the time after Clarice left polishing up her story and submitting it to the magazine. They'd given her an advance, but she'd had to front the travel expenses. With the article sent off, she filled out the paperwork for the travel reimbursement. The balance in her checking account was a little low. If the magazine was prompt, she'd be in good shape.

As she munched on her favorite sandwich, turkey and cheddar on focaccia, she was still upset about losing contact with George. She'd enjoyed the unusual companionship they'd developed. Also, because they'd been so focused on logistics, she hadn't been able to ask him lots of questions. *What was it like before he was reincarnated? How did he learn how to do the stuff dung beetles do? How long do dung beetles live, or did he even know?*

While walking back to her apartment, Judy tried to think of what to do. If he'd flown off somewhere, where would he have gone? After coming up blank for a couple of blocks, she realized it would be easy for her to find his Cleveland address or at least the address of his parents. A little more thought revealed her mistake. There would be no way they'd recognize him. Even if he jumped on one of their computers, he wouldn't have a dung ball to drop on the keys. It was just too improbable. If not home, where?

Finally, Judy had another thought. *Food.* He was a voracious eater. He'd told her he only went three or four hours between meals. Dung beetles were never very far away from elephant dung. He was either eating it or rolling it somewhere. Where would he find dung? If George had escaped from the airport, he'd have searched for elephant dung. *The zoo. That's where he'll be if he's still alive.*

George was despondent. He'd stared back at the woman with the thick glasses for a few minutes, but then she lost interest in him, so he investigated his surroundings. He was in a glass box. One end opened, but no amount of prying had any effect on the door. Next, he looked at the other end of his box. It was just a white wall, offering no way to escape. The left-hand side looked into another cage identical to his. It appeared to be empty. Finally, he looked at the side in which he'd seen the other dung beetles. Their box was longer than his, and he saw people looking at them through the far end of their box. *Sure, it was a zoo. People had to have a chance to see the exhibits.* He sat down, completely defeated.

Judy had never been to the Cleveland Zoo. She'd grown up in Toledo. Her phone told her it was about a twenty-minute drive this time of day. Driving to the zoo, she tried to figure out how to find George. She'd been incredibly embarrassed at the airport when the woman thought she was searching for a lost child, so she didn't want to call out his name. Finally, she figured, if he were there, he would be sure to recognize her. Also, she brought the little bag he'd traveled in. Maybe he'd smell it.

Judy parked at the zoo and followed the signs to the elephant enclosure. A couple of elephants wandered around lazily. Much to Judy's surprise, there were no obvious dung piles. Judy was sure these elephants produced dung. Though she smelled it, it was not evident on the ground. *Someone must clean up after them.*

Judy walked around the entire enclosure. Despite the small crowd, she always managed to be right beside the wall. She completed three rounds with no success. The only thing she discovered was a little barn. It sure smelled like elephant dung. It must be where they stored the dung they'd picked up.

As Judy was about to leave, she saw a zoo worker walking toward the barn. With nothing to lose, Judy went up to the man. "You guys have a lot of elephant dung in there, don't you?"

The man looked startled. "Yes, we do. I guess you smelled it?"

"You're right. It's a fairly strong smell." Judy paused and then continued. "What do you do with it? Does the zoo have dung beetles to feed?"

"Most of it goes to the back buildings. They make fertilizer out of it. You're right though, we do make a delivery to the insect house every couple of days. They have dung beetles. Apparently, they love the stuff."

Judy gulped. "Is it okay if I take a look at your dung pile?"

"I'm not sure anyone's ever asked before. Do you mind me asking why?"

"I know this sounds incredibly weird, but I lost my pet dung beetle."

"Your pet dung beetle?"

Judy stared at the man, not knowing what to say.

Finally, the man responded. "I guess if you have a pet dung beetle, it might have headed for our dung pile. I can open the shed for you."

As the man took out a key ring, he warned. "Get ready for a strong smell."

At the open door, Judy steeled herself and stepped in. He was right. The smell was strong. She looked over the dung pile and didn't see George. Also, if he'd been there, he'd have come flying out. Judy turned to the man and shook her head. "I don't see him."

As the man swung the door shut, he said, "You know, the morning crew told me they captured a dung beetle. Sometimes they escape from the cage up at the insect house. They always head here. I guess it's smart. They're not going to find any other place with their food."

"So, you say they took the beetle to the insect house?"

"Yeah. I guess it might be your pet."

Judy thanked him. There was a good chance the dung beetle caught this morning was George. She headed off in search of the insect house. It was easy to find the building and the dung beetle exhibit. Judy looked at the beetles in the glass cage. They all looked like George. She stood in front of the cage, giving plenty of opportunity for him to recognize her. None of the beetles, all of whom looked a little listless, seemed to do anything out of the ordinary. If she knew George, he'd be jumping up and down at this point. She walked away, discouraged. *What was she going to do?*

Judy sat on a bench, trying not to cry. The zoo was such a good idea, and then finding out about the dung beetle the maintenance guys had captured created so much hope. Now it seemed all hope was gone. She heard a strange noise, looked up and saw a woman getting out of a door leading to the space behind the insect exhibits.

Judy rushed up to the woman. "Do you work here?"

"Yes," the startled woman responded, adjusting the glasses on her nose.

"I'm looking for my lost dung beetle," Judy said. Then she realized how funny that must have sounded.

"What?"

Judy thought fast. "Let me explain. I work for a flea circus, and one of our star performers, a dung beetle, went missing. I was down at the elephant enclosure, and they told me they brought you guys a dung beetle this morning."

The woman looked at her skeptically. "You're right. They did bring in a dung beetle this morning. It wasn't one of ours. They were all present and accounted for, so I put it in quarantine. I don't know if you can tell if it's yours. They all look alike. Then again, you're the only one whose reported missing a dung beetle."

"Can I see him?"

"Sure, I can't see any harm in it. Still, I don't know the protocol. We can't give people animals just because they claim they belong to them." The woman unlocked the door she'd come out of and ushered Judy inside.

When they arrived at the cage George was in, he looked up and started to jump up and down.

Judy almost screamed, "George!"

"This is your dung beetle?"

"Yes, definitely."

"I don't know. Like I said, we can't just give away animals. Is there any way you can prove it's your beetle?"

"Watch. I told you George is one of the stars of our show. He can do all sorts of tricks." Turning toward the cage, Judy commanded, "Walk backwards, George."

He looked up at Judy, and she raised her voice. "I told you to walk backwards."

George caught on and backed up ten steps.

"See," Judy said to the woman, who looked amazed. "Roll over." He rolled over. "Fly up to the ceiling." He flew.

"Okay. I've seen enough. He's clearly your dung beetle. I've never seen anything like it. Do you have other insects who can respond to commands?"

Ignoring the woman's question, Judy asked, "Can you unlock the cage, please?"

The woman nodded, selected a key, and unlocked the small door. When the door was opened, George hopped onto Judy's outstretched hand. Judy opened the cloth bag and he climbed in. Judy thanked the woman profusely and scurried out of the space behind the insect exhibits as fast as possible.

Chapter Seven

JUDY COULDN'T HELP TALKING AS she walked to her car in the zoo parking lot. "I'm really happy to see you, George. It looked like you were happy to see me too. I didn't know if you were still alive. I finally figured out, if you were, you would have headed for the zoo. What did you tell me? A man has to eat. Anyway, you can tell me all about getting to the zoo and being caught by the maintenance guys and everything. My computer's at my apartment."

Twenty minutes later, Judy took George into her apartment. He looked around and sniffed. It was a two-bedroom apartment on the second floor of a set of garden apartments. The place was furnished with what he would have called IKEA modern. He thought the bright colors, an orange couch and a green side chair, looked nice. More than anything else, he wondered about the roommate. He was sure Judy wouldn't have rented a two-bedroom place for herself. What he smelled didn't please him, either. There was some animal living in Judy's apartment.

Judy walked to her computer, which was set up on the kitchen table. "Okay, how did you get to the zoo?"

`rode taxi`

"What do you mean? You wouldn't be able to hail a cab."

`hitched a ride`

"I get it. You hitched a ride on a taxi headed toward the zoo." Judy thought George was going toward the Y key when he suddenly flew off the keyboard. Jangles jumped up and swatted a few inches away from where he was in midair. Finally, George landed on top of the living room curtains, and Jangles parked herself under him.

Judy jumped up and grabbed Jangles. "No, bad cat!" she yelled as she took Jangles to Clarice's room and shut the door.

George flew down to the computer.

`don't like cats`

"I can see why. You were very quick, and it's a good thing you can fly."

`saw it coming`

"The cat belongs to Clarice, my roommate. The cat's name is Miss Bo Jangles. We just call her Jangles."

`get rid of her`

"No can do. We'll have to find a way for you two to coexist. There has to be a way. I wonder where you can stay. You need to eat that disgusting elephant dung. By the way, I still have some left over, and I know where they keep it at the zoo. I'll have to set up a place for you to eat and sleep in my bathroom. We can close the door so Jangles can't get at you, and I'll put her in Clarice's room when we're out here talking."

`get rid of cat`

"I heard you the first time, but I can't do it. She's Clarice's cat, and both Clarice and the cat are staying. Clarice and I have been roommates since our junior year at Ohio State. We work together well. Neither of us wants to change anything, particularly me. We can figure out a way to deal with Jangles."

`keep cat away from me`

"I hear you loud and clear. I have an idea. Let's go out and get a place for you to eat and sleep. We can arrange something to keep you safe from Jangles."

Judy offered the cloth bag to him, and he climbed in.

In the car, George wriggled out of the bag and rode on the dashboard. He wanted to see where they were going. "Okay, I see how the cloth bag isn't any fun. We'll have to figure out a better way for you to travel. While you don't want to be seen, you want to be able to see. I'll work on it."

Judy turned into the parking lot of a big-box pet store in a strip mall. "Hop in the bag, George," Judy said, holding it open. He entered the bag slowly.

In the store, Judy searched until she found the hamster cages. After looking at several options, she had an idea. She sat down and whispered to the cloth bag. "Listen, George, I'm going to get you out and show you some ideas. You're going to hop once for yes and two times for no. I want you to have some say in this."

Judy opened the bag, and George walked onto her hand. There were three hamster cage kits laid out so he could inspect them. *They all look alike,* he thought. *What am I going to do with the plastic tunnel?* He looked more closely and saw small differences. Truth be told, he really didn't have a clear opinion. *I'll tell her I like the biggest one.*

The cage he'd chosen was actually two clear plastic boxes. The smaller of the two was a cube, and the larger one was the size of two of the smaller ones. The boxes were attached to each other with a short, round tunnel made of clear plastic. There was a similar longer tunnel connecting the two boxes. The longer tunnel ran along the sides. There was a sort of chimney on each box, which, he guessed, acted as air vents.

In the car, Judy let him out of the bag, and he looked at the picture of the hamster cage on the box in the back seat. He wondered if he'd made a sensible choice. Because he'd been annoyed with Judy, he might have been too quick. He didn't like the whole idea of being confined in a hamster cage. He was used to coming and going as he pleased. Then again, he didn't like the idea of having to look out for the stupid cat all the time. *Though I guess I'll have to adjust, I don't have to like it.*

At the apartment, Judy banished the cat to Clarice's room and went into her bathroom to assemble the cage. When she'd finished, she held it up and faced George, who had been sitting on the rim of the bathtub. "Look at your plastic palace. I hope you like it."

Judy opened the little door, allowing him to crawl into the hamster cage. He wandered around, not liking what he saw. Judy went out, leaving him in the cage. A little frantic, he searched around for a way to escape. He stopped when he smelled food. Judy returned with one of the balls of dung left from the trip. She opened the door and rolled the dung ball into the cage. George felt a little better when he started to eat.

As he was ready to stop eating, he saw the cat coming. As Jangles investigated the cage, he hid behind the diminished dung ball. The cat's strange blue eyes bothered him. He could tell his hiding place wasn't any good when the cat reached out in an effort to paw him. Thankfully, the cage was sturdy enough to thwart the cat. George felt like sticking his tongue out until he realized he didn't really have a tongue.

After what seemed like a long time, the cat lost interest and ambled away. George felt very relieved. When he needed to sleep and eat, he'd be secure in his cage.

Five minutes later, Judy came in. She closed the bathroom door and headed toward the toilet. "Turn your back, George. This is the one problem with having your abode in the bathroom."

He complied. When he heard the flush, he waited for Judy to adjust her clothes and then started jumping up and down. "Okay, I'll get you out. Just a minute, I'll put Jangles in Clarice's room."

At the computer, George jumped on the keyboard.

`don't like cage`

"Tough buddy. You chose it, and it fits in the bathroom. Besides, Jangles can't get at you in there, and that's important. We can't keep the cat penned up in Clarice's room all the time. Speaking of Clarice, she's likely to be on TV in a few minutes. Do you want to watch?"

Judy turned on the six o'clock news. It had been a long time since George had seen any television. When Clarice came on, Judy shouted, "There she is, my roommate!" The story, about a potential teacher's strike in the Cleveland schools, wasn't very interesting. Still, Clarice looked good on TV. She was tall with coffee-colored skin and hair arranged in ringlets. George thought she was striking. Also, she asked the leader of the teacher's union some sensible questions. When Clarice's segment finished, George flew to the computer. Judy followed.

`black`

"Yes, Clarice is black. Friends used to call us chili and pepper, because of my red hair. Her being black doesn't bother you, does it? Because if it does, you can find yourself another hamster cage."

`just surprised`

"Like I told you before, Clarice and I have been roommates since college. She's my best friend. She knows all my secrets, and I know all hers, too. I know she's juggling two boyfriends, and she knows I don't have anyone to juggle. We've shared our dreams and consoled each other when our dreams were smashed."

`does she know about me`

"No, not yet. Clarice and I have only been together a few hours, and I thought you were gone then. Now we'll have to tell her. You're not the easiest person, or bug, to explain. I've been thinking about how to introduce you, and unfortunately, I haven't come up with any great ideas."

`just do it`

"Oh, we're Mister Nike, are we? Yeah, maybe that's what I'll do. I'll simply introduce you. I'll say, Clarice, this is George Wilcox, late of Shaker Heights. He's been reincarnated as a dung beetle. We met in Botswana, and I've brought him home to be our third roommate. He'll be living in my bathroom in a hamster cage. By the way, don't mind his elephant dung in the refrigerator. He eats a lot."

`I like it`

"Don't be silly. The whole reincarnation bit is really going to throw her. It took me a long time to get used to it. I'm not sure I know what to think even now. I mean, I've never run into anyone whose been reincarnated before. And I keep remembering all the flies I've swatted in my life and all the bugs I've squashed. It's just weird. You're weird. There's no way I can come out and tell her. She'll be sure I've flipped. She's a big-time church attender, and I don't know how reincarnation is going to fit with her religion."

`show her`

"You know you're not so dumb after all. It might work. I mean, that's the way you convinced me. What dung beetle can type? Sure, it's our best option. Let's try it when she gets home."

Chapter Eight

AT TEN O'CLOCK, CLARICE ENTERED the apartment.

"You're home early. I thought you were staying until after the eleven o'clock news."

"Thank goodness I was wrong. I actually got off at eight, and I went to Hank's to have a celebratory drink. I only stay late one night a week. It turns out most of the stories they show at eleven o'clock are reruns of the ones we do at six. They won't rerun mine. It was pretty lame."

"No, we watched it here. It was good."

"We? Oh, you mean Jangles. I'm surprised she sat still long enough to watch. She usually ignores the TV. You think she recognized me?"

"Actually, I was talking about someone else. I'll show you."

Judy picked up Jangles, sequestered her, and went to the hamster cage in her bathroom. She walked out with George on her right palm.

"What the hell! It's a bug! Judy, tell me you're not talking about how you and some bug watched me on TV."

"Come to my computer and let me explain." Judy sat down in front of the computer and Clarice followed.

The bug hopped around the keyboard as Judy typed.

`nice to meet you clarise`

"What's going on, Judy, and by the way, you misspelled my name."

"Look more closely, Clarice. I'm only typing when the bug, actually he's a dung beetle, points out the keys for me."

Clarice came closer. George and Judy typed more slowly this time, and she only used one finger.

`sorry about the spelling`

"Holy shit. How are you doing that?"

"I'm not. Both of us are. The dung beetle... whoops, he prefers to be called a scarab. He bows at the key he wants me to hit, and then I hit it. Before I tell you more, why don't you try?"

Judy stood up. "Sit here, Clarice, where you can do the typing. Just press the keys he indicates."

Clarice sat down with a skeptical look on her face.

"Tell Clarice your name."

`george wilcox`

"I'll be damned. I followed the bug, and he told me his name. What the hell's going on here? Judy, tell me what's going on!"

"Okay. You needed a demonstration before I gave you the whole story. One night when I returned to my tent from dinner, there was a message on my computer screen. It read, 'Don't squash me.' As I was reading the message, I saw George and this great big ball of elephant dung on the edge of my computer. He hopped up on the computer with his dung ball, raised the ball over his head, and typed something more. I don't remember... Wait, he wants to type."

`hi just hi`

"Yeah, I remember now. Anyway, I was completely freaked out. I thought someone was playing an elaborate prank on me, but it's not a prank. He had me Google him, and I discovered he's from Cleveland, actually Shaker Heights, and was murdered about a year and a half ago. He told me he's been reincarnated as a dung beetle. I brought him here because he wants to find out who killed him."

"The shit you say. Reincarnated as a dung beetle. I don't get it. How'd he remember his old life, and English, for God's sake? It's too weird. Tell me you're pulling my leg."

George ran to a key and nodded up and down. Somewhat reluctantly, Clarice followed his directions.

`it's all true`

"Judy, tell me this is some kind of trick."

"No Clarice, it isn't. Look, nothing up my sleeve," Judy said as she rolled up her sleeve.

"Empty your pockets."

"I don't have pockets. Do you want me to show you I'm not wearing a wire?"

"Yes, if you don't mind."

Judy stripped off her clothes. George jumped up and down on the keyboard, so Clarice went in position to type for him.

`yowzah`

Clarice laughed despite herself.

"Be quiet," Judy said as she put her clothes back on. "So, Clarice, you want to search the house to see if I have any co-conspirators?"

"You damn betcha!" Clarice headed toward Judy's bedroom.

"Hold on to Jangles if you bring her out of your room. Jangles and George don't get along."

Clarice called from Judy's bathroom, "I suppose you'll tell me he stays in this hamster cage?"

"You catch on slow."

Clarice came back holding Jangles. "There's no one else here. Is it really true, someone named George Wilcox has been reincarnated as a dung beetle, and he still knows who he is?"

"That's what we've been telling you."

"I'll be damned."

"Come here. I'll show you the two things I get when I Google 'George Wilcox, Cleveland.'"

Clarice read the short *Plain Dealer* story about the murder and the obituary. After she finished the obituary, Clarice turned to George. "It says you were twenty-four and died a year and a half ago. That would make you twenty-five or twenty-six, two years older than Judy and me. It also said you went to Oberlin."

`philosophy major`

"Okay, then you must have known Simon Paulson."

"Clarice has the hots for Simon."

"Shush, Judy! Did you know Simon?"

`simon peter paulson`

"Judy, it has to be true. How the hell did he know Simon's full name? I'm going to call Simon and find out what he remembers about George Wilcox."

The dung beetle indicated he wanted to type.

`we called him rabbi rock`

"Oh, it must have burned him up. He's about as Christian as you get, so calling him rabbi would bother him, and you made fun of his name, too. Rock for Simon Peter. He's the associate minister at the church I go to. He and I get into lots of arguments. He's sure every word in the Bible is true. In my view, he's been brainwashed. I always wondered how he made it through Oberlin the way he thinks."

"And I've always wondered how you two like each other the way you argue."

"Don't be pointing fingers, Judy. I've heard some big arguments you've had with Brad. I know for a fact you're still in love with him. Unfortunately, you can't seem to get along with him right now."

"Touché."

`lots going on here`

"Yes, there is, and I expect you'll learn all about it in due time," Judy said. "Right now, we should shut down for the night. It's past my bedtime. I rescued you from the zoo, bought you a house, and introduced you to Clarice. Enough for one day."

"And George, I'm going to be checking up on you with Simon. I wonder what they called you at Oberlin."

George jumped up and down.

`keep me secret`

"He's right, Clarice. We should be really careful about how many people we tell about him. The last thing he wants is to become a curiosity. We can't have news cameras and lots of publicity. He has to be a big secret. For right now, you shouldn't be asking questions about George."

"Okay. I'll hold off. I just know the reincarnation business would blow away that Bible thumper Simon. I really want to tell him."

"Not right now. The whole thing is so unbelievable; you'd never convince him. Look at how difficult it was for you to understand what's going on. If we ever tell people about George, we're going to have to be very careful how we do it. The whole thing's unbelievable."

"I see. Jangles and I are going to bed. We can talk about it more in the morning. What a day. I thought my new job would be the most interesting thing going on. Wow, was I wrong."

Chapter Nine

THE FOLLOWING MORNING, JUDY AND Clarice met at the kitchen table. Judy had taken George the last of the dung balls for breakfast, so he was in his hamster cage. Jangles, who was on Clarice's lap, seemed to have lost interest in the beetle, at least for the time being.

Judy started the conversation over coffee. "I have an idea of how to proceed. I don't have any writing assignments now, but it's okay. The reimbursement for the safari travel will come in soon. I was thinking of saying I was writing a story about people who've experienced sudden loss. It would probably get me in George's folk's door. He might want to see them."

"Maybe, but I don't see how it fits. I thought he was interested in trying to find out who murdered him. Isn't that what you told me?"

"Yes, you're right, and this is part of it. I want to learn more about him. Lots of murders are about personal things—jealous lovers, family squabbles, business problems—things like that. We have to know more about George to find out if any of those issues are involved."

"Gosh, I thought you'd want to be more direct. I should be able to find out who on the police force worked on his murder. My big brother, Lewis, is a lieutenant with the Cleveland police. I'm sure he could ask. I was thinking of telling him I have a friend who's researching a story on cold cases."

"Great idea. I remember Lewis from graduation. Sure, the police must have a file on George's case. Maybe there will be something useful there. I didn't realize how helpful being a freelance writer is. I don't even have to pretend. A story about cold cases is plausible, and I can write about anything I want. Well, anything I think I can sell."

"I don't have your freedom. I'm going to the station this morning, and they're going to give me my assignment for the day. I hope, eventually, I might get to do an investigative story, more than a one-shot deal. Right now, it looks like it will be a steady diet of interviews like the dull one last night or me standing in front of some burning building or big car wreck."

"You'll be at the anchor desk soon, keep plugging."

"You're sweet, Judy. Don't hold your breath."

"Let's change the subject. I have to figure out how to carry George around. He really doesn't like the little cloth bag we used when we were on the planes from Africa. He wants to see what's happening, and I don't blame him."

Clarice thought for a minute. "You need a way to carry him so he can see. At the same time, you don't want people to wonder why you've got a bug crawling on you."

"Exactly."

Clarice stood up and went to her bedroom with Jangles tagging behind her. Judy picked up the breakfast dishes, rinsed them, and put them in the dishwasher. After she'd put the toaster away and wiped the counter, Clarice returned, twirling a black pendant on a chain.

"This should do it," Clarice reported, showing the pendant to Judy.

"I can't wear anything like that, Clarice. It's too big. You can wear big jewelry. I'm four inches shorter than you. It would look odd."

"Do you have a choice, Honey? Don't worry about fashion, worry about practicality. This should work. Maybe you don't remember it. Some crazy guy in college gave it to me. He didn't stay around too long, just long enough to give me this necklace.

She continued, holding the pendant in front of Judy. "See, the filigree box opens in the back, and you put a colored marble in it. It's really a nice idea because you can change colors. It came with six different marbles. It should be big enough to hold him. He's black, so it would be difficult to really get a good look at him. It's perfect."

Judy took the pendant and looked at it closely. "I'll shorten the chain, and unless I'm running, he won't be bounced around too much. Let's see what he thinks."

"Do it quick, I have to get dressed and go."

Judy dampened a paper towel and went to get George. When they returned to the table, Judy and Clarice explained their idea to him, and he quickly jumped on the keyboard.

`willing to try`

Clarice opened the pendant, and he walked in. Judy shut the little door and put the chain over her head. It hung down too low for her taste, so she pinched the chain to hike it up.

"Walk around the living room and come back to me."

Judy walked around the living room and then went to check the mirror in her bathroom. When Judy finally returned. Clarice declared, "I can't really see him in there, it just looks black. Quick, take it off, so we can get his reaction."

`way better than bag`

"Can you see all right?" Judy asked.

`yes but sides limited`

"Geez, he's picky," Clarice commented. "I'd say it's a winner. Did you think it looked okay, when you checked yourself in the mirror?"

"I'll be able to wear it, though I'll have to be careful what else I have on. I can see how some of my outfits might really restrict his side views. Still, we can make it work."

"Great, I have to change and fly out of here."

Judy shortened the chain, and right after lunch she headed out the door with George in the pendant. Her first stop was the zoo. She brought a couple of Tupperware containers she hoped to fill with elephant dung. She was in luck when she reached the elephant enclosure. The same guy she'd talked to yesterday was working near the little barn.

Judy walked up to him. "Hi. Remember me, we met yesterday? I'd lost my dung beetle, and you were right. He was the one somebody took to the insect house. I have him now, and I need to be able to feed him. It was easy to get elephant dung in Africa, not so much here in Cleveland. Are you able to sell me some?"

"Look miss, I remember you, and I'm glad you have your beetle. We're not supposed to sell the dung. Like I told you yesterday, we take some to the insect house, but most of it gets made into fertilizer."

Judy stepped close to the man and let him see a twenty-dollar bill she had in her hand. "I don't need much. It's only one beetle. No one will miss it."

"If you have two of those, we can do business," the man replied, glancing around.

"Deal."

Judy was of two minds about her purchase of the elephant dung. On the one hand, she thought, *poop should be free.* On the other hand, she was pleased the guy hadn't been a stickler for the rules. As she walked toward her car, she noticed a little elephant dung on the outside of one of her containers. She detoured into a rest room to wash off the bits of dung. When she was finished, she put the containers up to her nose and was pleased with the results. She couldn't smell any dung.

In the car, George soon recognized they weren't headed back to Judy's apartment. She hadn't told him where she planned to go. He knew she'd made a phone call while he was eating lunch. Unfortunately, he didn't hear any of the details. He suspected it had something to do with where they were headed. This pendant thing worked well for him when they were in the zoo. In the car it was less than ideal. Mostly he saw the steering wheel. He wished she'd allow him to ride on the dashboard again. He'd had a really good view when he'd ridden there.

Judy entered a public garage and parked. George didn't know where they were, somewhere downtown. "We're going to a Starbucks, George. We have some time to kill before our next appointment."

He wanted to ask, "What appointment?" There was no way—no computer. He'd have to ride in the pendant and see what happened.

As a human, George had always liked the smell in a Starbucks. Now it wasn't anything special. He decided it was only fair. He was sure elephant dung would have had an unpleasant odor to him when he was a human, but the smell was one of the great parts of the visit to the zoo. While he knew Judy had her phone out, his view down was limited, so he couldn't tell what she was looking at. Busy with her phone, Judy dawdled over her fancy coffee. George was bored. Finally, Judy walked slowly to her car.

On the road again, even with his limited view, he could tell they were headed to the east side of Cleveland. When they entered Shaker Heights, he became alarmed. *Is she taking me home?* He heaved a sigh of relief when they passed the apartment building where he'd lived for his last two human years. Then he was nervous all over again as Judy turned toward the house where he'd grown up. He was almost apoplectic by the time Judy parked in front of his parent's house. He was furious with Judy. *How could she spring this on me without telling me?*

Judy rang the doorbell of the Dutch Colonial, and George saw his mother open the door. "Hello. You must be Miss Clayton who called.

You're right on time."

George was surprised. His mother looked older than he'd remembered. Her hair had turned gray, or maybe she'd stopped coloring it. She'd always been thin. Now she looked downright skinny.

The two women went into the living room, and Judy sat on the new brown leather sofa. George remembered being a little annoyed when his parents had replaced the furniture he'd grown up with. It was stupid. There was no reason for him to be attached to pieces of furniture. It was perfectly sensible for his folks to get new stuff.

Judy spoke up. "Thank you so much for meeting with me, Mrs. Wilcox. Like I told you on the phone, I'm a writer working on a project I'll be submitting to a magazine. The topic is sudden loss. You lost your son George suddenly over a year ago."

Right then Judy saw a group of framed photographs on the mantel across the room. "Oh, is that him?"

George's mother brought her one of the photos. It was Judy's first view of George the human. He was good looking, with sandy hair, blue eyes, and a nice smile. George recognized it as the photo from his senior year in high school. "He was a handsome young man," Judy remarked, giving the photo back.

When Mrs. Wilcox was seated after replacing the photo, Judy continued. "Can you tell me what losing him suddenly was like?"

"I'm glad it's been a while. I wouldn't have been able to give a coherent answer at the time. Though lots of people wanted to console me then, I just wanted to be alone. Anyway, I guess the first thing I'll say is—right at the start I didn't believe it. I mean he was so full of life, and then it was snuffed out."

"I'm sure it was difficult."

"Yes, it was. Like I said, George was full of life. He had a big personality. In many ways, when he was growing up, he dominated family time. The life of the party—that was our boy. He liked attention and knew how to get it. Not in a bad way, mind you. People gravitated toward him."

"Sounds like quite a guy. It must have been difficult to lose him."

"To tell you the truth, my husband, Harold, and George had a big falling out, so we hadn't seen much of him in the year before he died. Harold thought he was wasting his life working for the detective. That was part of it."

"Was there something else?"

"Yes, it was his girlfriend, Monica. Harold and Monica didn't get along the couple of times we saw her. Harold can be a little stuffy, and Monica appeared to be too wild for his tastes. Let me get back to your question. Sudden loss is very difficult. When we lost my mother, it was expected. We had time to prepare. Losing George was different. It just happened, boom. We didn't have time to prepare. It was harder on Harold than me. I know he wanted to repair their relationship, but he never had a chance. Their last words were harsh. It really took a toll on Harold."

"Unfortunately, what you're talking about is common." Judy was winging it. "Death isn't ever planned. With something like a protracted illness, you have a feeling anything you say might be your last words, so you moderate. Any relationship has its ups and downs, and a sudden death can be poorly timed."

"Well said, young lady. I guess you've been thinking about this subject for a while."

"Yes," Judy lied. "I understand not believing it when you first heard. When did it start to be real for you?"

"I guess when the memorial service finished. Before the service there were all the details: the funeral home, getting the minister, the church, the flowers, and the announcements. Friends and family came to visit. After the service, when George's sister left, life had to go on. And it had to go on without my son."

"And you didn't have any idea about how he would have wanted things to go."

"Yes. Again, with my mother, we even knew the hymns she wanted at the service. With George, we knew nothing."

Judy thought the woman was going to tear up, but her sadness passed. Judy continued. "I guess you have to make decisions like do we cremate, or do we get a burial plot, without any sense of what he would want."

"Oh, we had him cremated. We have a family plot where we inter the cremains of family members. It wouldn't have surprised him. I'm just saying all those details kept me busy. His death didn't become real until it was all finished."

When a man came in the front door, Mrs. Wilcox went up to him and gave him a chaste hug. "Miss Clayton, this is my husband, Harold."

Judy shook the outstretched hand.

"Miss Clayton is researching a story about sudden loss, and I've been telling her about what it was like when George was killed."

"I'm sorry Miss Clayton," Harold Wilcox said. "I can't be any help. It's still too raw. I don't want to talk about it." With that, he walked out of the living room.

Judy stayed for another fifteen minutes asking questions. She felt like a fraud, asking questions and taking notes for a story she wasn't actually planning to write. Still, she remembered one of her writing professors saying there were no bad experiences. Even the ones you didn't enjoy might be fodder for a good story.

George had mixed emotions as Judy sat chatting with his mother. He was mad at Judy for not telling him where she was taking him. He was trapped in the stupid pendant. Even if he wanted to leave, and he did when his father came in, he was stuck. At the same time, it was nice to see his mother and the house. The whole thing was confusing. He finally decided what he'd demand when they returned to the apartment. He'd tell Judy he wasn't ever hopping in the stupid pendant again unless he had a thorough briefing about where they were headed.

Chapter Ten

WHEN THEY RETURNED TO THE apartment, Judy tried to put George in his hamster cage. She didn't succeed because he flew to her computer. He waited impatiently for her to come type for him, but Judy didn't come right away. Instead, she headed to the refrigerator with the newly acquired elephant dung, retrieved Jangles' food, and fed her.

George jumped up and down.

Finally, she walked to the computer. "What are you so excited about?"

`don't ever do that again`

"What, take you to see your parents?"

`no surprise me`

"Oh, I see why you're upset. In this case, I'm not sure you would have agreed to go see your parents. I learned a great deal. Your mom told me she hadn't seen you much the year before you died. Partly I guess because you and your father had a falling out. I also learned about a girlfriend, Monica. Why didn't you tell me about her?"

`just tell me where next time`

"Okay, next time I will. Promise. What about Monica? Was it serious? Did you live together? Why didn't your father like her?"

`too many questions`

"Okay. Was it serious?"

He moved to the N key.

"Did you live together?"

He went to the Y key.

"Anything else to add?"

`I broke up with her`

"When?"

`a week before I was killed`

"So, should we be investigating her?"

George paused and then slowly walked to the Y key.

"I'll take the slowness of your response to indicate you're not really sure."

This time he made it to the Y key faster.

"Okay. I'll need her full name."

`monica daley`

"Good, I have something to investigate. You must be hungry. I've got the new dung. Let me take you to your cage so you can have dinner. Did you notice Jangles didn't even wake up when we came in?"

George hopped on Judy's hand. *Sure, I looked for the cat, particularly when I was flying to the computer. The cat makes me nervous. I don't think the cat has become used to me at all. I just think it was sleepy.*

After she'd put him in his cage, Judy returned with a large spoonful of dung. Soon he was busy rolling it into a ball. *Why in the hell do I do this*, he thought. *I'm only going to eat the stuff.* Apparently, instincts were strong. He wasn't able to stop shaping the dung into a ball and rolling it around the cage before he started eating.

Meanwhile, Judy fixed herself a sandwich and started trying to find Monica Daley. As she'd feared, checking the internet, she found several Monica Daleys in the Cleveland area. Eliminating those under sixteen or over forty cut the list considerably. She decided to investigate the five remaining Monicas.

One of the Monicas was in a wheelchair and thirty-five years old. Judy didn't figure she'd be the one George's father objected to for being too wild. Judy eliminated her. The next Monica was studying in a PhD program at Case Western and the Cleveland Clinic. She was in the right age range. Judy kept her in the pool. Next came a Monica who was first runner up in the Miss Cleveland pageant. There were lots of pictures of her. She was a brassy looking blonde with a spectacular figure. At the time of the pageant, she was listed as a community college student. Judy thought she might be George's type. She definitely belonged in the pool. The fourth Monica appeared to weigh close to three hundred pounds and lived in a far west suburb. Judy didn't think so. The final Monica was a clear possibility. Judy found she'd been a student at the College of Wooster when George was at Oberlin. She worked in the advertising department for the *Plain Dealer*.

With the list of Monica Daleys pared down to three, Judy went to see if George had finished dinner. When she arrived at the cage, she saw the floor had a thin coating of elephant dung. George sat in one corner munching on a small ball of dung.

"Don't tell me you've been rolling your food into a ball," Judy said, holding out a wet paper towel for him to wipe his feet.

At the computer, George wanted to type right away.

`couldn't stop myself`

"Oh, you mean with the dung ball. I guess you have plenty of dung beetle in your habits. It means we're going to have to clean your cage pretty often. It's going to reek soon. Enough of that. I have to figure out which Monica Daley was your girlfriend. Move to where you can see the screen well."

George flew to Judy's shoulder.

Judy put up the information on the PhD student Monica, and George flew down to the N key. Next Judy showed him the beauty pageant girl, and he flew to the Y key.

"So, you picked beauty over brains."

`so what`

"Don't get so touchy. Lots of guys would make the same pick. She is a very good-looking young woman. She's a little younger than you—at least it looks that way. The picture of you showed me you were good looking, too. The two of you must have made a handsome couple."

`high school picture`

"I thought maybe. Since you and your parents were sort of estranged before your death, it's not surprising they didn't have a more recent photo. Actually, I guess my parents don't either. Once you're out of high school, the regular photos stop. And my folks are in Toledo, not Cleveland. I don't see them often. Tell me more about Monica."

`airhead`

"Not a nice thing to say about your girlfriend. Is that why you broke up with her?"

`partly untidy lazy airhead`

"Oh, I get it. You two were living together, and she didn't provide any intellectual stimulation. On top of that, she was sloppy and lazy. Nothing worse than a lazy, sloppy roommate. How long did you live with her?"

```
about a year
```

"I'm sorry it didn't work out. You learn things living together you can't know based on dates." George jumped up and down.

```
sex was great
```

"You knew about the sex from dates. I mean, you didn't know how sloppy she was, and you didn't know she expected you to clean up her messes."

He went to the Y key.

"So, let's cut to the chase. She may have been involved in your murder. She was most likely angry with you when you broke up with her. I bet she'd been the one breaking up with guys, not the other way around. What did you do, move out, or give her an ultimatum to move out?"

```
gave her two weeks to move
```

"Interesting, so she was still living in your place when you were killed. It must have been a tense time. Living in the same place after you'd broken up. I can see how you wouldn't throw her out on the street. I guess she was looking for somewhere to move?"

```
not that I noticed
```

"Sounds like you weren't very pleased with her. And I suspect she wasn't too pleased with you either. Breakups can be tough, and breakups involving people living together are probably especially tough."

Just then Clarice came through the front door. "I have something for you, Judy," she called.

"I have stuff to show you too. George and I went to visit his folks."

"It must have been nice for him. You didn't tell them about his current manifestation, did you?"

"No, and I'm not sure he liked the trip. He was mad at me for a while."

"Oh, George," Clarice cooed. "Was it tough seeing your parents and your old house?"

George didn't budge.

"I learned something from the trip. Our boy had a live-in girlfriend. He broke up with her the week before he was killed. She should be the first person we investigate."

"Wait. You were so excited about your trip with George that I haven't had a chance to show you what I have. I called my brother Lewis, and he was glad to have an investigative reporter, at least that's what I called you, look into unsolved cases. He told me they are short on personnel, so they end up with quite a few unsolved murder cases. He gave me a copy of the paperwork for unsolved cases from the last two years. I checked; George's case is in this." Clarice pulled a stack of papers out of her carry bag.

"Great idea, and it might even make for a good story. Show us what you have on George."

Clarice shuffled through the papers and handed Judy three pages. George flew up to Judy's shoulder to read the police report. The start was grim. A young white male was found in a car on Quincy Street. He had been shot in the back of the head. The man carried a wallet identifying him as George Wilcox who lived in the Garfield Apartments in Shaker Heights, unit 903. None of the people the police interviewed on Quincy Street recognized the car, which was registered to Mr. Wilcox. And none of them had heard anything unusual the night before. The medical team determined the shot had been fired at close range at least ten hours before. This was followed by some medical mumbo jumbo about how they determined the time of death.

Before she turned to the second page Judy commented, "Pretty clinical so far."

The second page described the police effort to find information about the victim. First, they notified the next of kin. They called George's mother at home and went to see her. Based on information she provided, the police learned the deceased had worked for the Acton Detective Agency. The police went to see Gregory Acton. Mr. Acton was visibly upset when the police told them of the murder. He told the police he didn't have any idea where his colleague was supposed to be the previous evening. Very often the two of them worked independently. Acton allowed the police to look through Wilcox's files. There was no useful information. The agency didn't have any clients on Quincy Street.

The next section of the report described the visit the police made to Mr. Wilcox's apartment. His roommate, a Monica Daley, described as a young white female, was surprised when the police told her of the reason for the visit and broke down crying. When she finally calmed herself, she told the police she loved George. She'd been very concerned when he didn't return from what he'd described as a night-time stake out for his job at the detective agency. She had been about to call the police because she hadn't gotten a response on his cell phone in the morning.

The report gave brief descriptions of interviews the police had with known associates of Mr. Wilcox. The mother, his employer, and his girlfriend provided the names. None of the people interviewed had any useful information. The final page reported on the forensic examination of the car. It appeared to the examiner that the deceased had been killed elsewhere and then driven to Quincy Street. Also, the car had been thoroughly cleaned. There was nothing in the car at all. The search for the bullet came up empty.

"Not much," Clarice said.

Judy nodded, and George flew down and hopped on the keyboard.

`monica was lying`

"Yes, we were just talking about her. They'd broken up a week before the killing. She was still in the apartment because he was nice enough to give her two weeks to look for another place to live. Here, I'll get her picture up for you to see."

Judy found the picture of Monica Daley and showed it to Clarice. "What's the word he used?" Clarice asked. "Yowzah, that's it. George, she's a babe."

"He told me she was an untidy, lazy, airhead. He broke up with her. And it's not the story she told the police. We should look into her more closely."

"And we'd better find out about the stake out Monica mentioned. George, what was going on?"

`can't remember`

"Really, you don't know anything about the case you were working on?" Judy asked.

Though he'd been trying to remember what he'd been doing the day he'd been killed, he wasn't able to dredge up a memory. Things seemed to go blank sometime on the day before he was killed. His inability to remember anything from the critical afternoon bothered him.

`don't remember anything`

"Too bad," Clarice said. "I guess our efforts will have to focus on your old girlfriend. Maybe something will come back to you. I'm going to crash now. It was a tough day at the station for me."

Chapter Eleven

THE NEXT MORNING, CLARICE, JUDY, and George conferred over breakfast. Judy asked, "Where can we find Monica today? It's Friday."

`hardware store where she works`

"What kind of girl works in a hardware store?" Clarice asked.

`attracts male customers`

"I get it," Judy said. "The first runner-up in the Miss Cleveland beauty pageant would be a real asset for a hardware store. I bet she doesn't dress in baggy overalls."

`bingo`

"Men are so shallow!" Clarice exclaimed.

"Whoa girl. You're not above dressing provocatively. I've seen some of the outfits you wear. You know, like the purple number you wore on your first date with Jay. It certainly wasn't baggy overalls."

"You can't hide the merchandise."

"So which hardware store had the idea of hiring a babe to attract customers?"

daley's 87 street

"Daley's, does it belong to her father?"

uncle

"Clarice, do you know how long you have to work today?"

"This is my late night. I'm low on the totem pole, so I get the late night on Fridays. Don't count on me for anything tonight. I'm coming home and crashing."

"Okay, I was thinking a girl like Monica might be going out on Friday night, and maybe we'd be able to follow her. I would have liked to have had you come along. I guess I can handle it by myself."

what about me

"Of course, you're coming along. I guess we'll go to the hardware store, and I'll pitch my story about sudden loss. It will be interesting to see what she says."

I can fly

After a pause, Clarice spoke up. "I see what he's saying, Judy. He used to be a detective, and he's little. You could use him like a scout. Take him somewhere and let him out. He can fly around and see what he finds. Take your laptop so he can report to you in your car. I can see how he'll be a real asset in an investigation."

George stood by the Y key.

"What if someone comes at him with a fly swatter or something?"

"Our boy is smart enough to avoid any weapons. Still, there will be risk involved."

Judy interrupted. "You were about to say—no risk, no reward, weren't you?"

"Precisely. You're trying to catch a murderer. They aren't going to come up to you and tell you they did it."

"Sure. So is Clarice right, George? Do you want me to let you out in the hardware store while I talk to Monica? Then we can compare notes in the car."

He hurried to the Y key.

"First, you'd better eat breakfast. I'll get you a spoonful of dung, and I'll go take a shower."

Forty-five minutes later, George and Judy left Clarice getting ready for work and drove toward the Daley hardware store. It was the tail end of rush hour, so it took quite a while. They were able to park in the store's parking lot. The building looked relatively new. It was in better shape than the rest of the stores on the block.

With George in the pendant, Judy walked into the store. It was easy to spot Monica because a gaggle of men surrounded her. Judy went to the back of the store by the fertilizer and grass seed to let George out of the pendant. Judy looked around. No one was paying them any attention.

"We'll meet here. Come when I've finished talking to Monica."

George flew off. Judy sure hoped this would work. It was maddening to have such a cumbersome way of communicating. It would be so much easier if they could talk. She thought, *He was good at coming back when he had to fly to avoid security at the airports. He'll probably be good here too.*

Judy wandered around the store, which seemed to be well stocked. Big box stores like Lowes and Home Depot were stiff competition for local hardware stores. Despite the competition, it looked as if Daley's was thriving. Judy guessed Monica might well have something to do with the success. She certainly attracted the guys. Judy realized why. She had on a very tight pair of yoga pants and a skimpy top showing ample cleavage. Her long blonde hair finished the look nicely. It certainly seemed to work on the customers.

While Judy planned to buy cleaning supplies, she didn't want to get them before talking to Monica. There was some chance Monica would agree to do the interview right away, so Judy wanted to be able to take notes. She started toward the girl when she saw her break away from the group of men she'd been talking to. Monica headed to the rear of the store. Judy was at the other side of the store and unable to head her off before Monica made it to a room in the back.

George hid behind a display of string trimmers. He remembered the store very well. He'd picked Monica up from work lots of times. There was a time when he'd been annoyed with the way she so openly flirted with the customers. She'd always told him to calm down. Her uncle paid her good money to be nice to the customers. He remembered saying he understood. Nevertheless, he'd never liked the arrangement.

He had a good look at Monica as she walked toward the break room. *Wow, I almost forgot what a babe she is.* He flew along the wall, tracking her. When she opened the door to the break room, he ducked in and hid on top of the lockers. He knew the room. He'd done some smooching with Monica there on several occasions.

Monica went into the little restroom attached to the break room. When she returned, she sat down in one of the chairs and put her feet up on the table. *The spike heels she was wearing were probably killing her feet.* As she seemed to be getting settled, the door opened. George was shocked to see Bill Sawyer walk in. *What was he doing here?* Monica swung her feet off the table and kissed Bill. He saw Sawyer fondling her breast as the kiss lasted.

When they separated, Monica asked, "What are you doing here? Me and you weren't supposed to hook up until six."

"I have an hour before my next client, and I remembered you had a break coming. You seem happy to see me."

"Well, I am. Still, you shouldn't be in the store. My uncle would kill me if he saw us here. Customers aren't supposed to come in this room."

"The door's closed."

"Someone might see you coming in. Now get out, you're not supposed to be here. I'll see you tonight."

"One more little kiss."

George watched the two of them and was sure what he was observing wasn't a little kiss. When she was alone again, Monica spent some time repairing her makeup and rearranging her outfit. George was happy to realize he wasn't bothered by what he'd seen. He'd always known Bill was attracted to Monica. So were lots of other guys. Sawyer was a little more obvious than most, trying to chat her up even when he was there. When he'd complained, Monica told him he had nothing to worry about. Still, he wasn't surprised Bill had pursued Monica after he'd died. Five minutes later, he flew out when Monica opened the door. She seemed to notice him but didn't do anything about it.

Judy was waiting when Monica came out of the break room and went up to her. "Excuse me, are you Monica Daley?"

Monica looked a little startled. She wasn't used to being accosted by women. Men yes, women no. "Yes."

"I'm sorry to bother you at work. I'm a freelance writer working on a story on sudden losses, and I understand you lost your boyfriend, George Wilcox, suddenly. Do you mind answering some questions?"

Monica paused, looking uncomfortable, so Judy went on. "Look, we can do it somewhere else if it's inconvenient here. It might take five or ten minutes."

Monica spoke up after she looked toward the front of the store. "I shouldn't talk to you here. My boss wouldn't like it."

"Somewhere else then? I could meet you when you're off duty. It really won't take long."

"I get off work at six, and me and my boyfriend are going out to Margarita's for a drink. I guess we might be able to talk there, say around six-fifteen."

"That would be wonderful. I'm awfully sorry to have barged in on you like this. Thanks."

As she walked toward the front of the store, Monica was stopped by some guy, and Judy saw her turn on the charm. Judy went to get the floor cleaning stuff and then to her planned meeting spot with George. He flew down and landed on her out-stretched hand. She loaded him into the pendant.

In the car, Judy opened the pendant, and George walked out and flew to the computer keyboard sitting in the passenger seat. "Learn anything?" Judy asked as she fired up the computer.

`I know her boyfriend`

"Interesting. We're going to meet him this evening. She wouldn't do the interview at the store. Her boss wouldn't approve. Anyway, she agreed to meet at six-fifteen at a bar called Margarita's. The boyfriend will be there."

`I know the bar`

"Good. Let's go back to the apartment. We have some time until we are scheduled to meet Monica, and I don't want anyone seeing us communicate this way."

They had lunch when they returned to the apartment, and then George told her what he knew about Bill Sawyer. As far as he knew, Bill was an insurance salesman. He worked in his father's insurance office. Either he sold a lot of insurance, or there was family money. He drove a Mercedes, and Sawyer talked about extravagant vacations he'd taken, like cruises and trips to Japan. Judy had the clear impression George didn't like Sawyer. She figured it was normal. The guy had moved in on his old girlfriend.

At ten minutes past six, Judy walked into the bar section of Margarita's.

She saw Monica sitting with a guy, presumably Bill Sawyer, at a table for four. The guy stood up when Judy walked toward them.

She said, "Judy Clayton," and shook the guy's hand.

"Bill Sawyer, and you already met Monica."

"I'm so sorry to be breaking into your date. Like I told Monica, this shouldn't take long."

Monica nodded and said, "Take a seat. I told Bill about you. He knew George too. Have some chips and guacamole if you want."

George had a good view of both Monica and Bill when Judy sat down. The whole thing was unsatisfactory. *He was there, but he wasn't. Even if he knew the perfect thing to say or the perfect question to ask, he didn't have a way to participate.*

Judy checked out Bill Sawyer. He was a nice enough looking guy, nothing spectacular, maybe a little overweight, sort of soft looking. He was a nice dresser. A sharp crease in his khakis and an expensive looking shirt with colorful checks indicated he paid attention to the way he looked. Or maybe it was just when he was trying to impress Monica. Judy realized she had no idea how long they'd been a couple.

"No chips, thanks. Like I told you at the store, I'm a freelance writer working on a story about sudden loss, and you were living with a guy, George Wilcox, who died suddenly. According to the police report, you were very broken up about it. Tell me about it. How did you deal with the loss?"

Monica looked alarmed—a little unsure how to start.

Bill jumped in. "I knew George, and the police report was right. His death tore Monica up."

Judy tried to shift the focus to Monica. "George's mother told me her first reaction was disbelief. What about you?"

Monica finally spoke up. "It was incredibly hard. Me and him had been living together for almost a year. I felt incredibly lucky. He was real popular. I was lucky to be his girlfriend. I thought he was going to propose. I loved him, and I probably would have said yes. Then it was all cut off. It was hard to deal with it."

George started to squirm. *She's such a liar. Why is she telling this story? There was no way I was thinking of proposing, and she knew it.*

Bill interrupted again. "I happened to be across the hall when the police came, and I went to console her."

Monica took Bill's hand across the table. "Yes, Bill, you were wonderful."

Judy plowed ahead. "Was his death related to his work? I mean, working as a private detective might have been dangerous."

"I don't think so. Maybe. Actually, he didn't talk about his work much."

"So, his murder came completely out of the blue."

"Yes, one day everything was wonderful, and then your whole world gets turned upside down. I'm not sure I know how I made it through the first weeks. Bill was a great help, and slowly I healed. I can tell you it would have been easier if I'd been included by his family. Me and them never got along. I sat with Bill in the last row at his memorial service."

Judy asked a couple more questions before saying her goodbyes. She didn't obtain any useful information. It was very clear Bill Sawyer had moved on Monica right after George had been shot. It looked like he was a more interesting suspect than Monica. What didn't make sense was Monica's claims she and George were so much in love. *Maybe her ego wouldn't let her tell anyone a guy would break up with her.*

Chapter Twelve

THE NEXT MORNING, THEY FILLED Clarice in on what they'd discovered about Monica and Bill.

"So, Bill is the better suspect?" Clarice asked.

"Yes, he lived one floor below. I found it unusual he was right outside Monica and George's apartment when the police came to tell Monica about the killing. How could he know what was going on? It looks suspicious. George told me he'd been interested in Monica for a long time. When they were dating, she told him not to worry."

"I expect Monica was already trying to land someone," Clarice said. "George was breaking up with her. Maybe she was already cheating on him with this rich guy, Bill. Did you have the feeling she was being unfaithful? Particularly after you broke up with her."

`maybe isn't the guy the last to know`

"Clarice might be right, George. If Monica had a notion things weren't going well with you, my guess is she's the kind of girl who can get a guy on the hook when she wants to. Was she going out with someone when you started dating her?"

He went to the Y key.

"Tell us about it."

```
her guy got drunk so I consoled her
only first runner up
```

"Oh, I get it," Clarice responded. "It's every guy's fantasy—consoling the girl who didn't win the beauty pageant. George, you dog. You swooped in when the other guy blew it. You offered a shoulder to cry on. Then one thing led to another, and you were Monica's beau right from that moment. Smooth."

```
close not that simple
```

"It proves my point," Judy commented. "Monica isn't the kind of girl who spends much time without a boyfriend. When things started to sour with you, she probably set her sights on Bill and his money. I can't say he looks very appealing, but Monica would be attracted to the money."

"Aren't we all, a little bit anyway. There's a problem with this line of thinking. We are talking ourselves out of Bill as a good suspect. If he was going to inherit Monica when George kicked her out, why would he bother killing him?"

"Maybe Monica was so mad at George, she wanted Bill to kill him. That way he'd prove he was worthy. Nothing like committing a murder to show you're serious about someone. And it would appeal to Monica. She'd have something to hold over Bill. George is probably the only guy who's ever broken up with her. Maybe she was feeling a little down and wanted more security in the new relationship. If she tires of Bill, she might still like his money. She would be able to blackmail him."

Judy stood up and paced around the living room and then returned to the table. "I'm not sure all the speculation is getting us anywhere. We only know a couple of things. First, Monica is a liar. She didn't tell the truth, to the police when they told her about George's death or to me yesterday. There's no way he was in love with her. They broke up, and he was kicking her out of his apartment. Second, we know Bill always had the hots for her, and he hooked up with her right after the murder. It's not much to go on."

Clarice rose and stretched. "Did you get the mail yesterday?"

"I completely forgot about it. Do you want me to go down and get it?"

"No, I'll go."

George watched the cat track Clarice to the front door. When Jangles was not allowed to follow out the door, George got nervous. With Clarice out of the apartment, the cat seemed to pay more attention to him. He didn't like it.

Clarice came back to the apartment excited. "I have something for you, Judy."

"What? I never get any mail."

"It's from Brad." Clarice held out an envelope.

Judy grabbed the envelope and ran into her room.

George jumped up and down, and Clarice came to help him.

`what's up who's Brad`

"Let me fill you in. Brad is Judy's soldier boy. The way I understand it, Brad was a friend of Judy's older brother. Brad and the brother are two years older than Judy. Anyway, from a very young age, creepy young if you ask me, Judy had a thing for Brad. He didn't pay any attention to her until she showed up at Ohio State. Then they started to date. She was a freshman and he was a junior. It got real serious real fast. They had a lot of common background. The only conflict they had was about Brad's ROTC stuff. Judy's not enamored of the military, and she didn't want Brad to go that direction. While they had some big fights, Brad stayed in ROTC and was commissioned at graduation. The funny thing is, they didn't ever really break up. They still write some, and they've seen each other a few times like at Christmas in Toledo. I wonder what this letter's about. Brad's in Afghanistan. At least, that's the last place I heard about."

A few minutes after Clarice finished her explanation, Judy walked out of her bedroom with an odd look on her face. "He's coming to visit, and he'll be here tomorrow."

"Tomorrow?"

"Yes, the mail from Afghanistan doesn't get here very fast. I have to clean up. What do I do with the cage? How do I explain the elephant dung in the refrigerator? Will Brad fit on the couch in the living room? I wonder why he's coming. He hinted he had some big announcement."

"Slow down girl, you have too many questions. He'll fit on the couch, at least if it's where you want him to sleep."

"I don't know."

"We'll cross that bridge when we come to it. Your questions about George are tougher. Let me just say I'm not moving his smelly cage in my bathroom. I'd move it into your bedroom unless there's a good chance Brad will be there. Did he say how long he'd be staying?"

"No. Oh my God, he'll be here tomorrow."

"I know you're excited. When's he getting here?"

"He asked me to pick him up at ten at the airport tomorrow morning. He's going to call tonight in case I didn't get the letter. I'm glad I did. I can be calmer when he calls."

The remainder of the day saw Judy madly cleaning every corner of the apartment. George felt very left out and somewhat annoyed. He, Clarice, and Judy had a good thing going. Until the letter from this guy Brad, they'd been focused on solving his murder. Now all progress seemed to have stopped. Also, he'd been the center of attention. Now he was in the way. He didn't like being a problem. *I guess I like being a novelty,* he thought. *A problem, not so much.*

Clarice told Judy she'd take George to church with her the next day. If they were at church, neither of them would be in the apartment when she and Brad returned from the airport. They spent a long time trying to figure out how to get a mid-day meal for George. After a search, Clarice found a small, shallow Tupperware box in a kitchen cupboard. She decided she'd put some dung in it and hide herself in a restroom between the service and the church lunch. Judy thoroughly cleaned the cage and put it on the far side of her bed.

For dinner they ordered Chinese delivery from their favorite place and stayed in. A Saturday night in the apartment was unusual for them, Clarice in particular. Her one boyfriend was away at the training camp for his professional football team, and the other one was still getting over one of their arguments.

When they'd finished eating, Judy spoke up. "I'm nervous as can be. You know, as much as I've tried, I've never been able to get Brad out of my head. It was so wonderful when we were dating in college. Now I don't know. This letter sounded different. He always used to tease me, asking me to come join him wherever he was. There was none of the teasing. I'm afraid he's going to tell me he's found someone else. He's too much of a gentleman to do it with a letter."

"Don't read too much into it. This letter was cryptic, if you ask me. I've read some of his other letters. They were more straightforward. Whatever happens, it will be good. If he is going to finally break up with you, it will be hard. In the long run, it might be better. You two have been playing footsie for so long, it's time for you to… what's the expression… fish or cut bait."

"I can't be philosophical about it. I don't want to break up with him." Judy teared up. "I don't know how I'd live without the dream of Brad."

Clarice came around the table and hugged Judy. "Whatever happens, I'll be here for you."

Judy stood up from the table and fled to her bedroom. Fifteen minutes later, they heard Judy's phone ring. While Clarice thoroughly expected Judy to come out and report on the call, she didn't show. Clarice had to tiptoe into Judy's bedroom to put George in his cage. Judy was sleeping soundly, so she didn't have any trouble.

The next morning, Judy was incredibly nervous. She left for the airport way before Clarice thought she needed to. At ten, with George in the pendant, Clarice headed off to church. George had never been to an African American church service before. His parents were Presbyterians, and he'd gone to church with them. In college, he attended church much less regularly. His Presbyterian upbringing didn't prepare him for what he saw. There's no way there had been any spontaneous outbursts of "amen" and "preach it, brother" in any service he'd ever been to. While he thought the theology behind the sermon wasn't anything to write home about, he thoroughly enjoyed himself.

Clarice managed to feed him after the service. Lunch for Clarice came next. Clarice had lots of friends, and they all came up to say they'd seen her on the evening news. George enjoyed seeing his old college classmate Rabbi Rock when he came to talk to Clarice. While he'd seen him up at the front of the church, he hadn't had a good view, and Simon hadn't had a big role in the service. George sensed Simon really liked Clarice. Still, there was a little reserve about her. It seemed like she wasn't sure she was ready to forgive him for something he'd done recently.

As they drove home, Clarice told George she wasn't sure what they'd find. Judy was so wound up about this visit, she didn't know what would happen. "Stay in the pendant and enjoy the show," she advised him.

Like I have a choice, George thought.

As they entered the apartment, he glimpsed Brad Curry before everything blacked out during the hug Brad gave Clarice. When he had a better view, he saw Brad was a good-looking guy with short Army-style blond hair. He was about five ten or so and wasn't wearing a uniform.

Clarice and Brad caught up with one another—Brad telling her about a mutual friend he'd run into, and Clarice telling him about her new job.

While Brad and Clarice talked, Judy sat in silence, holding Brad's hand and giving him an adoring look. From what he could see, he was sure Brad hadn't come to break up with Judy. The big news Brad told Clarice was he planned to leave the Army in a month. He was visiting to use up the last of the leave he'd accumulated.

The more George looked at Brad, the more he thought the guy was certainly jumpy. He couldn't sit still. He was up and off the couch several times, once to get a drink of water and once to look out the window. It continued as the three friends talked. He also had some odd twitches. Though he disguised them fairly well, George saw them.

The most alarming thing George learned was Brad planned to stay for at least a week, maybe longer. Last night, they'd planned to keep him a secret during Brad's visit. There was no way they'd be able to keep it up for a week or more. Maybe they had enough food for him; he didn't know. Surely Brad would notice the hamster cage. It was right beside Judy's bed, and given the look on Judy's face, he was pretty sure she'd be sharing the bed with Brad sometime during the week, maybe tonight.

Judy must have had the same thought. She got up and walked to her computer on the kitchen table. "Come here Brad, I have something extraordinary to show you. Clarice, you come too and bring exhibit A."

When they were all assembled, she continued. "As you know, I recently came back from a safari in Botswana. I brought an amazing thing with me. Clarice, show Brad what's in the pendant."

Clarice opened the pendant, and George walked out onto the laptop's keyboard.

Brad looked confused. "You brought a bug from Africa?"

"Hold the questions for a while, Honey. This isn't just any old bug. It's a dung beetle. Actually, he prefers to be called a scarab."

Brad broke in. "How…"

Judy gave his hand a squeeze. "Let me explain. George, that's his name. George has been reincarnated as a dung beetle, and he still remembers his previous life."

"You're crazy," Brad blurted.

"Let me tell you, I thought so too," Clarice explained. "Wait Brad, we can show you it's true."

"How the hell…"

"George, say something to Brad."

He hopped on the keys and Judy typed for him.

`welcome to cleveland brad`

"How does that show me anything?"

"Look closely, I'm only pushing the keys he's indicating. Say something else, George."

This time Judy waited so it was clear George had indicated the key before she typed.

`it's true`

"How are you doing that?"

"You sound like me," Clarice said. "I didn't believe it either. I was sure Judy was spoofing me. I even made her strip to show she wasn't wearing a wire. Judy, let him type. It's what convinced me."

"Just type what George indicates with his little nods."

Brad replaced Judy in front of the computer with a skeptical look on his face.

`judy wonderful girl`

Brad stood up in utter amazement. "What the hell?"

"Ask him a question," Clarice prodded.

"Why did you pick these girls?"

`luggage tag said cleveland`
`clarice part of package`

"I get it," Judy said. "He had been looking around for someone from Cleveland, and he saw my luggage tag. Brad, let me tell you how I met George. One night I came to my tent and there was a message on my computer. It said, 'don't squash me.' When he had my attention, I saw him lift his big dung ball and drop it on keys to say something else. While I was sure it was some kind of prank, it wasn't. This little beetle is George Wilcox from Shaker Heights, and he was killed a year and a half ago. One of the things he had me do was Google him. He knows a lot about George Wilcox, and it all checked out when we got here. It's amazing."

Brad stood up and walked to the couch. After a brief pause, Judy followed. "I know it's a lot to swallow, reincarnation as a dung beetle isn't what you'd expect. Still, we couldn't hide it. I don't want to start our new relationship hiding anything from you."

Brad chuckled. "Things are changing for me too, but I've got nothing like this. It's really weird."

Judy and Clarice filled Brad in on what they knew about the murder. It took quite a while with all the details they had from the police report, George's memory, Judy's talks with his mom, and Monica and Bill.

"So, you know quite a bit," Brad commented. "Unfortunately, you don't really have many real leads yet."

"No, it's frustrating."

Chapter Thirteen

GEORGE WOKE UP WHEN IT was dark in the apartment. His cage was being carried out of Judy's room. Whoever was carrying him didn't hold the cage completely steady, and with nothing to hold, he found himself rolling around. *What the hell*, he thought. The cage steadied when whoever it was finally put it down.

When the light from the computer screen gave him a chance to see what was going on, he saw Brad was carrying his cage. After getting Word up on the screen, Brad opened the cage door, and he walked out and flew to the keyboard.

"What's it like to die?" Brad whispered.

`don't remember`

"When did you remember who you were? I mean, when you were a larva, or when you were a full-grown beetle?"

`full grown`

Brad left the computer, and George saw him go to look out the window. Returning to the computer Brad asked, "Was it sudden or did it take time? Remembering, I mean."

He paused before starting to type. He didn't have a distinct memory of waking up as a dung beetle. At the same time, he didn't remember much of the time when he felt like he was both a dung beetle and a human. He remembered rolling one of his imperfect dung balls and starting to wonder what the heck he was doing. He started to type.

`not instant but fast`

"Were other dung beetles reincarnated humans?"

`no way to tell`

"Makes sense. I don't suspect dung beetles have a way of communicating with each other. Do they?"

`if they do nobody told me`

"Fair enough. So, what made you decide to find Judy? I guess it wasn't Judy specifically. You were looking for someone headed to the states. I guess Cleveland. And what made you think of dropping your dung ball on the keys?"

`too light had to communicate`

"I see. You weren't strong enough to make the keys work. I thought you guys are strong, aren't some of the dung balls bigger than you are? I've seen videos of dung beetles rolling big balls of dung and lifting them. I'm surprised you weren't able to make the keys work."

`strong lift weak push`

Brad got up and checked the windows and the rest of the apartment. George was amazed at how silently Brad moved around the apartment. When Brad returned to the computer, George indicated he wanted to type.

what you do in afghanistan

"I was a platoon leader with a company trying to help the Afghani army. It was a bonehead move when we befriended some of those warlords. Many of the guys the Afghanis sent us to train were real lowlifes. Guys who were not good enough to be in any Army. While we were trying to get those guys in shape, some other guys, Taliban loyalists I guess, were ambushing us and putting IEDs in the road. I was scared the whole time. We lost some really good guys. I wonder if they're dung beetles now."

Brad paused, thinking about what he just said. "If they ended up dung beetles, I'd have liked to have seen the look on some of those guy's faces. Many of them were very devout Christians and being a dung beetle isn't their idea of heaven."

hoping just a stage

"You mean like purgatory?"

George went to the Y key.

Brad did another walk around the apartment. It was starting to get light, and he spent quite a while at the window. When Brad returned to the computer, George was ready to type.

ptsd

"Is it obvious? Yeah, you're right. I started to get real jumpy a couple of months ago. I'd seen it happen to other guys. It's so weird over there. All the pressure. Guys dying. And all for what? I started to jump at my own shadow, and I guess you saw me scouting out the apartment. I haven't had an uninterrupted night's sleep in a long time. It's the big reason I'm getting out of the military. Actually, they're giving me the gentle shove. I'm being allowed to get a regular discharge. If I fought them, I'd be getting a medical discharge."

`any treatments`

"I've been to some talk therapy, and it helps some. The shrink who ran the program told me I wasn't the worst case he'd seen. While I might recover and be normal, there are no guarantees. The thing holding up my discharge now is the determination of disability. I'm going to be getting a rating. Most people with PTSD have some behaviors they can't get rid of. Actually, with me it's the stuff at night. I hide it fairly well during the day."

`mostly`

"Okay, so you had some suspicions. Maybe Judy does, too. I guess I should tell her. I really care for her. I guess love her. It's not fair to her if I try to hide something this big."

`bingo`

George watched as Brad stood up again and did a little tour of the apartment. He wondered if he'd given the right advice. Brad didn't look like the kind of guy who was used to admitting weakness of any kind. Still, he thought Brad should tell Judy. It was clear Judy was head over heels in love with him, and she needed to know. When Brad returned, George indicated he wanted to type.

`no expert`

"Neither am I. You're right. Judy needs to know. I'll be involved in some kind of therapy for a while. She needs to know about it. And I don't plan on spending any more nights on the couch. If I have to get up and stalk around the apartment while I'm sleeping in her bed, I'd better tell her. I guess I want her to know why I'm weird.

"Let's change the subject. What do you know about the night you were killed?"

`I was working`

"Judy or Clarice told me you don't remember that day. Maybe we can figure something out. If you were a private detective, you must have been doing work for someone. Maybe you were trying to get the goods on a cheating spouse. Maybe you were trying to find a missing person. I guess I don't know much about what private detectives do."

`notebook missing`

"Right, I remember, and you told us you wrote down your assignments and notes in the notebook and only gave your boss summary reports at the end. It seems weird to me for you to be so independent. Unless it was a big detective agency, it doesn't seem plausible."

`very loose outfit`

"Weird, all I'm saying is it's weird. Let's change the subject again. So far, you and Judy have only interviewed your parents, your old girlfriend, and her new boyfriend. It would be sensible to try to interview your enemies. There must have been some people you've crossed at work or at school or in other ways. Are there any people you can think of? I mean, while you may not have thought some arguments were anything big, the other people might have had a very different reaction."

`monica's old boyfriend`

"Makes sense. You moved in on his girl, and she's a real fox. At least that's the way I heard it. I'd say he should be a suspect. What's his name?"

`paul schreiber`

"Okay, he should go on the list. Who's next? There have to be other people you crossed. Maybe not like stealing girlfriends. Other things."

George thought about Brad's request. He thought of himself as a fairly laid-back guy. Though he had friends from college and lots of acquaintances, he couldn't come up with anyone who he'd call an enemy. It was the same thing from high school. Maybe his old high school girlfriend would fit. She'd tried to get back together with him when he came to Shaker Heights after Oberlin. He'd flat turned her down. He guessed he hadn't been very nice to her. She might qualify as an enemy. Brad looked impatient.

`old girlfriend`

"Name?"

`sandra locket`

"Good, we have two suspects. It's enough for a start. Think about it, George. You were murdered. Someone had to be really pissed with you to murder you.

`maybe work related`

"Maybe a cheating spouse caught you snooping. Right now, we've run into a dead end there. You can't recall anything about what you were doing the night in question. It's perfectly possible it was a previous case."

He thought back to his cases. When everything went right, the pictures told the story. He made reports to his boss, not the divorce lawyer, so his name didn't come up. The whole idea was for the suspects not to have any notion he had been following them or taking pictures. He didn't like dwelling on his failures. Finally, it came to him—the car dealer. He certainly saw him and was incredibly pissed.

`philip mcknight`

"So, he's a husband you caught cheating, and he might have it in for you. Right?"

George nodded next to the Y key.

"This is good, there are three names to look at. I guess I've just assumed I'd be allowed to help Judy with your problem. I never asked. I hope it's okay. The whole thing seems very important to Judy."

"Did I hear my name?" Judy asked as she walked out of her room.

She was dressed in her pajamas. As she walked over, Brad stood and hugged her.

"Talking to George, I see."

"Yes, he's a good listener. Not much of a talker. A good listener. We've been talking about the investigation of his murder. We've come up with three suspects—the guy who he stole Monica from, his old high-school girlfriend, and one of the guys he found cheating on his wife."

"Wow, you've made progress. I should have thought about the guy he stole Monica from. He told us the guy was drunk at the critical moment when Monica needed support, so he swooped in. Clarice's idea was he was living every guy's dream—consoling one of the losers in a beauty pageant. Monica was first runner up for Miss Cleveland. No doubt the guy was steamed when he got over his hangover. Who else do you have?"

Brad was about to show Judy the names when he realized "ptsd" was not far above the names. He closed the computer before Judy saw anything. "Let's get some coffee. I seem to remember you're a little happier in the mornings when you've had some coffee."

"Good idea."

George watched the two walk into the kitchen area and wondered if it was going to work out between them. He worried about Brad's PTSD. *It might be a real problem for them.*

Chapter Fourteen

GEORGE WAS A LITTLE ANNOYED when Brad seemed to want to take charge of helping him. Though he knew Army officers were take-charge guys, part of him resented it. The four of them, mostly the other three, decided Philip McKnight, the car dealer who'd caught him spying, was the most likely person to investigate. Clarice argued Monica's old boyfriend, Paul, wasn't as likely because of the time between George's offense and the killing was too long. By the same reasoning, Sandra was put on the back burner too.

"Let me see what I can find on the internet," Judy said.

She typed in 'Philip McKnight, Cleveland' into Google and came up with several entries. She decided to go to the oldest one first. It was a wedding announcement from five years ago, complete with a picture. The article described the marriage of Philip McKnight and Missy Jaye. It gave all the typical details about the bride's dress. There were relatively few details about Philip, except he was from North Olmsted and was employed at Jaye's Chevrolet. The picture showed a smiling young couple who looked very happy with each other.

George jumped on the keyboard.

```
married boss's daughter
```

"Looks that way," Brad commented. "The two of them look really young, maybe in their early twenties. The date on this story is five years ago, so you must have been trying to catch him cheating on Missy. Being caught cheating on his boss's daughter would be devastating for the guy. It looks like he lost his job as well as his wife. Let's see what we can find."

Judy scrolled through the stories, finding nothing. It turned out several of them were about a different Philip McKnight. Finally, she found a story about a shakeup in the management at Jaye's Chevrolet. Someone named William Burgess was promoted to Assistant Manager of the dealership. He was replacing Philip McKnight, who was leaving the company. Arthur Jaye, the founder and president of the company, had a lot of nice things to say about Mr. Burgess. He didn't say anything about McKnight.

"Look at the date," Brad exclaimed, getting up excitedly. "If I'm doing my math right, it's less than a month after George was killed. It fits."

"Your math is right, Brad," Clarice said. "I have to go to work now. I'd say you two should pump George for more details about what happened with Philip McKnight."

"You're right. What can you tell us?" Judy asked. "I'll type for you."

```
cheated on wife
```

"We thought so. Try to give us more information. Who did he cheat with?" Brad asked.

```
secretary dolly something
```

"Wow, a wife named Missy and a paramour named Dolly. Wasn't this guy interested in any women with real names?" Judy asked.

"Wait a minute, Honey. Isn't it unfair to blame the girl for her parent's choice? You can't help what your parents name you."

"At least Missy is clearly a nickname. If I'd been given that nickname, I'd have ditched it as soon as I had a chance. Clearly before any marriage."

ok judith

"Brad, don't you dare laugh."

"You typed it," Brad responded, giggling despite himself.

Judy abandoned the keyboard and aimed a playful slap at Brad, which he blocked as he grabbed her. They both wound up on the carpet, rolling around and laughing. George watched them and noticed how jealous he was. He felt good about finding Judy and being in Cleveland. While everything was going well, it wasn't the same. He was still a dung beetle.

Judy and Brad left George on the keyboard and went into Judy's room. He knew two things. First, he knew what was likely to happen between Brad and Judy. Second, he knew he'd have to watch out for the cat. Before he was able to tell whether his first hunch was right, he knew his second one was. The cat was making stalking moves toward the table. Not taking any chances, he flew up to the top of the curtains.

An of hour later, Brad and Judy came out of the bedroom looking very pleased with themselves. When they came near the table, George flew down to the keyboard.

don't leave alone with cat

"Oh gosh, I'm so sorry, I forgot," Judy said. "Brad, I should have told you. Jangles doesn't get along with George. She tries to attack him any chance she gets. I had to put her in Clarice's room the first day, and Clarice corrals her when she's here. It's a good thing he can fly."

"I didn't know dung beetles could fly."

"They can, and it's come in handy. I let him loose in the hardware store where his old girlfriend Monica works, and he was the one who found out about the new boyfriend. Also, we were worried about airport security on our return from Africa. He flew by the security, so it was no sweat."

"I can see how his flying ability and his size will come in handy when we look into Philip McKnight. He was a detective before, and I guess he can be again—a dung beetle detective."

"Let's fix lunch and then we can figure out how to find Mr. McKnight. Also, George has to eat."

At lunch, he still formed a ball and rolled it around his cage. Brad and Judy were watching, but he wasn't able to stop what he was doing. Brad asked where Judy procured his elephant dung. Judy gave a long explanation, including the story about how they were separated as they exited the Cleveland airport, and how she found him at the zoo.

When the lunch dishes were done, Brad retrieved George from his cage and headed toward the computer. Judy intercepted him with a wet paper towel and told him to have George wipe his feet before he went to the keyboard.

"Okay," Brad said when they were all in place. "How do we go about this? We need a way to find Philip McKnight."

George indicated he wanted to type.

`bill collectors`

Though Brad looked puzzled, Judy perked up. "I get it. He's suggesting we pretend to be bill collectors. It would be easy for us to approach Jaye Chevrolet to ask if they had an address for Philip McKnight who listed them as his employer on a loan application three years ago. Something along those lines? Right?"

George went to the Y key.

"Cool. We'll need to fake some ID badges. It won't be hard. Quick, search for bill collectors in this area, and we'll use a name that's close. I can print up something real official looking. We can get them laminated, then scuff them up, and we'll be ready to go."

"You're really into this!" Judy exclaimed, getting up and putting her arms around Brad.

"Yes, I am. Now get moving on finding bill collector names."

When Judy sat at the computer, George directed her.

`tell him not troop`

Judy paused for a moment, then laughed. "George says you shouldn't be giving me orders like I'm one of your troops."

"Okay. Point taken. Will you please find the bill collector names?"

Judy smiled and turned to the computer. She found several bill collectors and looked at a couple of their webpages. They chose the Haggerty Agency whose logo featured a large H. Brad took the computer and mocked up an ID card with a large boldface H for the Harcourt Agency. He made two cards, one with a male name and one with a female name. When he was happy with what they looked like, he shrank them to the appropriate size, and Judy showed him how to work the printer.

When they had a couple of copies, Brad was ready to head out the door. Judy stopped him before he made it to the door. "You're not dressed like a bill collector. Do you have anything better?"

"Oh, you mean like a coat and tie?"

"Yeah, something more business-like. You're going into someone's workplace and asking questions. You need the right outfit."

"Now we have two stops to make—one to laminate the IDs and one to buy me some clothes. That it, Boss?"

"I'm no more the boss than you are."

After they made their two stops, they drove to Jaye Chevrolet. Brad parked, and Judy and George got out and went into the show room. They'd decided to disguise the fact they were together, so Brad stayed in the car for five minutes. They wandered around looking at the new cars and when they had a chance, the secretaries. George didn't recognize the woman in the pictures he'd taken of Philip. A little later, Brad walked in.

Brad went up to the receptionist and flashed his newly scuffed up ID.

"I'm Bill Philips, with the Harcourt Agency, and I need to find one of your employees."

The receptionist, who couldn't have been out of high school long, looked unsure of herself. "Who are you looking for?"

"Philip McKnight. He listed you guys as his place of employment on a loan he took out with one of our clients."

"Oh, Mr. McKnight no longer works here."

Brad tried to look disappointed. "Is there anyone here who might know where I'd be able to find him?"

Pausing for a moment, the receptionist responded, "Yes, yes there is. Miss Jaye works in the front office. I can see if she's busy."

Miss Jaye, Brad thought. *She must be McKnight's ex. She probably dropped his name after she divorced him.*

The receptionist stood and indicated for Brad to follow. Judy and George saw them going into the offices and wondered what the heck was going on. Judy got tired of brushing off salesmen, so she decided to go to the car to wait for Brad.

After Judy'd been in the car for a while, she looked at her watch. "He's been in there for almost ten minutes. What the hell is he doing?" When there was no response, Judy laughed at herself. *I'm acting like George might respond. Of course, he can't.*

Five minutes later, Brad came out with a piece of paper in his hand. "You wouldn't believe who I just talked to."

"Philip McKnight."

"No, his ex-wife, Missy. She works here with her father. She gave me an earful about Philip. As well as her definite opinions. I have his address, his current place of employment, and also the name of the secretary he was cheating with. Missy thinks they're living together. It was amazing how much she was willing to tell a complete stranger."

"It was the tie, Dear."

"Whatever, I'd say we were a big success," Brad proclaimed as he started the car.

As they drove off the dealership's lot, Judy spoke up. "Now what do we do? Our bill collector routine worked excellently. We have his address and even more. Now we should figure out a way to approach him. I mean, if we were the police, we'd ask him, what were you doing on a certain night, or we'd get a warrant and search his house. We're not the police. We need a strategy. Any thoughts?"

"I guess you're right. While I was thinking we would look at the house where he lives and the place where he works, I didn't have a firm plan."

"Okay. Let's see what we find. Maybe we'll come up with some ideas when we're on the way. Let me see those addresses, I can put them in my phone."

After Judy entered the address of the car lot where McKnight worked, she opened the pendant and George walked out and flew up to the dashboard.

"Since we're going to be driving for a while, he likes riding there better."

"I can see how it makes a difference. We might actually get out at the car place. I turned in my leased car before I went to Afghanistan, so I'll need some wheels. I can start my search there. You'll have to put him away when we're looking at the cars."

When they arrived at the address, they almost missed the used car lot. It was a big step down from Jaye Chevrolet. There were probably fifteen cars and a little office. Most of the cars were on sale, according to the signs on their windshields. Brad pulled into one of the three customer parking spaces. As they parked, George flew down to Judy's hand, and she put him in the pendant.

They wandered around the lot for several minutes before Philip McKnight came out of the office and approached them. George thought he looked like a used car salesman, cheap suit and all. He looked a little heavier than he remembered—not fat, just heavier. As he came up to Brad, George saw they were about the same height.

"What can I help you with?" Philip asked.

"I'm getting out of the Army soon, and I'll need something. I'm starting to look. I'd like a sedan, nothing too big or too expensive."

"Come right this way."

Philip showed Brad several cars. Judy trailed along, acting interested. Brad tried to get Philip to open up about himself with little success. He revealed he'd been working at the lot for eight months, and he trusted the owner. As he emphasized, the lot had been in business for twenty years and always stood behind its cars. When Brad asked him what he did before he worked for this lot, McKnight was evasive. After a half hour, Brad thanked Philip for his help, and the three of them drove away.

Brad asked Judy to put in the address for Philip's house. "I'm not sure we'll learn anything there. At least we should look."

"This is where George can really come in handy," Judy commented. "Though it would look suspicious if we went looking into the windows, he can. It's even possible he might be able to crawl into the house somehow. Get close, and we'll let him out. All we have to do is figure out a rendezvous spot and an approximate time."

When they reached the address, they found an unimpressive ranch style home from the forties or fifties. The lawn was a mess, and the house needed a new roof.

As Judy was opening her window, Brad commented, "This is several steps down from the house of an Assistant Manager at a car dealership."

"No doubt. Okay, George, we'll park by the neighbor's house in twenty minutes."

George flew out Judy's window. His nose was assaulted by the smell coming from the house. It was wonderful to have a keen sense of smell in Africa. It didn't help so much here. He flew up to the big window to the right of the door. The curtains were parted, so he looked inside. As he suspected, it was the living room. It had a couch, two chairs, and a big TV. He thought the TV might be the only thing Philip kept from the divorce. The next window, probably a bedroom, revealed a closed curtain. Closed curtains frequently thwarted him as a private detective. At the back of the house, he hit the jackpot. The glass was out of the window there and the cardboard patch wasn't secure. He was able to scramble through and get into the house.

He found himself in a bedroom currently being used as a junk room. There was a pile of cardboard boxes in one corner, a bicycle, which didn't look like it had been used in a while, a couple of pieces of broken furniture, and a stack of papers. Luckily, he was able to make his way under the door to the hallway. The bedroom with the closed curtains was nothing special. The bed was big, probably a king, maybe another thing Philip took from the divorce. There were clothes scattered on the floor, all male as far as he could see. He flew past the bathroom. He couldn't make himself look inside because it smelled so awful. He ended up in the living room. From there, he followed his nose into the kitchen. It was a mess. Either Dolly wasn't much for housework, or she didn't live there. There was a small den or office across from the living room. It had a very cluttered desk and an overstuffed chair. There was a small porch off the den. He didn't know what he'd learned or how much time it had taken, but he felt like leaving.

As he was flying through the living room, the front door opened. George flew to the hallway.

Philip was on his phone as he walked in. George heard Philip clearly. "Dolly darling, please reconsider. You know I love you. The house seems so empty, and I feel so empty. I'll never be rough with you again."

He didn't hear what Dolly was saying. Finally, Philip responded, "Listen, let me take you out to dinner tonight. Seven o'clock at the Metropolitan. You don't have to make any promises. We can just talk."

Philip paced as he listened, then he smiled. "Great, see you then."

Philip disconnected his phone and headed toward the kitchen. George hoped he was going to clean up. He didn't stick around to see. He made it into the spare bedroom and escaped under the cardboard cover on the broken window. When he flew around the house, he didn't see the car with Brad and Judy. He landed on a tree branch close to where he thought he was supposed to meet them.

After ten minutes, he understood why they hadn't shown up. Brad and Judy would be afraid of Philip recognizing their car. He was a car salesman, and they were probably trained to notice the cars prospective clients were driving. It would often help them put the car they were trying to sell in context. *If they were afraid to come here, where would they be?*

He flew to the next block. At the first cross street, he saw Judy's car parked on the side and flew in the window.

When he landed on her hand, Judy spoke up. "Oh George, I'm so happy to see you. Luckily, we were behind Philip and saw him go into his house. Brad didn't want to wait near his neighbor. Phillip might recognize the car. You should also note Brad told me you'd be smart enough to realize what happened and smart enough to find us. He was right."

Chapter Fifteen

AT HOME, BRAD AND JUDY quizzed George. "Tell us what the house was like," Brad asked.

`messy bachelor pad`

"So, Dolly doesn't live there anymore?"

He went to the Y key, and then indicated he had more.

`phoned dolly tried reconciling`

Judy asked, "Did you get any details?"

`dinner 7 tonight metropolitan`

Brad stood and started one of his patrols around the apartment. "Judy, do you know the Metropolitan? I presume it's a restaurant."

"No, let me look it up."

After a few minutes, Judy reported, "It appears to be a nice enough place. Come look."

Brad came over, and George flew to Judy's shoulder. They saw pictures of an upscale restaurant featuring lots of ferns in planters separating the tables. There were also hanging plants overhead.

"The patrons must feel like they're eating in a jungle," Brad commented. "Want to try it out?"

"Aren't you afraid Philip would recognize us?"

"Yeah, he might. It wouldn't be a big deal. Coincidences happen. We'd be able to laugh about it. There's no reason to be concerned."

"Okay, and it will be a great place for George to eavesdrop on their conversation. When they're seated, I can drop him off in one of the plants. As you mentioned, the place looks like a jungle. He'll be able to spy on them for their whole dinner. What about it?"

`sounds great`

Brad took charge at this point. "Good, he's on board. Now I need to talk with you, Judy. Let's go into the bedroom. Give him something, so he is well fed before we go to the restaurant."

Judy put George in his cage, which still sat on the kitchen table, and gave him a big spoon full of elephant dung. He started forming it into a ball. It was crazy. For some reason, he had to do it. As he rolled the ball around, he watched Brad and Judy head into the bedroom. By the tone of Brad's voice and his overall nervousness, George knew this was going to be the PTSD talk. He was curious about how Brad was going to approach the topic. It wouldn't be easy, and he wondered how Judy would take the news. Given Brad's restlessness and occasional twitches, she might already have a clue.

A half hour later, Judy came out of her room looking serious. She walked to the refrigerator, took out two beers and returned to the bedroom without giving George as much as a nod. *At least they're still talking*, he thought.

An hour later, both of them came out. Judy had changed into a dress, and Brad had removed his tie. They were recognizable as the two people who'd been car shopping. Judy came up to the cage and opened the door.

After leaving his cage, George wiped his feet and washed around his mouth on the wet paper towel Judy offered.

"Great, George," Judy said. "We need you to remove all the evidence of elephant dung. If you're going to be lurking near where people are eating, we don't want them to smell you. I wore this dress because it has a sash. You can hide in the sash and then jump off when we get near Philip and Dolly's table. I'm not going to wear the pendant tonight. It's too distinctive. I'll put you under the sash when we get to the restaurant. We've made reservations for six forty-five, so we'll be there before Philip and Dolly."

Brad came up to George. "Judy and I had a long talk. Now she knows about my PTSD, and she has decided not to kick me out. She's going to come to a couple of my therapy sessions. I thought you'd like to know."

Brad sat down, ready to type.

`you're lucky guy`

"I know I am. She's absolutely wonderful." Brad put his arm around Judy, who'd come up beside him.

"I want to go through it with Brad. He's going to make a full recovery."

`write story about it`

"George! You're so clever. It would make a great story. I'd do it first person. PTSD is a huge problem in today's military. While I guess it was a big problem before, it wasn't recognized. Researching for the story would make it easier for me to help Brad. It's perfect."

She turned to Brad. "You wouldn't be bothered if I followed his suggestion, would you? I'd let you see the story before it went to any publisher."

Brad seemed a little hesitant. Finally, he spoke up. "I guess that's what I get for falling for a freelance writer. Sure, but I'll hold you to your promise to let me review the story before it gets published."

At six-fifty, they pulled up to the restaurant. In the parking lot, Judy loosened her sash, and George burrowed in. Judy looked down and tightened the sash a little. "No one can see you. Everything is working."

Brad asked for a table near the door and sat so he had a view of both the door and the interior of the restaurant. When they were seated, Judy excused herself and went to the restroom. As she expected, she did not see Philip or Dolly.

She returned to the table and sat down. "They aren't here yet."

"We're five minutes or so before their seven o'clock reservation. I didn't order anything for you to drink. The waitress told me she'd be back when you returned. The menu looks interesting."

The waitress returned to the table just as Philip and Dolly came up to the hostess. They didn't notice Brad and Judy as they followed the hostess to a table a couple of rows away.

Brad said, "Why don't we go up to Philip and say what a coincidence it is to see him. You can sidle up to the plants near their table, and George can jump out. Move him to the side so it won't be difficult for him."

Judy thought she looked weird as she adjusted the sash. No one seemed to notice.

When they returned to their seats from the somewhat awkward conversation with Philip and Dolly, Judy was sure George had made his escape from the sash onto the plants where they wanted him.

George looked through the leaves at Philip and Dolly. He didn't really recognize Dolly. He hadn't had a chance to take any pictures of her from this close. She was a little trashy looking—blonde hair with visible dark roots, too much eye makeup, and very bright lipstick. Her most prominent feature was her large breasts, what his friends would have called *bazooms*.

For the first part of his stay, they didn't say much. They ordered drinks, a Tom Collins for Philip and a whiskey sour for Dolly, and then looked at the menu. After they ordered, they sat in silence. The silence continued as they started on their drinks.

Finally, Dolly spoke up. "Look, you wanted this dinner. Tell me why I should take you back. You hit me. A woman would be a fool to stay with a man who'd hit her. I should know. I've seen what my mother has to put up with."

"Hitting you was a huge mistake. I'd had a terrible day at the lot. A whole bunch of people like the bozo who came up to introduce himself. They just want to look around. They aren't really interested in buying. I waste so much time with guys like him. I'd even done three test drives during the day and didn't sell a thing. You have no idea how frustrating it can be. And then you didn't have dinner ready. I snapped. I'll never do it again."

"That's what they all say."

"Ever since the private detective took those pictures of us, my life has been going to hell. You're the only good thing that's happened to me in the last two years. I can't go on without you. I swear, I'll never hit you again. Come home with me. I've cleaned it up for you. I know I have a temper. I also know how to control it."

Dolly laughed. "I know all about your temper. Actually, it started with the private detective. I remember when you came back from trying to catch him. You were so mad you were shaking. What would you have done if you'd caught him?"

"Beat him up for sure. I wanted to kill the guy at the time, and I might have. I tried to find his name. Even though I tried hard, I never found him."

"I saw your temper again when your wife kicked you out. To tell you the truth, I've always been a little afraid of your temper. I thought it was okay because it wasn't ever directed at me. Until last month."

"I'm better now. And I know what a big mistake I made. I love you, Dolly. You have to come back to me."

"We'll see."

Silence returned and continued when their meals had been delivered. George had probably learned all he needed. Philip wasn't a good suspect. *He didn't even find out who I was.* It was boring watching them eat. He turned around and saw the people getting up from the table behind him. A few minutes later the table was bussed and cleaned. He turned to Philip and Dolly. Philip was still trying to get her to come live with him again, and she seemed to be giving in. She had a whole list of ultimatums for him, and he caved, agreeing to all of them. Since things looked better to him, it was clear Philip was eager to get out of the restaurant. When they got up to leave, George turned around again.

A family with young children was getting seated at the vacant table behind him. As he was turning in their direction, a little girl shouted, "Look, there's a bug in the plant!"

The little girl's father turned to look at George and started to get up.

George panicked and flew off and dove into one of the hanging baskets. A couple he flew over saw him, and the man made a swipe at him with his napkin. Several people seemed to have seen him, and they were shouting and pointing. A tall waitress was heading his way. He didn't feel safe in the hanging plant. Too many people saw him go in. When he heard someone pulling a chair close to where he was hiding, he flew out of the plant. He had to weave around the people who were trying to swat him with their napkins. Finally, he made it toward Brad and Judy's table. Thinking quickly, Brad stood up and opened the door, allowing him to fly out. He made it to the car and settled on the hood.

Thirty minutes later, Brad and Judy came out and let him into the car.

Judy remarked, "You caused quite a commotion in there. Though I'm sure you're not interested, people congratulated Brad for having the good sense to open the door. The restaurant comped us dessert. I shouldn't be eating desserts. In this case, I didn't put up any resistance. The creme brûlée was good."

George tried to calm down. He resented Judy taking the whole thing so lightly. He'd been incredibly scared. Some of those people came very close to him with their napkins. Judy and Brad probably didn't know how difficult it is to fly when people are interrupting the wind patterns by waving things. The whole incident was disturbing, and here they were laughing as if nothing had happened.

While he was steamed at Brad and Judy for their attitude, he wondered if he wasn't a little bit to blame. He was sure the little girl only saw him because he moved. It was a lesson learned. Actually, he already knew to avoid movement when he was hiding. Something moving is much easier to spot than something sitting still.

Chapter Sixteen

CLARICE WAS THERE WHEN THEY returned home. "Where were you guys?"

George waited patiently while Brad and Judy filled Clarice in on the day's events: deciding to investigate enemies, finding Philip's workplace and his home, eating at the same restaurant as Philip and Dolly, and his narrow escape from the waving napkins.

At the end of the briefing, Brad turned to George. "Did you find anything out before you were spotted?"

`not him`

"How do you know?" Clarice asked.

`mad at me couldn't find name`

"Incredible!" Judy exclaimed. "How did you find out? You weren't at their table long before you were spotted. I thought he was trying to get Dolly back. How did you figure out he wasn't the one who killed you?"

`temper he hit her`

"I might be able to piece it together," Brad said. "So our boy Philip hit Dolly, because he has a bad temper. And Dolly found out about the temper when Philip saw George taking pictures. One of them brought it up. He wrote, 'mad at me' up there."

George went to the Y key.

Brad continued, "So, Philip told Dolly he never found George's name. It means he couldn't have killed him. Somehow it came up in a discussion about Philip's temper. That's my guess."

`close enough`

"Wow Brad, you and George are simpatico!" Clarice exclaimed.

"Looks like it," Judy said. "It must be a male thing. They had quite a discussion last night. For a while, George knew more about Brad than I did."

"We've straightened that all out now, haven't we?" Brad commented, giving Judy a hug and a kiss.

"Get a room, you two!" Clarice said, laughing. "The way I see it, while we have one suspect we can scratch off the list, we still have a long list. We don't know about Monica, and what's his name, her new boyfriend, the guy George stole Monica from, and his old girlfriend from high school."

Judy extracted herself from Brad's embrace. "Clarice is right. The list is long. Who should we investigate next? You should choose, George."

`paul schreiber`

"He's Monica's ex, the one before you took over, right?" Brad asked.

George went to the Y key.

"Okay, let's see what we can find out about Mr. Schreiber. I'll Google him."

George flew to Judy's shoulder, and the other two hovered. Judy found quite a few entries for Paul Schreiber, Cleveland. The first was someone who sang in a rock band.

"Is this the guy?" Clarice asked, pointing.

George flew to the Y key.

"Whoa, he stole a rock star's girlfriend. Our boy must have had some moves."

"I wouldn't call this guy a rock star, Clarice," Judy said. "I've never heard of this band, The Wilted Roses. It looks like they're local, and there's nothing in this piece about them having any records. I'll Google the band name."

When Judy found the band's website, they discovered she was right. The band was four guys and a girl, all from the Cleveland area. The girl was the lead singer. The guys—two guitars, a backup singer, and a drummer—had spikey hair, clothes with unlikely vents, and sported numerous tattoos.

"Which one is Paul?" Brad asked.

`drummer`

"Let's listen to one of their songs," Clarice suggested. "They have a couple of demos you can click on. See, at the bottom of the page."

When the song finished, Judy spoke up. "The girl can really sing. Still, it doesn't work. The guys tend to drown her out, especially the lead guitar. I doubt they're destined for stardom."

"I agree," Clarice remarked. "If I was giving advice, I'd tell the girl to ditch these guys. You're right, she can really sing. I didn't recognize the song. Do you suppose one of them wrote it?"

"We're drifting off course here, ladies. It was easy to find Paul, and we can find where The Wilted Roses are playing. Their website listed upcoming performances."

"Yes, here it is," Judy responded. "They are appearing nightly for the next two weeks at someplace called the Road Station. Does anyone know where it is?"

"Yeah, I know it," Clarice volunteered. "It's on the east side. It's basically a bar, kind of a rough one. It's claim to fame is continuous live music after six. I've been there once. For a place advertising live music, the acoustics are pretty horrible. It's one of those places where it's impossible to carry on a conversation."

"We've been here in the past," Brad said. "When we figure out how to talk to Paul, we need a good reason to bring up George. As Judy mentioned before, we're not the police, so we can't just go up to people and ask them questions about a crime."

"Let's sleep on it," Judy said, grabbing Brad's arm and hauling him toward her bedroom.

"Are you sure you're going to sleep?" Clarice chortled.

"None of your business."

The next morning, Judy and Brad arranged to meet Clarice at the Road Station at nine-thirty that evening. Clarice told them the place wouldn't be too busy then. It was a late crowd.

The day dragged as far as George was concerned. Judy coaxed Brad to shop for more civilian clothes, and they left him behind. Staying in his cage so he wouldn't have any troubles with Jangles, he spent several hours trying to reconstruct the days leading up to his death. He didn't have any luck. He was unable to remember the case he was working on. It was a complete blank.

Before they left that evening, Brad changed into some of his new clothes, a nice French blue shirt and khakis, and Judy put on a pair of tight pants and a flashy top.

"What do you think?" Judy asked. "Don't we look like a couple of people going out to a dancing place? I can wear the pendant with this top."

In the car on the way, Brad spoke up. "Judy is going to use her freelance writing bit tonight."

"Yeah, I'm going to pitch a story about rock bands. I'll tell them there are lots of stories about bands who've made it. I'm going to say I'm writing about bands before they're a big success. It'll appeal to their ego. I can't say I'm doing a story about struggling bands. I have to make them believe I'm sure they'll be discovered."

It seemed sensible. George guessed he knew Paul had always wanted to be in a band. The Wilted Roses must have happened after he'd died. In truth, he'd been more interested in Monica than Paul when they'd first met. He didn't know him very well.

The parking lot for The Road Station was a big dirt field. There were no lines drawn. Still, the parked vehicles were more or less in rows. With George in the pendant, Brad and Judy walked toward the bar. They heard a band with its amps turned up before they were anywhere near the door. The band wasn't The Wilted Roses. When they entered, they learned the Roses were the next act.

"They're over there," Judy remarked as she nodded toward the side of the stage.

When the band stopped to scattered applause, silence descended. Brad and Judy seated themselves, again at a table where Brad had a good view of the room and the door. George thought it had something to do with his PTSD.

"Clarice isn't here yet," Brad commented.

"No, and this isn't the right time to approach the band. They look busy getting ready for their set."

A waitress came to take their drink orders. They ordered a small pitcher of beer, three glasses, and nachos. Judy knew the nachos would please Clarice. About fifteen minutes later, The Wilted Roses started playing. If anything, George thought their live performance was worse than the demo they'd listened to last night. Clarice arrived during the third song and dove into the nachos.

When the band finished their set, Judy joined a small crowd around the lead singer, Ginger Nichols. She was clearly the talent in the group, though the lead guitar guy did the introductions to their songs. In the pendant, George found it hard to really see anything because of the crowd of people.

Finally, Judy made it to the front of the crowd and spoke to Ginger. She pitched the idea of the story about as-yet undiscovered rock bands, and Ginger was intrigued. When Ginger understood what Judy wanted, she called over the lead guitar guy and explained the idea to him. Judy emphasized the importance of interviewing all members of the band, so the guitarist wouldn't think the story was just about Ginger. Following some discussion, they arranged for interviews at two the next day, an hour before the band's regular rehearsal. Judy wrote down the address and thanked them before rejoining Brad and Clarice.

While Judy had been talking, George caught a few glimpses of Paul. He seemed to be sharing his break with a good-looking, skinny, dark-haired girl. George only had fleeting views of her. It was frustrating. Just when he spotted Paul and the girl, Judy had turned so all he was able to see was the singer, Ginger. When the lead guitar guy came up, he had another shot at Paul and the girl. Then Judy moved again. He was disgruntled by the time he and Judy returned to the table.

Brad, Judy, and Clarice decided they'd leave when their beer was finished. Before then, a guy came up and asked Clarice to dance. She accepted and strutted out onto the dance floor. George watched Clarice dancing and was glad Judy was wearing the pendant. He would have been bounced to death on Clarice.

Two songs later, Clarice returned and told Brad and Judy she was going to join a group at another table. Brad and Judy said, "No problem. We're ready to leave."

In the car, Brad gave a big sigh. "Let's not go there again, okay Honey?"

Judy was busy taking George out the of the pendant. "I know. It was too loud. I thought you were getting really anxious."

"It was the noise and all the people, particularly toward the end when it filled up. It's going to be a while before I'll be comfortable in a place like that. I get nervous when I'm in a situation I can't control. I made myself sit there. I suspect you noticed I was sweating up a storm."

"I'm so sorry, I should have thought about it more."

"No, it's not your fault. I thought it wouldn't be a problem. I guess I was wrong. Let's say it's a lesson learned."

Chapter Seventeen

WHEN CLARICE WALKED OUT OF her bedroom the next morning, the others were at the kitchen table.

"Did you find boyfriend number three?" Judy asked with a smile.

"No, get me coffee. I need to move it. I'm already in jeopardy of being late. Any real news to report?"

"You know it all," Brad said as Judy stood up to get the coffee.

"Yeah, Judy's going to interview the band in the afternoon. Did George have any useful comments?"

"Not really. He told us it appears Paul has another girlfriend, and she doesn't look anything like Monica. That's all really. The place last night wasn't good for gathering information, too loud and too crowded."

"Okay, I'll see you tonight. I'm going to grab something at the Starbucks close to the station." Clarice put down her cup and headed toward her room.

Brad spent the morning on the phone trying to straighten out the paperwork he needed to complete for his discharge. When he finally succeeded, he learned he'd have to go to the recruiting office to sign some forms the officials were going to fax there. He and Judy conferred and decided he'd have to take an Uber. Brad couldn't be sure he'd be back before she had to leave for her interview.

After Brad left, George climbed on the keyboard, and Judy came to see what he had to say.

great guy

"I guess you can tell I agree with you. But I'm worried about him. PTSD is a tough diagnosis. I don't believe he has the worst case. Still, he was up wandering around the apartment several times last night. Maybe scouting is a better word than wandering. While he doesn't expect to find anything, he can't stop himself."

like me rolling my food

"It's not the same thing. Well, maybe it is. You don't seem to be able to stop rolling your food into a ball and fouling up your cage in the process. Could you stop, if you really tried?"

don't know

"My hope is Brad will be able to overcome PTSD. You'd think the effects of the trauma would dissipate over time. I'm going to look up the research to find out if I'm right. He just returned from Afghanistan. You, on the other hand, are a weird mix of human and dung beetle. There's no research to look up."

Judy switched to the internet and started to look up PTSD. Though some of what she found reminded her of Brad, much of it didn't. She wasn't aware of any flashbacks or nightmares, but she wasn't sure. Also, he seemed to be generally well adjusted, except for patrolling the apartment at night and maybe where he wanted to sit in crowded places. As far as she could tell, he didn't seem to be turning into an alcoholic. She was happy to find she was right. Often PTSD improved over time. Sometimes it didn't. It was disturbing to read about instances when

PTSD symptoms appeared quite a while after the trauma.

George, who'd been reading along with Judy, saw her switch to Word. She wanted him to be able to respond.

"Looks complicated to me. There are a large number of possible symptoms under the broad heading of PTSD. While Brad has some of them, he hasn't exhibited any of the most serious ones."

`yet`

"Don't be so pessimistic. While some of it is scary, he'll go to therapy. I believe he can lick it. The worst cases are ones where the person doesn't get help until way late. Brad was smart enough to know he was getting into trouble, and he's sought help. It was probably difficult. The standard military approach is to suck it up and not complain. I'm proud of Brad for resisting the standard approach. We'll get through this."

`good luck`

"Thanks, some luck would certainly help. Now we'd better eat lunch so we can make it to our interviews at two o'clock."

The address Ginger had given Judy turned out to be a slightly rundown-looking two-story house in an older neighborhood. It clearly needed a paint job and some of the shutters weren't hanging straight. The garage door was open, revealing it was the site of the band's practices. There was a drum set, some guitars on stands, amps, and speakers. There were three cars parked in the driveway. None of them were recent models.

At two on the dot, Judy approached the front door with George in the pendant. Ginger opened the door and invited her in. The first thing Judy saw in the house was the stairs to the second floor. Following Ginger, she turned left into the living room. Two of the guys in the band were there, sitting on a couch. Ginger offered Judy a seat in an overstuffed chair. As Judy sank in, she realized Paul wasn't one of the two band members present. The lead guitar guy, the one who played too loud, wasn't there either.

Ginger did the introductions. "Judy—it's Judy, isn't it?"

"Yes, Judy Clayton."

"So, this is Jim Henderson, he's our base guitarist, and this is Sammy Kindall. He does back-up vocals. Somebody has to make me sound good."

Judy shook hands all around and decided she'd start even if the whole band wasn't assembled. "I'm writing a story focused on new promising bands. It's easy to find stories about bands who have made it. Not many are written about bands before they get popular. I want to write a different story. I work freelance. I've been successful getting my stuff published in magazines. So, let me start with my first question. Who organized The Wilted Roses?"

After a pause, Ginger spoke up. "I guess we did—me and my brother Clint. He should be here in a minute or two. We liked music, and the band he played in broke up. Too many big personalities. Anyway, we decided to try to start a band about a year and a half ago. We knew these two from bumming around clubs, and they knew Paul. He's the drummer."

"Schreiber's always late," the backup singer, Sammy, commented.

"Who writes your songs?" Judy asked.

"I do," Ginger replied. "The guys improvise on the arrangements. It's a collaboration. We start off with a basic melody, and then in practice, we change it up until we have it right."

At that point, the front door opened, and Clint Nichols came in. Judy guessed Clint was Ginger's older brother, maybe by four or five years.

Judy continued with the next question. "Was it difficult to get bookings when you were starting out?"

Clint answered, "I had some contacts from other bands I'd played in. They helped. My little sister can really sing, and the rest of us are good too. At first, we didn't play very big places. Now things are looking up. You saw us at The Road Station. It's a big place. You get lots of exposure there."

As her questions continued, Judy got the impression Clint was the alpha male in the band. He was older than the others and jumped in with the answers. He even interrupted the others, rudely, Judy thought. When she finished her general questions, Judy asked to interview each band member individually.

In her separate interview with Ginger, Judy tried to gently hint she would be better off ditching the guys and going out on her own. Ginger was flattered by the line of questioning. In the final analysis though, it was clear in life, as well as on stage, she was dominated by her older brother. As she was finishing with Ginger's interview at two forty-five, a car pulled up outside. *I hope that's Paul Schreiber*, Judy thought. She had been starting to wonder if he'd ever show. While the interviews were mildly interesting, she'd arranged the whole thing to talk to him.

Judy was relieved when Paul came in the front door. After Paul was introduced to Judy, the others went to the garage to get ready for practice, so his being late worked to Judy's advantage. Judy and Paul were the only ones in the living room. George, who was getting thoroughly bored with the interviews, perked up. Paul hadn't changed much since he'd seen him last.

Judy asked Paul her normal set of questions very rapidly and then turned to something different. "I understand guys in rock bands have good luck with the ladies. I saw you with a nice-looking girl last night. Is it true?"

Paul looked a little sheepish. "I guess so."

"Someone told me you used to go out with a beauty queen."

"Your information is good. Yeah, Monica, she was a real babe. I dated her before I was in this band."

"Did you break up because of the band?"

"No, it was nothing like that. She was in the Miss Cleveland pageant, and at a little get together before the pageant, this guy, George Wilcox, spiked my drink, and I passed out. I woke up with a terrible hangover to find Monica was incredibly pissed at me. Wilcox had been there for her when she didn't win. She was only first runner up. She dumped me."

"Sounds terrible. Are you sure this guy spiked your drink?"

"Yeah, a friend of mine told me Wilcox was bragging about it a couple of months later. I always suspected something. I can hold my liquor."

"Sounds like this Wilcox guy was a jerk. Did you do anything to try to retaliate?"

Just as Paul was about to answer, Clint came barging in, yelling at Paul to get in the garage for practice. Judy was left with nothing to do as Paul rushed off to obey Clint. She didn't know what to make of Paul's claim about George spiking his drink. There wasn't any reason for Paul to be lying to her. She went out the front door and listened to the band through the garage door. The door's interference didn't really help the music, but it did dampen the sound, which Judy thought was a blessing.

On the drive home, Judy thought about what she was going to say to George when she made it to the apartment. *How will I react if he says he did spike the drink? Would it make any difference in the quest to find his killer?* Judy didn't know what to think.

George had questions too. *Should I confess to spiking Paul's drink? Would Judy believe Monica was in on it? The whole thing was so convoluted.* He didn't know how to proceed. He considered bluffing his way through it. He could say Paul was lying. In the end, he decided to tell the truth. He wanted to be straight with Judy.

Brad was at the apartment when they returned. After giving Judy a kiss, he announced, "I finished the paperwork. I'm a couple of steps closer to my separation from the Army. It feels good. How was your trip?"

"Until the very end, it was a waste of time."

"I don't get it."

"Let's extract George from the pendant, and I'll explain. Please grab me a drink of water."

Brad brought the water and came to sit by Judy, who was positioned in front of the computer. George sat near the keyboard.

"I went through the charade of interviewing the band. Some of it was interesting. Clint, he's the lead guitarist who plays too loud, is Ginger's older brother, and he dominates the band. While I sort of hinted to Ginger she'd be better off without him, it didn't go anywhere. Basically, The Wilted Roses are like a lot of other bands practicing in garages and playing occasional gigs. The interesting part came when I interviewed Paul Schreiber. He claimed George spiked his drink at a party before the beauty pageant. It's how George was able to move in on Monica. Is he right?"

`yes`

"Why'd you do it?" Brad asked.

"To get the hot girl. Isn't it obvious?" Judy replied.

`about to break up anyway`

"So, your claim is you were simply speeding along something destined to happen in any event," Brad conjectured. "The spiked drink just made certain it would look like Paul had let Monica down big time. It was the nudge she needed."

"Yeah, nudging her into your arms," Judy responded.

George heard the hostility in Judy's remark. He knew he was in hot water with her.

`she told me she liked me`

"That's no excuse for sabotaging her boyfriend. I have a difficult time feeling any sympathy for your position in this."

`ask monica about it`

Judy was about to respond when Brad put his hand out stopping her. "Are you saying Monica knew you were going to spike the drink, so she had an excuse to dump Paul?"

`exactly`

Silence descended for a few minutes. Finally, Judy spoke up. "You know we can try to verify your surprisingly shaky story. I mean it seems so farfetched. Monica tells you to spike Paul's drink, so he misses the pageant, and it looks like he's not supporting her. Frankly, I don't believe she's smart enough to be that devious."

`it's the truth`

"I can see where you're coming from, Judy. While I've not met Monica, I remember you told me George eventually dropped her because he claimed she was an airhead. What he's describing is perhaps a bit too sophisticated for an airhead."

George headed to the keys to respond.

"No, I'm not typing for you," Judy said. "We're going to have to figure out how to straighten this out. So far, I'm not buying your story."

That night George didn't sleep any better than Brad. He was really stung when Judy had refused to type for him.

Chapter Eighteen

THE NEXT MORNING, JUDY AND Brad told Clarice about George spiking Paul's drink before the beauty pageant and his claim Monica was in on the deal.

Addressing George, Clarice said, "It's all pretty farfetched. And the way I see it, even if it was all Monica's idea, you're not off the hook. It was just plain unfair to Paul. Mean. If Monica wanted to break up with him and hook up with you, why didn't she come out and tell him?"

"Clarice is right, George," Judy added. "I can't see how it's being Monica's idea helps your case. You should have told her to suck it up and dump Paul."

He didn't know how to respond, so he sat there with the girls and Brad staring at him. Following an uncomfortable silence, Judy sat down in front of the computer. "Are you going to say something? I cut you off last night. Maybe I shouldn't have. I was just disgusted."

`I made a mistake`

Silence returned. It was Brad who finally spoke up. "I don't know about you two, but I guess I'm willing to accept what he typed. Pretty girls can convince a guy to do stupid things. Wasn't it you, Clarice, who accused him of living the dream—getting to console the loser in a beauty pageant? You're right. It's something a lot of young guys would have jumped at."

"Yeah," Clarice responded. "And if Monica had won, he'd have the chance of being the boyfriend of Miss Cleveland. You're right, lots of guys would spike someone's drink or maybe even worse."

"Still, he wasn't right to do it," Judy concluded. "I don't care how beautiful Monica was, he did a really underhanded thing. It's part of the reason he's a dung beetle now. If he'd been a better human, he might have been reincarnated as an eagle or a lion or something more majestic than a dung beetle, even a dung beetle who wants to be called a scarab."

"Does it work that way, Judy?" Clarice asked. "The better person you are, the better your chances of being reincarnated as some cool animal?"

"I don't know. While I'm not sure, I think that's how it works with Hindus."

"I was about to say no offense intended," Brad said. "I guess it's not right, George. Given your current incarnation, if it works like Judy's suggested, you might have worse secrets than the one we've uncovered."

Judy and Clarice looked at him strangely, so Brad continued. "So, he's a dung beetle now. The way I see it, he's fairly low on the totem pole. Suppose, if he was a super person, he gets to be an eagle. I haven't thought this out all the way. Still, it seems like there are lots of slots between eagle and dung beetle. It seems maybe he'd be a crow, a cow, or a fish or something if the only thing he did wrong was spike Paul's drink. Dung beetle is too severe for only one misstep."

"I see what you're saying, Brad," Judy commented. "We're probably better off not trying to extrapolate too much. Maybe being a dung beetle is good. Maybe some people get to be worms or pond scum like amoebas or are never reincarnated at all. We don't have much to go on here. All we can conclude is—he was no angel."

`agreed I'm no angel`

"We're all onboard with your conclusion, George," Clarice said. "Also, it appears Monica's no angel either. She engineered or at least strongly encouraged the spiking of Paul's drink. A couple of days ago we thought maybe she'd talked Bill into killing you. There's a similarity there. We think Monica can be awfully devious."

"You're right, Clarice, we haven't eliminated her or her boyfriend Bill," Judy responded.

"How about George's old high school girlfriend, Sandra something?" Brad asked. "We haven't found out anything about her. I say we should look at all the possibilities before looking at anyone a second time."

`locket`

"He's right, Sandra Locket."

"Of course, he would know his old girlfriend's name," Judy commented. "I'll see what shows up for her on Google."

Sandra Locket, Cleveland, generated several Google hits, most involving shooting competitions. George verified his Sandra Locket was the shooter, so Judy opened one of the entries. Sandra Locket was listed as the winner of the women's pistol competition. Several of the other entries were similar. While Sandra didn't always win, she was often near the top. One of the stories about a big competition had a picture of the three women who placed the highest. The women were posing behind gigantic trophies. All the women looked a little funny, because they had sound suppressing earphones on. Sandra, the second-place winner this time, was a nice looking, short, brown-haired girl with the ability to smile nicely for the camera.

"Look at those outfits," Brad exclaimed. "They look like NASCAR drivers with all those product endorsements."

"She's a gun nut," Clarice commented. "Did you know about the guns?"

dad owns gun store

"I remember the police report said you were shot at close range," Judy reported. "A medal winning pistol shooter wouldn't have had to be close. It doesn't quite add up. Then again, maybe she wanted to be doubly sure she didn't miss. Why take a long shot if you can get a shorter one?"

"Also, we know she had a gun available," Brad added.

"Probably lots of them. Having a gun is no big deal, Brad," Clarice remarked. "Almost anyone can get ahold of a gun these days. Ohio's not the wild west, but procuring a gun isn't difficult at all."

"I bet it's not as bad as Afghanistan. One of the scariest parts of the whole deal was everyone and his brother had a gun. We were always afraid one of the new recruits would turn his rifle on us. Even though the Afghani army vouched for the recruits, you never knew. I feel safer here. Maybe I shouldn't."

Judy put her arm around Brad and hugged him tight. "Things here are much better than Afghanistan, I'm sure. Clarice is right. It's easy to get a gun. At least in gun stores you have to pass a background check."

"I'm surprised at how many people fail those," Clarice commented. "I did a story on it once. In 2017, over a hundred thousand people were unable to buy a gun because they failed the background check. Most of them were ex-cons. They're not allowed to possess guns."

"Still, they can get ahold of one on the black market," Judy said. "If you knew the right place to go, you'd be able to buy a pistol without going anywhere near a gun shop or a background check."

"We've drifted off topic. We're all agreed we should look into Miss Locket, right?" Brad asked.

"Yes, you should," Clarice answered. "Wait a minute. It's easy for me to say. I have to head off to work. I guess I should say—I recommend it."

"I concur with Clarice's recommendation," Judy responded with a smile. "First, we have to go to the zoo to get him more food. We have a little left, not much. On the way, we can try to figure out how to approach Sandra."

`fresh stuff would be nice`

At this point, Clarice hurried off to get dressed for her day.

Brad spoke up. "Also, we need to know where we can find Sandra. Do you know anything about where she works?"

`lj guns and ammo`

"I suspect the L stands for Locket. You told us her dad owned a gun store. Judy, can you find an address for the place?"

"I'm on it."

"Now I have to figure out what to wear. It's going to take me a while to get the hang of civilian life. In the Army, particularly in Afghanistan, it was the same outfit every day. While I had several sets of clothes, they were all the same."

"Brad, stop complaining. You're going to wear khakis and a shirt. The only real decision you need to make is which shirt. Even there your options aren't plentiful. Now in my case it can be really difficult, particularly because I have to choose an outfit I can wear with the pendant."

After Clarice left for work, Judy loaded George into the pendant and left it on the table. She thought he'd be safe from Jangles while she went to get dressed. It turned out to be a mistake. As soon as Brad and Judy went into the bedroom to dress, Jangles jumped up on the table and pawed the pendant. George was terrified. He was trapped. When the pendant went on its side, it scooted on the tabletop. Jangles pounced on the pendant and grabbed it between her paws. Just as George was sure he was going to be bounced all over the place, Judy came out half-dressed and swatted Jangles. The cat jumped down, and Judy grabbed the pendant.

"George, I'm so sorry. I thought I was being so smart. Putting you in the pendant was to protect you. It for sure and certain backfired."

Judy took George out of the pendant and asked, "Are you all right?"

`get rid of cat`

"We've already discussed the cat situation, and we're not going to get rid of her. I'll be more careful. I promise I'll always put you in your cage before I leave you alone with Jangles. You're safe in there, aren't you?"

`safe enough`

◇◇◇

At the zoo, Judy didn't find the guy she'd purchased the dung from before, but she was able to make a deal with one of the other maintenance men. This time, she only had to pay twenty dollars for the same amount of dung.

On their way to the little shed housing the dung, the guy was talkative. "We have a new elephant on loan. It's there in a separate enclosure," he said, pointing to a small elephant. "It means we'll be harvesting more dung. You can count on a steady supply."

"Thank you so much," Judy responded.

At the little barn, Judy tried to scoop the freshest looking dung into her containers. Despite the fact it all looked foul to her, some of it was moister than the rest. She was able to fill both containers. These two containers, and what they had left over, should last George for quite a while. Before they went to the car, she detoured in the restroom to rinse off the containers and the spoon. She didn't want to smell like elephant poop.

It was a long drive to LJ Guns and Ammo, so Brad and Judy stopped at a small restaurant to grab lunch., Judy took one of the containers into the ladies' room to feed George. "There's nowhere in here for you to roll your food into a ball, Buddy. You're going to have to suck it up and eat out of the Tupperware."

He climbed in and started to eat. This dung smelled a little funny, and it tasted funny too. It was much spicier than he was used to. He wondered if the zoo's new elephant was an Indian elephant. *Maybe an Indian elephant's dung would be much spicier*. He wasn't pleased.

When everyone had finished lunch, they drove to the gun store. It was impressive. It sat on a big lot, maybe two thirds of a city block. The store was painted weirdly, bright yellow with camouflage trim.

"Sandra's shooting outfit has the same color scheme as the building," Brad commented.

"You're right. How are we going to do this?"

"We'll have to play it by ear. We don't know whether it will be easy to get to talk to Sandra. I'd say this is a scouting mission. We may not even see her. Let's let George out when we get in, and the three of us will see what we find."

Judy scoped out the place and headed toward the archery section. She let George out there and told him to meet her by the crossbows in fifteen minutes. Meanwhile, Brad wandered toward the guns. Judy didn't see anyone who fit Sandra's description, so she wandered around looking at the camping gear. She had no interest in looking at guns. She saw Brad was in a conversation with one of the salesmen.

After looking at one of the pistols the salesman had recommended, Brad asked about all the trophies sitting on shelves above the racks of guns. The salesman was clearly proud of the trophies. "Our owner and his daughter, Sandra, are responsible for most of them. Sandra works here. Today's her day off. She's a crackerjack pistol shooter. She's won trophies in national competitions."

Brad saw George flying toward the trophies, so he quickly asked a question about the pistol the guy had been showing him. Brad finally told the guy he'd think about the pistol and wandered around the store until he saw Judy head back toward the archery display.

In the car, Brad concluded, "That was a waste of time. The guy I was talking to told me this is Sandra's day off."

"I have to agree," Judy replied. "It's certainly not my kind of store.

Even if I had a gift certificate, I'm not sure I'd be able to find anything to buy. If we decide to go there again, you can go by yourself."

When they got home, Judy let George out of the pendant, and he flew immediately to the keyboard.

"What is it?" Judy asked.

`not sandra`

"How do you know?"

`at tournament`

After a pause, Brad spoke. "Oh, I get it. I saw you flying by those trophies. I couldn't read any of them. One of them must have been for a tournament on the day you were shot, right?"

George flew to the Y key.

"I can't get over how fast you interpret what he is saying, Brad"

"Just lucky. George, if the tournament was during the day, she still might have shot you at night."

`in denver`

"And if it lasted for several days, there's no way she'd be capable of returning to Cleveland at night to do you in."

`bingo`

"Okay, we can scratch Sandra off the list," Judy said. "Is there anyone else we should consider? Think about it. Brad and I are going out with friends tonight, so you'll have the apartment to yourself. Well, you and Jangles. You'll be in your cage with your dinner. You can roll it into balls to your heart's content."

When Judy gave him a big scoop of the new dung, he sniffed it. *Yeah, it's the Indian stuff again. Ugh, my stomach is just recovering from lunch.*

Chapter Nineteen

THE NEXT MORNING THE GROUP assembled again in the kitchen for breakfast, and Judy asked George if he'd come up with anyone else they should look at.

`richard singletary`

"Give us more," Judy urged.

`at work`

"Keep going."

`beat him out for promotion`

"I see," Brad said. "It fits. This guy might have been angry about losing out on the promotion. It's natural for him to resent the person who received a promotion he thought should have been his. Also, he might have been able to discover the case you were working on the night you were killed."

Clarice jumped in. "Wait, why was this guy mad at you? He should have been madder at the person who decided who should get promoted. You didn't do anything underhanded, did you?"

George went to the N key.

"Even if it was all above board, jealousy is a strong motive," Judy commented. "It may not be sensible. Still, like Brad said, often people resent the person who beat them out for a promotion. Then again, maybe it wasn't only emotion. Maybe this guy thought, with you out of the way, he'd get the promotion by default. I'd say Richard Singletary is a definite possibility. Did you come up with anyone else?"

still thinking

"All right, keep thinking," Judy responded. "Scoot over, and I'll see what we can find about Richard."

Judy's attempt to find Richard Singletary on the internet was frustrating. The first nine entries were nixed by George. Finally, he went to the Y key when she found an entry for the Acton Detective Agency. Richard Singletary was listed as Assistant Chief Detective and identified in a picture of the agency's employees.

Brad asked, "Assistant Chief Detective—is it the position you were talking about?"

George went to the Y key.

"He looks quite a bit little older than I thought you were," Clarice remarked. "It might have bothered him to lose out on a promotion to a younger guy. It makes him a better suspect in my eyes."

"Why were you promoted and not him?" asked Brad. "Do you know?"

college

"I get it," Judy responded. "You received the promotion because you were a college graduate, and he wasn't."

He went to the Y key.

"I don't suspect there were many college graduates at a detective agency," Brad commented. "You can qualify for most of those jobs with a degree from a community college. How many other college graduates worked at your agency?"

none

"It's all the more reason for this guy Singletary to resent George," Clarice commented. "A younger guy skipping over you just because he has a college degree can be really hard on a person. I know lots of guys who're sure no one learns anything useful in college. In some ways I can see where they're coming from. It might really get this guy going. Didn't you tell us you were a philosophy major at Oberlin? Losing out to a philosopher would make it even worse."

"Yes, it was philosophy," Judy responded. "Richard had motive enough. I've kept looking and I can't find anything else about him on Google. I guess we should go to the detective agency. Would you like to see your old place of work?"

George went to the Y key.

Later, with George in the pendant, Judy and Brad drove to the Acton Detective Agency. Acton had a six-room office suite in a suburban office park on the east side of Cleveland. They had decided to approach Gregory Acton, the boss, with Judy's story about doing a sudden loss article. Since they thought it was easier to stick to the truth than to construct too many lies, they were going to tell the truth about Brad—he was her boyfriend who was getting out of the Army. Stretching the truth just a little, they decided to hint Brad might be interested in a job in a month.

The receptionist, who had hunched shoulders and wore bright orange, directed them to Gregory's office without asking why they wanted to see him. At first Judy thought it was odd. On second thought, it was quite possible many clients would not want to state their business to anyone other than the detective. Gregory Acton was in his mid-fifties, about six feet tall with completely white hair. He smiled as he greeted them and then gestured for them to take seats as he returned to his desk.

George had a good view of Greg behind the desk. He was familiar with the office. There was only one change he saw. Greg had a new picture featuring his very attractive wife. George had never met her, but he remembered other pictures of her. This picture certainly stood out. Greg's wife, a leggy blonde in a skimpy bikini, leaned against Greg in some tropical location. George's eyes were drawn to a tattoo she had. It was a ring of stars circling her arm. The tattoo was distinctive because the size of the stars seemed to vary randomly. George had seen the same tattoo somewhere before. He couldn't remember where. He decided he'd better pay some attention to the conversation.

Greg was explaining his reaction to the loss of George. "It was sudden, and it really spooked all of us. He was clearly a rising star around here. In fact, I'd recently promoted him to Assistant Chief Detective. His death caused a big shake-up."

"Is being a private detective usually dangerous?" Judy asked.

"Not usually. Some of what we do involves providing protection to people, and at times, it turns out to be dangerous. We also deal with some irate spouses if they see us taking pictures of them being unfaithful. George was caught once. If the guy hadn't been slow and out of shape, George might have been in some danger. It was an abnormal situation, though. Most of what we do is really sedate."

Brad jumped in. "So, it was a real shock when one of your detectives was shot while he was on a stakeout? Has it ever happened before?"

"Not to this agency. About four years ago, another private detective was killed in a similar situation. It's rare. I don't know of another deaths, and I've been in the business for more than twenty years."

"If this is not too personal a question, how did you deal with the death?" Judy asked.

Greg leaned back in the chair. "You're right, it's a personal question. Anyway, I liked George. He was a college graduate, you know. The only one working here. I was starting to consider grooming him to be a partner if he kept at it. Then he was gone. It upset some of my plans.

Sudden changes aren't easy. I guess I was able to deal with it. I've been through other situations involving death. I was in the Persian Gulf War. I guess you're still dealing with the region."

"Yes," Brad answered. "I just returned from Afghanistan. We still have a few people there."

"Do you know what you're going to do when you get out, son?"

"No, I don't have anything lined up yet. I'm open to almost anything."

"Let me try to talk you into detective work."

Brad nodded, and Judy interrupted. "It seems like you two are about to have a conversation. Is it okay if I talk to other people on the staff? Most of them would have known George Wilcox, wouldn't they?"

"Sure. Abby, she's the receptionist, knew him, and Rich Singletary did too. The other two guys who would have known him are out on protection duty right now, so you can't interview them. Feel free to talk to the others."

Acton rose. "Let me introduce you to Abby. When you've finished with her, she can introduce you to Rich." Acton described what he wanted to happen and returned to talk to Brad.

Judy gave Abby the standard introduction to the sudden loss story. Abby told her she liked George, and she was incredibly broken up when she learned he'd been shot. She told Judy she understood detectives sometimes did dangerous work. Still, George's murder had been a complete shock to her. Selling her story, Judy asked some probing questions about how she dealt with the loss. As a result, she learned more about Abby than she expected.

George was surprised how much his death had affected Abby. It made him feel guilty, because he hadn't paid much attention to her when he was alive as a human. He guessed being preoccupied with other girls made him tend to ignore her, and he didn't find Abby attractive. Clearly Abby was looking at him. Her tale of real grief made him feel a like a heel. He should have been nicer to her.

Judy tried not the be impatient with the girl. Still, while she listened to her, she couldn't help thinking it was really Richard Singletary she wanted to talk to. Finally, Abby finished and took her to Richard's office and made the introduction.

Richard Singletary was surprisingly short. He'd been sitting around a table in the picture of the Acton staff Judy had seen on the internet. When he rose to shake her hand, Judy figured he was only maybe an inch or two taller than her five foot four. He had a short haircut. Judy thought he looked like a Marine.

"Like Abby told you, I'm doing a story about how people react to sudden loss," Judy said. "You lost a colleague suddenly, George Wilcox. I've talked to his parents, his girlfriend, and other people at the agency. Would you mind telling me how you reacted?"

"Gosh, it's been a while. I guess my first reaction was shock. I mean, it was so unexpected. I remember Greg calling us all together after he'd been interviewed by the police. His announcement of Wilcox's death came completely out of the blue. He asked if any of us knew what Wilcox was working on. No one had any idea. Shock, yeah my first reaction was shock."

"Did it make you feel different about your job? Did it seem scarier?"

"No, it didn't, because frankly I wasn't sure Wilcox's killing had anything to do with his job. It was personal."

"How do you mean?"

"Well, he had a complicated personal life. He had this fabulous live-in girlfriend, a beauty queen or something. He told me he was dumping her. To hear him tell it, he had another spectacular girl lined up. My guess is someone connected to one of those two girls did him in. I mean, he'd been juggling them for at least a month."

"So, his murder didn't have anything to do with the stakeout he was doing."

"I don't know for sure. The stakeout might have gone wrong. I don't think so. Like I told you, his social life was the source of his trouble. The girl he was going to hook up with after the beauty queen had a boyfriend."

Judy found his conjecture interesting. It was pretty far from the line of questioning she'd anticipated. In an attempt to get back on track, she asked, "Wilcox just was promoted to Assistant Chief Detective. Was there much competition for the job?"

"I didn't have any problem at all. Greg came in and told me he'd raise my salary, so I didn't get hurt by being skipped over. While I knew he liked Wilcox, he took care of me. I got the money and not the hassle. It's beside the point. You interrupted me. I was about to tell you this girl, Isabell something, had a boyfriend, Randal, I think. And on the day Wilcox was shot, he came looking for Wilcox."

"The afternoon he was shot. Why didn't the police hear about Randal's visit? It might have been important."

While Richard looked a little guilty, he stuck up for himself. "I didn't think anything of it. I didn't even know he was the girl's boyfriend at the time. I only learned about the relationship later. It wasn't any big deal. Whoever it was who shot Wilcox didn't leave any clues. They were pros. It didn't seem like this guy Randy had the ability to pull it off."

George didn't like the whole interview. Richard had contradicted himself. Either Randy and his love life were important, or they weren't. Also, he hadn't known Greg had given Richard a raise. Somehow it took something away from his pride at getting promoted. Finally, he had another girlfriend to explain to Brad and the girls. He hadn't brought up Isabell because he thought no one knew about her. Now he remembered telling stupid Richard. It was going to be a big mess when he returned home. He'd have to tell everyone about Isabell and Randy, and they'd probably not like what he had to say.

Chapter Twenty

AS THEY DROVE AWAY FROM the detective agency, George knew Brad and Judy were going to give him a thorough grilling when they returned to the apartment. The discussion in the car focused on Judy's anger at finding out about Isabell and Randy. Judy told Brad that George hadn't been straight with them, and she was upset. Brad tried to calm her with little success.

Judy marched to the computer when they entered the apartment. "George, I'm taking you out of this pendant, and we're going to have a long talk."

After he was extracted from the pendant, George went to the keyboard, ready to take his medicine—not happy, only ready.

"Why is this the first time we've heard anything about Isabell? Was Monica really the untidy airhead you've told us about, or were you dumping her so you could hook up with Isabell? You have some explaining to do."

Brad broke in. "You'd better give him one question at a time."

"Okay. Why didn't you tell us about Isabell?"

`thought not relevant`

"Well, that's clearly hogwash. Richard told us her boyfriend came looking for you on the day you were shot. He might have had every reason to be pissed with you."

`didn't know about randy's visit`

"You were stealing his girlfriend, right?"

`finished with randy`

"George," Brad asked, "did Randy know?"

`thought so`

He sensed Judy was still mad.

"How long had you been stringing two girls along?"

`a little over a month`

"What you were doing was unacceptable. I'm starting to wonder if Monica was telling us the truth when she told us she thought you two were still in love. You were still living with her while you were trying to get hooked up with Isabell. Did you tell Monica when you started dating Isabell?"

Despite knowing it wouldn't make him look good, he went to the N key.

"Did Isabell tell Randy about you?"

`she told me she would`

Brad took over. "This whole thing was a mess. You were breaking up with Monica, and Isabell was breaking up with Randy, and it was happening right before you were shot. George, you haven't been straight with us. We've been chasing all around looking at stuff not nearly as relevant as this. Why have you kept this a secret?"

He didn't know how to respond. Part of the answer had to do with the blank period near the end of his life. Some of what they wanted to know about was stuff he didn't remember. It was like his being unable to remember the case he was working on. He remembered a bunch of tense phone calls with Isabell, who was having trouble facing Randy. Then it all sort of faded out.

`close to murder hazy`

"I can see the problem a little," Judy commented. "Some of what we're talking about happened right before you were shot. Still, some of it didn't. If you were really interested in figuring out who killed you, you should have known Isabell and Randy were people we'd want to investigate. I just don't know how you thought it was sensible to leave them out."

"Judy's right. Whatever you've been hiding is going to come out now. We need to find out about Isabell and Randy. Can you give us full names?"

`isabell melendez randy ingersol`

Judy was switching to Google, so he flew up to her shoulder to see what she found. The first thing Judy discovered when she entered 'Isabell Melendez, Cleveland' was a notice a singer was going to be performing at a local night club.

"Is it her?" Brad asked.

George flew to the Y key.

"Wow!" Judy exclaimed. "She has her own website. Look at this picture, Brad."

George was terribly afraid the picture was going to get him in trouble again. He had heard about nothing other than the picture for a whole week from Monica.

Judy pointed. "Isabell looks like a pretty girl. Like her name suggests, she's Hispanic with big brown eyes and beautiful black hair. Wait, the couple behind her left hand grabbed my attention. It's George and Monica. I'm sure it's them."

"Is Judy right?" Brad asked. "You kind of have a dopey look on your face."

George knew the picture. He and Monica had gone to a bar where Isabell was performing. She played the piano and sang. He remembered thinking she was a knockout, and she sang nicely too. The camera caught an adoring look on his face. Monica, on the other hand, was giving him a mean stare. It wasn't the smiling beauty queen look at all. When she'd seen the picture after he'd suggested they should catch Isabell's act again, she was incredibly pissed.

George went to the Y key.

"The picture makes it look like you're really into Isabell. At the same time, it shows Monica isn't happy about it. I guess cameras don't lie. Were you dating both of them at the time?"

no first time saw isabell

Judy started with rapid-fire questions. "How long before you were dating Isabell?"

a month

"How long before you dumped Monica?"

another month

"How long before you were killed?"

less than two weeks

"Okay, we have the timeline," Brad concluded. "This all happened fairly late in your life."

my human life

"Fair enough, your human life. Anyway, it seems to me this girl Isabell and her boyfriend Randy are the first people we should have been looking at. I still don't get why we're just finding out about them now."

George didn't respond, so silence followed. Judy went to get some water for her and Brad, and then returned to the computer. "Let's see what we can find about Randy Ingersol."

Judy's search came up with five possibilities. George pointed her to Randy Ingersol, the singer. He too had a website. It wasn't nearly as nice as Isabell's. He seemed to specialize in children's songs and advertised his availability for birthday parties, bar mitzvahs, and similar events. He was a medium-height, pale-faced guy, with brown hair cut like one of the 1960s rock stars.

"Okay George, we're going to see Isabell's act tonight, and we're going to talk to her. You'd better hope what she has to say jibes with what you've been telling us. I'm still annoyed with you. You know that, don't you?"

He went to the Y key.

At six in the evening, they watched Clarice's newscast. As she had alerted them in the morning, she had the lead interview. One of the city council members had lobbied hard in favor of one of the bidders for a new city fire station. After the company he'd supported was awarded the contract, a reporter for the paper found out he was a part owner of the construction company. It was a clear conflict. In the interview, the council member tried to bully his way through. Clarice nailed him with questions. When Clarice called him on one of his half-truths, he became very upset and stalked out.

"That's my roommate!" Judy exclaimed. "Isn't she wonderful!"

George, who had one eye out for Jangles during the interview, agreed, however he had no way to indicate his approval.

On the other hand, Brad found a way to use the moment. "Yes, she was great. I always knew you demonstrated good sense in picking people to hang out with."

Judy raised her eyebrows. "You think so, do you?"

"Yes," Brad responded as he tackled Judy. George flew off Judy's shoulder as Brad approached. Brad and Judy ended up on the floor, rolling around laughing. Eventually, they came to a stop, sharing a deep kiss.

George thought this would be one of the times Clarice would have called out, "Get a room." It turned out they did, so he watched the rest of the news from the top of the curtains.

Later, they drove to the bar where Isabell Melendez was booked for the night. They arrived at eight-thirty, which turned out to be before most of the crowd. The bar had booths around the wall and small tables in the middle. It probably seated between seventy and eighty people. Brad and Judy were seated at a table two rows back from the piano. Isabell was starting her first set when they were seated.

From the pendant, George had a good view of Isabell. He also saw Brad, who'd positioned himself so he could see the whole room. He didn't look too jumpy. Still, George was surprised Brad had agreed to be so far from the door. Maybe the little romp he and Judy had during the second half of the news had relaxed him.

When he focused on Isabell, George felt sorry for himself with a shocking intensity. He'd really fallen hard for Isabell, harder than he'd ever fallen for Monica. With Monica it was mostly lust. Well, pride and lust. It was nice to be the guy with the prettiest girl in the room. With Isabell it was more. He'd been attracted by her voice and her looks. After he knew her better, things intensified. She was so bright and lively. He'd been deeply in love.

Brad and Judy seemed to be enjoying Isabell's show. Isabell played the piano and sang. Many of the songs she selected were songs they knew, and she had a very pleasing voice. Judy had planned to try to talk to her during her break. Unfortunately, she didn't manage it. When she Isabell had finished her last song, several people came up to talk to her. Judy was still toward the rear of the crowd when Isabell excused herself and walked backstage.

"You'd better be more aggressive next time," Brad commented, starting to get up.

Before Brad escaped, Judy replied, "Yes, and we'd better order some food. Even though we ate before we came, I can feel this drink. We may well be here for a long time, and I don't want to be tipsy when I'm talking to her."

"Okay," Brad said with a smile. "But food is going to foil my strategy to get you liquored up."

"It was a bad strategy, Buddy. I get really sleepy when I'm liquored up."

Brad and Judy shared a hug, and Brad signaled the server to ask for a menu. They ordered, and then Brad stood and strolled around the room.

Later, when Isabell announced the next song would be the last one of this set, Judy positioned herself so she would be the first one to come up to Isabell.

"I loved your songs," she said. "You have a great voice."

"Thanks," Isabell responded. She seemed surprised when Judy didn't move away.

"Isabell, I'm a writer working on a story about sudden loss, and I understand you lost a boyfriend suddenly, George Wilcox."

Isabell looked distressed. She took a step away from Judy.

Not letting her escape, Judy added, "We can do the interview later, maybe after your last set."

"Okay. Not now," Isabell responded, relaxing some.

"Thanks," Judy said as she retreated.

The encounter bothered George. Isabell seemed upset with the idea of talking about him, and he didn't like the way Judy appeared to bully her. Then again, it made sense. Judy really wanted to learn what had happened.

During her next set of songs, Isabell seemed to glance over toward Brad and Judy. When she finished her last song, Isabell received a long ovation. As before, a group of fans wanted to talk to her. When the last fan left, she held her open hand to Judy, who was half-way out of her chair, and mouthed "five minutes." Judy nodded and sat back down.

Brad pulled up a chair for Isabell when she reappeared from the dressing room. She'd changed into more casual clothes. The room had cleared out quite a bit, so Judy felt it would be okay to conduct the interview at the table. "Can you tell me what it was like to lose someone close to you suddenly?"

Isabell paused, collecting her thoughts, and didn't speak right away.

"Maybe I should explain a little more," Judy added. "I'm a freelance writer, and like I told you, I'm researching a story about sudden loss. I heard about George Wilcox being shot, and I've interviewed his parents, his boss, and some of his friends. I'm not going to use any names. I just need to know about your relationship and how you dealt with the loss. I know this might be hard."

"Good, I wouldn't want my name involved." After a pause, Isabell continued, "I didn't really know George very long. I'd say our relationship deepened very quickly. He'd already told his girlfriend to move out. We were in love. We hadn't made any big announcements yet. He had this girl, and I had a boyfriend I had to tell."

"When did you hear about his death?"

"It was the next day. I called his house, and his old girlfriend Monica told me."

"How did you react?"

"I was devastated. It came at a really low point for me. I'd made a terrible mistake. A mistake I was going to hide from George..." Isabell teared up and looked around nervously.

Silence descended as Isabell tried to get herself under control.

"Whatever it is," Judy said. "It seems like it's a secret you've been holding in. You'll be better off getting it out into the open."

George wished Judy wouldn't be so pushy. It was frustrating. There was nothing he could do about it. Brad started to be nervous, excused himself, and took off on one of his walks.

Coward, George thought.

"Okay. Maybe it would be better if I told someone. I had this boyfriend, Randal. Randy is the sweetest boy. Nevertheless, I loved George. I was having trouble telling Randy. While I knew I should just come out with it, I hadn't yet. On the night George was killed, Randy came storming into my apartment, shouting about George. He'd found out about us somehow. When I told him he was right, he broke down. I made a horrible mistake then. I took him in my arms to console him, and..."

"Oh my God!" Judy exclaimed. "You didn't sleep with him. Did you?"

Isabell nodded through her tears. "I told him it was one last time. I know I shouldn't have done it. He was so pathetic. I don't know."

Isabell broke down again, and Judy stood up and put her arm around Isabell. When the girl gained her composure, Judy continued, "So when you heard the next day George was dead, it must have been devastating."

"To say the least. I had so much guilt about the night before. Randy even slept over. When he finally left, I tried to phone George. I didn't get an answer. Eventually, I called the phone in his apartment in the afternoon and heard the news from Monica. I bawled for hours. It was the darkest day of my life. I still tear up about it."

"How long did it take you to get over it?

Isabell took out a tissue from her purse and blew her nose. "It was about two months before I stopped crying every day. I cancelled all my engagements and went into a deep funk."

“I’m so sorry my questions brought all this up again. It must have been horrible. I don’t know if I can use what you’ve told me in my story. There are too many unusual feelings involved. It’s not typical. If I do, I’ll be sure not to use your name, or identify you in any way.”

“Thanks, and maybe you’re right. It might have been good for me to tell someone about what happened. It’s been eating at me. I shouldn’t keep things hidden away.”

On the way home, Judy filled Brad in on what Isabell had told her. George found he was shaken by the experience. It was hard to see Isabell so upset and to hear she’d made love to Randy when she was supposed to be breaking up with him. The one last time bit didn’t feel right. Then again, he remembered how he’d still been making love to Monica well after he knew he was going to break up with her. The whole thing brought up confusing emotions.

Chapter Twenty-One

BRAD AND JUDY SLEPT IN the next morning, Saturday. When they finally dragged themselves to the table for breakfast, Clarice was already finished.

"Gosh," Judy said. "Wasn't last night your late night at the station? I thought you'd sleep in too."

"I'm so jazzed about my interview yesterday I had trouble sleeping in. It's the first time something I did for the six o'clock news was replayed at eleven. The whole thing is going to be big. The station told me it's been picked up by CNN, and I might get interviewed by the network today."

"We watched it. You were great, Clarice," Brad commented.

"Thanks. To tell the truth, it was easy. I couldn't have had a better guy to interview. He was so cocky. It was easy to bring him down. I was a little surprised when he walked out, but we had him dead to rights."

"I guess an interview like yours doesn't happen very often," Judy remarked. "Usually guys refuse to be interviewed on camera. They just refer you to their lawyers."

"You're right. This guy thought he'd be able to bluff his way through. He granted the interview because he was sure nothing would go wrong."

"Bad judgement on his part," Brad concluded.

"Extremely so," Judy added.

"Whatever, it's been a big break for me."

"Oh, Clarice. Brad and I aren't trying to take anything away from what you did. You were wonderful. It must have been difficult to keep your cool when the guy was shouting at you. You did a great job."

"Spectacular," Brad added.

"Thanks. Now tell me what you two were up to yesterday."

"Gosh, I'd better feed George. This is way later than I've fed him other mornings."

As Judy was returning, she heard Brad filling Clarice in on yesterday's trip to the detective agency. Judy broke in. "My interview with Richard Singletary was the most interesting part. He told me he didn't have any problem with the promotion. The boss gave him a raise, so he didn't lose anything financially. And he had some fascinating information. It turns out George had a girlfriend he hadn't told us about, Isabell Melendez."

"That dog. Was he juggling this other girl and Monica?"

Brad took over. "Yes, at least for a while. He told us the second girl, Isabell, was the one he really fell for. He told Monica about her when he gave her two-week's notice on the apartment. At the same time, Isabell was having trouble telling her boyfriend, Randy."

Judy interrupted. "We went to see Isabell last night. She's a singer, actually quite a good one. After her last set of songs at the Twilight Club downtown, I interviewed her. I used the story about sudden loss—same thing I did with George's mother and Monica. You wouldn't believe what she told me."

"I left, because I thought I was making Isabell nervous," Brad noted.

"Yeah, Brad had left, and she told me she was having trouble telling her boyfriend. On the night George was killed, she finally got up the gumption to tell him she was breaking up with him, and he started blubbering. Trying to console him, she put her arm around him, and one thing led to another."

Clarice blurted, "She didn't do one last time, did she?"

"You're right, and the guy slept over. The next morning, she realized the magnitude of her mistake and tried to call George. After not being able to get him on his cell all morning, she finally called the apartment and heard about the murder from Monica. She was devastated."

"I should say so," Clarice said. "She told a perfect stranger all this?"

"I was surprised, too," Judy answered. "She really seemed like a sweet girl, and she'd been keeping it all a secret. It was good for her to tell someone. I was a sympathetic listener, and Brad had left before she really opened up."

"George was there," Brad added. "It must not have been easy for him to hear it. He seemed fairly subdued when we made it back to the apartment."

"The way I see it, this girl Isabell and her boyfriend weren't the ones who committed the murder," Clarice concluded. "They were doing what they were doing the night George bought it."

"Yes," Judy added. "For some reason George didn't tell us about Isabell and her boyfriend. We found out about them at the detective agency. Whatever, Isabell's story gets them off the hook. Lots of other possibilities have been eliminated too. We're only left with Monica and her current boyfriend, Bill. We've told George, he needs to come up with some other suggestions."

"Let's see if he's come up with anyone," Brad said. "I'll go get him. I take a wet paper towel, right?"

When Brad deposited George on the keyboard, Judy asked the first question. "Have you thought of anymore people we should investigate?"

`stumped`

"You mean, there's no one else, you ever crossed?" Clarice asked. "There's no one else who would be mad at you. I find it hard to believe."

`what about you Clarice`

"It's not about me. I'm not the one who's been murdered."

"It's a fair question," Judy commented. "We're all close to human George's age. While I've made some people mad at one point or another, I can't remember anyone I made really furious—mad enough to do me in."

Brad responded, "The problem is, Judy, you may not know how other people take things. They might be much angrier than you ever knew."

"You don't know how empathetic our girl is, Brad. Judy is really keyed into other people's feelings."

"This isn't about Judy, Clarice," Brad countered. "It's about George, and perhaps he's not as empathetic as Judy. He's a guy, or at least was a guy. Often guys aren't as keyed into their feelings as girls."

"What do you say?" Judy asked. "Did you consider yourself empathetic?"

`as much as next guy`

"So not very much," Clarice concluded. "You need to keep thinking. There must be someone. Someone you really pissed off even if you didn't realize it. I know it's difficult. Think hard."

`I can think hard`

"You haven't shown me much, dung boy."

As George headed out on the keyboard, Judy lifted her hands from the keys. "Enough of this bickering. Don't be so hard on him, Clarice. We should cool it. George does have to think hard, and so do we. At this point, we still have Monica and her current boyfriend, Bill. As I remember it, we weren't able to decide which one of them was the best suspect. The point is we haven't eliminated either of them."

"You're right, Honey," Brad said. "We have to figure out how we can learn anything more about Monica and her boyfriend Bill."

"I wish I could help," Clarice added.

"I'm the only one Monica has met," Judy responded. "Maybe you and Brad should go to the hardware store."

"Yeah, I can see it." Brad added. "Also, I've been wondering how I can approach Bill. Maybe I'd be able to go see him with my story about getting out of the Army and needing insurance. Actually, I stopped my car insurance when I went to Afghanistan, so at least I will need car insurance."

"Brilliant, Honey, but it's Saturday. We'll have to wait until Monday. Today you and Clarice should go to the hardware store."

"If George goes, he'll have to ride somewhere else. The pendant is too conspicuous," Clarice added.

"We'll figure something out," Judy commented.

They headed to the hardware store after lunch. They'd arranged for George to ride on top of Clarice's head in one of the ringlets. As long as she didn't talk to any really tall people, he'd be hidden. Clarice was going to claim she knew a friend of George's and had heard about Monica. They hoped this would start a conversation that might reveal something. Even though it was a longshot, it seemed like their best idea.

Just as the three arrived at the hardware store, Clarice's cell phone rang. It was the station wanting her to come in for an interview with the network. Clarice knew they'd all heard the call, so she looked at Brad. "You're on your own, big boy. I have to have Judy drive me to the station ASAP."

"We'll come back and get you as soon as we can," Judy said.

They all exited the car. Judy switched to be the driver, Clarice sat in the front seat, and the girls drove off. Brad took a minute or two to collect himself and then entered the store. It wasn't difficult to spot Monica. He'd heard about tight pants and cleavage, and her outfit today was a repeat. She was talking to another customer, so Brad had a chance to plot his strategy. He wandered around looking at gardening tools and lawn mowers. There weren't many customers in the store, so Monica would likely be headed his way when she finished with the other guy.

When the other customer left, she came up right to him. "Hi, I'm Monica. Can I help you with something?"

Brad couldn't help noticing Monica's big smile. "Oh hello. I'm Brad, and I'm going to have to have a lawn mower. Can you tell me about them?"

With a big smile and a move that somehow amplified her cleavage, Monica responded. "Sure. The first thing I need to know is how much lawn you have to mow."

Brad was winging it all the way. "I'm looking at a house with a front yard about fifty by thirty, and a backyard is more like fifty by sixty. I'm not sure of the measurements. I bet I'm close."

Monica beamed. "That big a yard is on the borderline. If you were an older guy, I'd be showing you the ride-on mowers. You look young and strong, so no ride-ons."

"While I don't know how strong I am, I still feel young. Let's look at the ones I push."

"Where do you live now?"

There was no reason she needed to know. Brad guessed it was part of her attempt at charm. He played along. "I'm in an apartment now. I'm looking seriously at this house."

Monica twirled around and walked slowly down the line of lawn mowers, giving Brad a look at her rear end in the tight pants. When she made it to the lawn mower at the end of the line, she bent over at the waist and inspected the tag on the mower. Again, her butt in the tight pants was waving Brad's way.

When she straightened up, she turned around and started her sales pitch. "This mower is top of the line. It should make caring for the lawn a breeze. Some of the cheaper mowers can be difficult to push. This one has a power assist. While it will go slowly all by itself, you'll want to go faster. The power assist helps you. It can be very useful going up hills."

Brad squatted down and inspected the price tag. "This may be a little pricey for me. What do I give up if I move down from the top of the line?"

Even though Monica looked a little disappointed, she still smiled at Brad. "Well Brad, you lose reliability more than anything else. We have other mowers with the power assist. I'll tell you they aren't as well built as this one. Lawn mowers take a lot of abuse, and while there aren't frequency of repair numbers like there are on cars, you get what you pay for. Reliability is worth paying for."

While she was talking, she moved closer to Brad and put her hand on his arm, smiling up at him with her big blue eyes the whole time she was talking. Brad had to check himself. He wasn't there to buy a lawn mower. It was time to change the subject.

"Hey, didn't you say your name was Monica? This whole time I've been racking my brain because I had a faint memory about a beautiful girl named Monica who worked in a hardware store. Now I remember, you were George Wilcox's girlfriend."

Monica was a little taken aback. "Where did you know George?"

"At Oberlin. He was a couple of years behind me, and we hung out some. I heard about you when I saw him up here after he graduated. I was on leave then. I just got out of the Army a month ago."

Brad brushed his hand through his hair. "My hair hasn't even grown out yet."

Monica seemed to relax. Still, she looked around the store. Since she didn't see anyone who looked like a more likely customer, she turned to Brad. "It was too bad about George's murder. It was horrible for me at the time. We'd been living together for almost a year."

"I heard he was killed. Do you know how it happened?"

"He had this job at this detective agency."

Brad interrupted. "Yeah, he told me."

"So, all I can figure is somehow a case went wrong."

"The police didn't find anything?"

"I really don't know. They only talked to me once. All the details went through his parents. The girlfriend gets left out."

Brad touched Monica's elbow in a comforting way. "It must have been really hard."

"Some. Yeah sure, some. It was confusing more than anything else. Actually, George and I were having trouble, and I was about to tell him I was moving out. I never had a chance to do it."

"Oh, I'm sure it was hard. I mean, you had to have conflicting emotions. I mean about the killing."

"I guess this is going to seem harsh. I'm pretty sure he had another girlfriend, some nightclub singer. I had moved on, too. I'd started to see someone. Me and him are talking about living together."

"I guess you have to move on. I guess his getting shot avoided a messy breakup."

"You're right, it did. Enough of this, I thought you were here to look at lawn mowers."

Brad went through the actions of looking at the lawn mowers and watched Monica try all her tricks. She was good at sales and probably made the hardware store lots of money. As Brad went outside to call to arrange a place to meet, he wondered why Monica had told him a whole different story than she'd told Judy.

Chapter Twenty-Two

AS BRAD WAS ENTERING THE hardware store, the others were driving to the TV station.

"This is the first time I've been alone with you since Brad came. You were sure wrong. He wasn't coming to break up with you. It looks like the opposite."

"Yes, and I'm gloriously happy about it. He has a rough road ahead. He wants me by his side."

"A rough road… I don't understand."

"Wow, we haven't been alone with a chance to talk. Brad has PTSD. It's why he's getting out of the Army. He told me, if he tried to stay in, they'd have forced him out with a medical discharge. Anyway, I don't know how serious his PTSD is. I do know it's not good. Surely, you've seen how jumpy he is. He's forever getting up and walking around. It's like he's checking out the apartment. He has no reason to check things out. Still, he can't help himself. Also, he's up at night doing the same thing four or five times each night."

"I guess I wondered. I didn't think it was bad. PTSD. Wow, PTSD can be serious."

"We're going to see it through together. I plan to go to some of the therapy sessions. I might even make it my next writing project. I can make part of the story a first-person account."

They drove in silence for a few minutes before Judy spoke up. "Let's not worry about Brad now. This is your big moment—a network interview. You aren't dressed for it."

"No sweat. There's a dress I took in when I started working. It's stashed away for just this kind of thing. Also, we need something to change into after we do a weather story. You can be stuck out in the rain sometimes. While I haven't had to use the dress yet, it's there for something like this interview."

"What will they ask?"

"I'm not sure. It's a friendly interview, so they may prep me on the questions. I'm afraid I'll wind up on the cutting room floor. A lot of video never gets used in the network evening news. It depends on what else is happening today, and, if it's a slow news day, the chances they'll use something like my interview go up."

George found it interesting to be riding in Clarice's hair. While his view wasn't very good, he liked listening to the two women. When Judy arrived at the station, she let Clarice out, telling her she'd find a parking place.

"Go to the newsroom. I'll tell them you're coming."

George held on tight when it became clear Clarice was going to run up the stairs to get to the newsroom. Clarice went up to a secretary or receptionist or something. "Where do they want me for the network interview? I have about twenty minutes."

"Oh, hi Clarice. Go see Joel, he knows the details."

"Oh, a girlfriend, Judy, drove me. She's a red head, you can't miss her. She should be coming up soon."

"I'll find her a place to sit."

Clarice headed down a hallway to Joel's office. He was the producer of the local evening news show. His door was open, so Clarice knocked on the doorway. "I'm here."

"Great, Clarice. You have enough time to go to wardrobe and make up. I don't know who's going to be doing the interview. It might be the anchor or one of the other reporters. They'll ask a bunch of questions and then pick the ones they want for the national news. It's a great break for you."

"Okay, I'll go change and get made up. Where do we do the interview?"

"We'll use the main set. We have the cameras and lighting there already. And we can get your interview wrapped up before we need it again."

"Great. Thanks, Joel."

"Knock 'em dead, Clarice."

George held on tight again as Clarice sort of jogged down the hallway. At the end of the hallway, she made a couple of turns and opened a closet. She rifled through until she found a red dress in a plastic cover. She took the dress, hustled down the corridor, and went into a dressing room.

He began to wonder if Clarice had forgotten about him in her rush to get ready. It seemed like it. She took off her jeans and top before slipping the red dress over her head and zipping it up. He would have loved to have a chance to type "yowzah." Unfortunately, he was in no position to type.

Clarice stood in front of a full-length mirror to look at herself. She turned several directions and seemed pleased with the results. After the inspection, she looked at her watch, put her discarded clothes in a little closet, and walked out.

Down another hallway, Clarice entered an open door to the makeup room. She greeted a girl who was dressed in a green smock. "Hi Marlene. I guess they told you I have an interview, so make me look good."

George started to get nervous when Clarice sat in a chair like a barber chair. He was sure the makeup lady, Marlene, would see him. He was almost certain she was eventually going to fuss with Clarice's hair. He prepared to fly. Somehow, he'd find either Judy or a way out. If he'd been thinking ahead, he would have paid more attention. Now he was sure he'd have to fly. Since he hadn't had a great view, he wasn't sure which direction.

Marlene put a bib on Clarice—sort of like the kind of thing a dentist puts on a patient—and started working on Clarice's face. George felt terribly exposed. He was going to have to fly soon. He decided to take off when the makeup person's back was turned.

A few minutes later, Marlene said, "I'm finished with your makeup, now let's take a look at your hair."

George took off. There was no time to wait for Marlene to turn around.

Marlene shrieked, "There was a bug in your hair!"

Clarice blurted, "Oh, George."

George didn't stick around long enough to hear how Clarice explained herself. He was too busy trying to figure out which way to go. He went down the corridor and ran into a dead end, so he turned around. He saw the makeup room as he flew past. He didn't pause to see if there was any commotion. Next, he found himself on the news set. He recognized it from watching TV. He landed on a curtain to assess the situation. He wasn't sure he'd be able to hide where he was, but he also didn't know where to go next.

After Clarice's hair was done, she found Judy in the lobby reading a magazine.

Surprised to see Clarice, Judy said, "You look great. Is the interview finished?"

"No, it hasn't started yet."

Clarice came up close to Judy and switched to a whisper. "Our friend flew off somewhere. I forgot all about him, and the makeup girl was about to do my hair."

Judy had a stricken look on her face. "Golly, I forgot all about him, too. I'm sure he'll show up. He's fairly resourceful."

Clarice headed off, hoping Judy was right. She decided George could take care of himself. She didn't need to be worried about him during this interview.

From his perch on the curtain in the newsroom, George saw people arriving. The first guy was a camera man, who fiddled with the camera. Next was a lighting guy, who adjusted some lights. Next Clarice came in looking good in her red dress. A couple of people from the station arrived after her. It didn't appear they had any particular function. He guessed they just wanted to see the interview. It wasn't very often one of the station's reporters was interviewed by the network. He decided he'd better not fly with so many people around, so he stayed put. As he'd learned in the restaurant, the key was for him was to remain stationary.

The interview took quite a while, and George couldn't tell which parts of it would make the final cut. He was sure Clarice was right, lots of it would never be used. He thought Clarice did a good job, but she appeared to be getting tired toward the end. When everything was finished, the people left, and he was able to fly again, he decided not to try the door Clarice had entered through. It most likely led to the dead-end hallway with the makeup room. While he didn't know where the other door led, he had to try it.

After several wrong turns, George heard Judy and tried to follow her voice. Eventually he smelled her and was able to fly on to her shoulder. Judy jumped. "Oh, there you are. We were worried."

"What?" asked the receptionist.

"Oh, nothing," Judy said as she opened her purse for him to crawl in.

Clarice came out five minutes later. "I can't find our friend anywhere."

"He found me, so he's safe and sound. Ready to go?"

"Yeah, call Brad and tell him we're coming."

"He's already called. He's found himself a coffee shop, so he's not hurting. How did the interview go?"

"I have no idea. They asked lots of questions. I don't know if they'll use any of them on the evening news. We'll have to watch."

At the car, Judy let George out to ride on the dashboard. It was a vast improvement over Judy's purse. It was dark in there, and there were lots of strong smells, not all of which were pleasant. He found he was hungry and tired.

George hopped onto Clarice's hair when they stopped at the coffee shop. He found it difficult to get comfortable. Apparently, the makeup person, Marlene, had sprayed a bunch of sticky stuff on Clarice's hair. He had trouble moving to a good spot.

Judy walked to Brad's table while Clarice hung back a little. Judy gave him a hug and kiss. "You okay, Honey? I'm sorry it took us so long."

"No problem. I was able to read some news stories on my phone. You girls get something to drink, and I can recommend the pastries."

When they were all settled, Judy asked, "Learn anything from Monica?"

"Not really. I talked to her all right. She's an A-one flirt, I'll tell you. I expect she sells lots of guys more stuff than they need. She started me out with the top-of-the-line lawn mower."

"Lawn mower?" the two women echoed.

"Yeah, I told her I was strongly considering a house with a big lawn. I didn't know what else to say, and I guess it worked. Anyway, after we talked about lawn mowers, I told her I knew George from college. The funny thing is, she didn't give me the same story she gave you, Judy. She told you she was deeply in love with him and was devastated when he died. I didn't get anything similar. She told me they were breaking up. She said he had another girl, and she had another guy. I guess it was Bill."

"Wow, she told you a whole different story," Clarice commented.

"Maybe she acts differently with guys," Judy remarked.

"No, the questions she was asked were different," Clarice said. "We learned all about the importance of the question in my communications class in college. The answer you get depends on how you ask the question. Judy, you told her you were writing about reactions to sudden loss. She wanted to make it seem like it was a big loss. Brad didn't say anything about loss, so she didn't need to emphasize it. She's a pleaser. She wanted to give you what you wanted, so she reacted to the question."

"There may be something to what you're saying. My guess is she's a liar—plain and simple," Brad responded.

"I'm inclined to believe Brad," Judy commented. "We can't rely on anything Monica says."

"How was the interview, Clarice?" Brad asked.

"I don't know. It was very disjointed. Since they were going to edit it down a whole bunch, they asked lots of questions. I don't know what they'll use, and I'm preparing myself for the possibility they'll drop the whole thing."

Ten minutes later, they left the coffee shop. In the car, George extracted himself from Clarice's hair with some difficulty. He was glad he had six legs because two of them were hard to get out of Clarice's hair. He hoped he hadn't pulled any hair. Clarice didn't seem to register any discomfort, so he guessed he'd succeeded.

On the way home, Clarice and Judy told Brad the story of forgetting George. They told him they didn't know where he was during Clarice's interview. Clarice explained, "I felt like a fool when Marlene, she does our makeup, told me she was about to work on my hair. George, of course, was paying more attention than I was, so he flew off somewhere."

"After Clarice's interview was over, he flew onto my shoulder. I was waiting in the lobby."

When they arrived at the apartment, Judy went right away to get some food for George. As he started forming the dung into a ball, Judy said,

"I'm so sorry we forgot about you at the news station." She realized he was unable to respond. Still, she felt it was important to say something.

When George had finished eating, Judy came with the wet paper towel. Then she took him to the computer to give him a chance to type. The three humans huddled around the computer, and Judy asked, "Where were you after you flew off of Clarice?"

`panicked`

"I'm so sorry George. I should have thought about you and taken you out to Judy before makeup and hair."

"Yes, I'm sorry too. I have to admit I forgot all about you being in Clarice's hair."

George had had enough time to calm down, so he typed,

`ok`

"So, back to my question. Where did you go?"

`newsroom curtain`

"Oh, so you witnessed my performance?"

He went to the Y key and then had Judy type.

`very nice`

"Why thank you. Now you're making me feel bad about calling you dung boy before."

"Good, we've all made up now," Brad remarked. "Clarice, are you going to call your family to tell them to watch the network news?

"You think I should? They might not run my interview."

"Brad's right. You should call them."

"I will, and it's time to let Simon off parole. I'll call him too. I might even invite him to come meet his old college friend tomorrow afternoon.

I'm sure it will be fun."

`looking forward to it`

The network news ran a short segment showing some of the original interview and two of the questions Clarice answered in the afternoon. Brad and Judy jumped off their seats and gave Clarice a high five. George, who had been sitting on Judy's shoulder, flew up to his perch on the curtains. He didn't want to get injured during any of the celebration. He was sure hugs would follow the high fives.

Clarice's cell phone started to ring, and she went off to talk to her family. "They recorded it!" she called out to Brad and Judy.

Brad, Judy, and Clarice went out to celebrate. They left George at home in his cage. It was okay with him. He needed some rest.

Chapter Twenty-Three

AFTER BREAKFAST SUNDAY MORNING, BRAD surprised Judy by suggesting they go to church. "You never went to church when we were in college. Why now?" Judy asked.

"I know," Brad replied. "Since I've been having trouble, I've started going some. The Army has some interesting chaplains."

"Sure, I'll go. Which denomination? My folks were Methodists. They hardly ever went. We even missed some Christmas and Easter services."

"Let's try a Lutheran church. The chaplain I liked was a Lutheran. My folks weren't anything."

"I'll hop on the internet and see where we can go. Clarice will get a big kick out of this. She goes every Sunday and bugs me about not going. Her church is some kind of Baptist. George went with her last Sunday when I was picking you up at the airport."

Judy was right. Clarice was surprised Brad and Judy were going to church. They assembled by the computer to find out what George wanted to do.

```
clarice pendant
```

"All right with you, Clarice?" Judy asked. "Wearing the pendant two weeks in a row won't bother you, will it?"

"No, I'm honored he wants to go with me. It will be good preparation for his meeting with Simon this afternoon."

"Brad, Clarice's church has a luncheon every Sunday, so she and George won't be home until about two. While we can go out to eat somewhere, we want to be here when she brings Simon."

"Who's Simon?" Brad asked. "I think I heard his name last night."

"He's one of Clarice's many admirers. Clarice and Simon are an off-and-on item. Lately, they've been off. With this invite, Clarice is angling for on again. The surprise is George knew Simon in college. Clarice is sure the notion of him being reincarnated as a dung beetle will really freak Simon out."

"Yes, I am," Clarice commented. "Simon is the assistant minister at our church. He and I argue all the time. He believes every word in the Bible is literally true. While I keep telling him there's a difference between inspired and literally true, he doesn't buy it."

Brad felt ill-prepared to enter the conversation, but it didn't stop him. "Hasn't the Bible been translated at least a couple of times before it got to the English we use?"

"The argument, which is a good one, won't work on Simon. I've tried it."

Judy jumped in. "How will he react to George's reincarnation?"

"I can't wait to see," Clarice responded. "He's going to take a lot of convincing. It will knock him for a loop. He has very firm beliefs about what happens to someone when they die. I don't think being reincarnated as a dung beetle is anything he's ever contemplated."

"Doesn't make him any different than most people," Brad said.

"It'll be different with Simon, believe me," Clarice commented.

Brad and Judy returned from the Lutheran church before Clarice and fixed themselves lunch. They hadn't enjoyed the service. The minister spent too much time making them feel bad about what they were doing. What's more, not a single member of the small congregation came up to greet them.

George knew what to expect at Clarice's church this time. He concentrated on Simon Paulson's role in the service. The head minister did all the heavy lifting, and Simon did minor stuff—the call to worship, the offering prayer, and introducing a couple of hymns. Clarice received a great deal of attention after the service. Lots of people had seen the network news interview and wanted to come up and congratulate her. She finally had to excuse herself to get to the bathroom for George to eat. At the luncheon Simon claimed a seat beside her, and it was clear he was happy to share some of the attention showered on Clarice.

Given a closer look at Simon during the lunch, George thought he looked better than he remembered. Though it was difficult for George to tell, he thought Simon had grown an inch or two. He hadn't been particularly tall in college, so George was surprised when it was clear Simon was considerably taller than Clarice, even in her high heels.

When they'd finished lunch, Clarice and George brought Simon to the apartment.

"Great to see you," Judy said as she gave Simon a brief hug. Then she gestured to Brad. "This is my boyfriend, Brad Curry."

Simon shook Brad's outstretched hand. "Clarice has been telling me about you. She told me you just returned from Afghanistan. That must have been tough."

"You're right. It wasn't easy. As I understand it, you're not here to meet me. There's another member of our group you should meet."

Simon scanned the apartment with a puzzled look on his face.

Clarice let him twist in the wind a bit and then relented. "Come sit at the table, Simon. This is something you'd better take sitting down."

Everyone went to the table. Judy sat in front of the computer with Clarice and Simon flanking her. When everyone was seated, Clarice opened the pendant, and George walked out and hopped on the computer.

"What's going on?" Simon asked, looking very startled.

The three in the know smiled. Finally, Clarice spoke up. "You already know this bug, Simon. Since you obviously don't recognize him, he'd better reintroduce himself."

George went to the keyboard.

```
hi I'm george wilcox
```

Simon looked at Clarice. "What's going on? Why is Judy typing this nonsense?"

"Look closely, Simon. Judy is only typing the letters the bug is indicating. Slow down and use one finger so he can tell what's going on."

```
remember me
```

"I repeat. What's going on?"

"Here, switch places with me, Simon," Judy offered as she stood up. "It's the only way Clarice or Brad would believe what's going on."

Reluctantly, Simon moved into Judy's seat.

"Ask him a question," Clarice suggested.

"Are you a hoax?"

```
no I'm george wilcox
```

Simon looked up from the computer and addressed the group. "How are you doing this?"

Clarice responded, "We're not, Simon. It's no trick. Your old college friend George Wilcox has been reincarnated as a dung beetle. Excuse me, as a scarab. Anyway, he found Judy when she was on a safari in Botswana."

Simon stood and started to pace around the apartment. "Clarice, I don't know how you are doing this, and I don't like it. George Wilcox was shot. I went to his memorial service."

"I know it's hard to believe," Brad replied. "I know you're convinced this is some kind of prank. Believe me, it's not."

"Listen, Simon," Clarice said. "Is there something only George Wilcox would know?"

"Maybe."

"Ask him about it."

"I remember a late-night discussion he and I had in the dorm. We were in a philosophy class together. I was very skeptical of Kierkegaard's ideas, and one of them really set me off. I bet your bug doesn't know which one it was."

"You want me to type?" Clarice asked.

"Sure, go ahead. You won't know the answer either."

`subjectivity is truth`

Simon started to shake, so Clarice stood and put her arm around him. "It can't be," he stammered. "He was the only one there, and you certainly weren't there."

"I had trouble believing it too. It took me a long time. I accused Judy of all kinds of things. Finally, I understood it's true. George Wilcox is this dung beetle."

"Reincarnation?" Simon seemed befuddled. "I don't know what to think."

George jumped up and down.

"He wants to type," Judy said.

"I'll do it," Clarice responded.

`john 14 verse 2`

"In my father's house are many mansions," Simon quoted.

After a pause, Clarice spoke up. "I get it. He is trying to say the passage leaves lots of territory unexplained. Some of the mansions might be right here on earth. George found himself in Africa."

"I can't understand why my God would do such a thing," Simon lamented.

`don't limit your God`

"Sounds like him. He was always telling me to expand my view of God."

Simon rose again and paced around the room. Clarice went to him and took him in her arms. "It's what I've been trying to say all along, Simon. You've should loosen up. You and the God you talk about are too uptight. Leave some room for doubt. You don't have to know everything."

Simon extracted himself from Clarice's embrace and started to pace again. Clarice came and sat with the others. They sat in silence.

Finally, Simon came and sat down. "It's a lot to take in. I still can't believe it. Judy, can you tell me how it all happened?"

Judy gave Simon the full explanation about how George had approached her in Botswana, and the others chimed in with explanations of how they'd become convinced he was who he said he was. Simon sat back and listened. After everyone finished, he finally spoke. "I guess there's no way I can't believe it. It's just so weird! I guess Clarice is trying to tell me it shouldn't shake my faith. I'm not sure I understand."

"That's my point," Clarice interrupted. "You don't have to understand everything. It's the whole point of faith. There are some things you aren't going to be able to figure out. There are some things you have to take on faith. The search for ultimate truths is going to be fruitless. It's what we've been arguing about for so long."

Simon shook his head and smiled. "I need time to sort out my thoughts."

After a pause, he continued. "Who would have thought it would take a bug, a dung beetle, for me to see what you've been trying to say for so long?"

Clarice took his hand. "Don't be hard on yourself, Simon. Maybe I'm not very good at explaining myself. Communication is a two-way street. I'm glad we're understanding each other a little bit better."

George indicated he wanted to type, and Judy sat down at the keyboard.

clarice great girl

"I guess he was talking to me," Simon responded. "And he's right."

"Yes, sometimes he's right," Judy commented. "Not always. He can be wrong, and not very helpful at times."

"So, have you made any progress on the mission he picked out for you?" Simon asked.

Judy, Brad, and Clarice explained the saga of trying to find out who killed George. When they'd finished, Simon summarized what he'd heard. "So, the long and short of it is you've eliminated just about everyone he's suggested. You're almost back where you started. The only thing I can suggest is going to the scene of the crime. Doesn't Sherlock Holmes learn a great deal by investigating the crime scene? Also, in this case it might jog George's memory."

Brad jumped up. "Great idea, Simon. We have the crime report. It lists the place where he was found. Why didn't we think about that?"

"What do you say, George?" Judy asked.

I'm game

The group broke up then. Clarice and Simon begged off and drove to the church where they'd left Simon's car while the rest of the crew took off to investigate the crime scene. They were sure they weren't Sherlock Holmes. Still, maybe they'd find something.

Chapter Twenty-Four

THEY DROVE TO QUINCY STREET, which was in the Cleveland Heights section of the metro area. They took the computer in case George wanted to type. The police report listed the names of the Quincy Street neighbors who had been interviewed and gave their addresses, so they knew where to start.

George sat on the dashboard, giving him a good view. Much of the territory they drove through was familiar to him. A few minutes after they'd turned away from the lake and started to climb, he saw a house. For some reason, it seemed familiar. He almost jumped up and down to alert Brad to stop, but he didn't.

They turned right and then right again onto the section of Quincy Street they wanted. Halfway down the street, they saw a vacant lot adjacent to one of the addresses they were headed for and across the street from another.

Brad pulled over and stopped. "This would be the most sensible place to abandon a car containing a dead body. A killer would want to avoid dumping the body in front of an occupied house. This vacant lot would be the spot. You bring two cars, drop off the car with the body and get picked up by the other car. It probably happened in the middle of the night. None of the people living nearby would have known anything about it."

"It would take two people. I guess it's thoroughly possible. Should we get out and look around?" Judy asked.

"Sure, and let George fly around to see if anything comes back."

"Good idea." Judy opened her door, and George flew out.

George flew up to a tree branch about ten feet above the car. He felt strange being where his body had been found. Actually, this wasn't returning to the scene of the crime. This was returning to where his body was found. If the police were right, the crime happened somewhere else. Still, the police might be wrong, so he started to look around. Nothing seemed familiar. He saw Brad and Judy trying to play Sherlock Holmes. He didn't think they'd find anything.

George decided to go look at the house they'd passed on the way. *There was something familiar about the house. It's not a strong memory; on the other hand, I don't think it's nothing, either.* He knew he should probably alert Brad and Judy about checking out the house. Since communication was so cumbersome, he decided to just go.

He flew through the vacant lot on Quincy Street and by the house facing the other street. As he'd hoped, he was right across from the house he wanted to check out. As he flew toward it, he had a better view than he'd had in the car. Since the house, an impressive contemporary, sat below the road level, all he'd seen from the car was a little of the deck and a lot of the roof. Now he could see more of the house. The house sat on one edge of a large lot the owners kept natural. The house was a little sideways to the street, giving it a nice view and considerable privacy. He flew over the deck, noting the hot tub, and tried to peek in the windows. After he'd flown around the entire house and looked in every window, he decided no one was home.

George flew up to a tree branch to rest. While he was unable to shake the idea this house was important somehow, he couldn't figure out why. *If I'd encountered this house as a human, I'd have had a very different view.* He flew out toward the street, went down to what he thought was his human eye level, and landed on another tree branch. He looked at the house again. His view now was more like it had been from the car. Mostly he saw deck and roof. He moved away from the street to get a different view. From this position he saw more of the deck and part of the hot tub as well as lots of roof.

Before flying back to Brad and Judy, he looked at the address, 1287 St. Clair Road. *For some reason, it might be important.*

Judy looked impatient when George flew to the roof of the car. "We've been looking for you and calling. We didn't see you anywhere, and you didn't come. Let's get into the car to give you a chance to tell us where you were off to."

In the car, Judy fired up the computer and George hopped on the keys.

`laptop on lap`

"Very funny," Judy said, a little exasperated. "Yes, the laptop is on my lap for a change. We want to know if you found anything, and where did you go."

`already dead here`

"He's right, Judy," Brad commented. "The police report said they thought he'd been shot somewhere else, and the body was driven here."

"What about the second part of my question?"

`house 1287 St Clair`

"I'll put it in my phone," Brad said. When he found the address, he continued. "It's right around the block from here. It was easy for you to fly there. Why? What made you interested in the house?"

not sure faint memory

"Let's take a close look," Judy suggested. "Maybe looking at it again will jog his memory. Memory is a weird thing. I'm not surprised he can't remember being shot. I've been thinking about it. Even if he saw who did it, the trauma involved might well have interrupted the implanting of a memory. And I guess other things happening that day might not have been transferred to the part of the memory he retained. At least it's my guess. He told us he's not able to remember the case he was working on when he was shot."

Brad started the car and made a U-turn on Quincy Street, went to the end of the block, and turned left. Another left turn put him on St. Clair Road right beside 1287. He slowed down.

"It's a nice-looking house," Judy commented. "I'm not sure I'd want to have to get out of the driveway on a snowy day. It looks pretty steep."

"Fair enough," Brad replied. "It has a nice deck with a hot tub. It's set up for outdoor living in good weather. I like the woods off the deck. The guy doesn't have any lawn to mow." After a pause, he continued, "Look at the size of the chimney. It must have a big fireplace, so it will be cozy in the winter. I wonder who lives there. Is there any way of finding out?"

As Judy was preparing to reply, a car behind them honked. Brad pulled over a bit so the car could get by.

Judy finally had a chance to reply. "There should be. Clarice would know. We can ask her when we get back."

"She might not be finished with Simon. Though I'm not sure, it looked like they might spend most of the afternoon together."

"Could be."

George kept trying to figure out what it was he remembered about the house on St. Clair. He'd had a similar reaction when he'd seen the tattoo on Greg's wife's arm. He had a fleeting memory he was unable to get to really come into focus. *Were the two things related?* he wondered.

In the end, he found it very frustrating. Most of his memories were very clear. He'd always prided himself on his good memory. Having a good memory made school easy. Now there was an important part of his life he couldn't remember. He didn't like it.

When they returned home, the apartment was empty. Judy set the computer on the table in its normal spot. Looking around to determine where Jangles was, George sat down next to the keyboard.

Judy sat at the computer. "Anything come to you when we drove by the house?

He flew to the N key.

"Let's see what you can find out about the house," Brad suggested.

Judy Googled *1287 St. Clair Road, Cleveland* and came up with several entries. It turned out the house had changed hands several times. One of the real estate companies had a virtual tour of the house still up.

After watching the tour, Judy asked George if any of it jogged his memory.

He went to the N key.

Just then, Clarice and Simon came in. Judy noticed changed body language. She was sure Clarice and Simon had reconciled. When Simon wasn't looking, she gave Clarice a wink. Clarice smiled and returned the wink.

"Did you find out anything by going to the scene of the crime?" Simon asked.

"No, we came up empty," Brad said. "As George pointed out, according to the police report he was most likely dead by the time he was taken to where his body was found. It wasn't really the scene of the crime. The only interesting thing was that he thought one of the nearby houses looked familiar. Unfortunately, his memory is hazy. We're looking to see what we can find out about the house."

"Yeah, it's a nice house. Look at the real estate ads for it. They have lots of pictures."

After they'd seen the photos of the house, Clarice spoke up. "Looks like a nice place. I like contemporary designs, particularly this one. The big deck and hot tub are probably great when it's not freezing outside. Do you know what he remembers about the place?"

"He hasn't been able to tell us anything," Judy responded.

"Is it okay if I ask him a question?" Simon asked.

"Go ahead."

"Is it the inside or the outside of the house you remember?"

`deck hot tub`

"Good question, Simon," Brad remarked. "His answer's consistent with him being a private detective. His boss told me they spend a lot of time looking for wayward spouses. His last case might have involved him snooping on someone on the deck or maybe in the hot tub."

"Right, George?" Simon asked.

`don't know`

Simon looked puzzled, so Judy explained. "He doesn't recall much starting about a day before he was murdered. We think the trauma from the killing interrupted those memories being implanted. Maybe the memories are only there in fragments, so the house seemed familiar. Unfortunately, nothing is clear for him. While we hoped seeing the house again might make things clearer, it hasn't seemed to work."

"I see," Simon replied. "That makes things much more difficult."

"Yes," Clarice said. "It's a little like trying to complete a puzzle with a few critical pieces missing."

"What are you two doing for dinner, Clarice?" Judy asked.

"I don't know. We haven't talked about it."

"I say we should go out. When we were driving this afternoon, we passed the Mountaintop. I haven't been there in ages, and I'd like to go back. Want to come with us?"

"What do you say, Simon?" Clarice asked.

"Sounds nice," answered Simon. "I've heard of the Mountaintop, but I've never been there. It's supposed to be good, so sure I'd like to go. Before we go, I have some questions for George. Is it okay if I ask him?"

"In a minute. Let me find the phone number, so I can get us a reservation," Judy responded.

Judy found the phone number for the restaurant, and she stood up to let Simon sit in front of the computer.

`let me off at 1287`

"He means tonight before we go to the restaurant," Brad commented. "It's a good idea. He is much more likely to have a chance to see the people who live in the house in the evening. With as many windows as the house has, he'll be able to spot the people. It might restart his memory."

"Sounds like a plan," Judy responded. "I was able to get a table for four at seven-thirty."

"Okay, we're set," Simon said. "Now, I have some questions for you. First, what do you know about the time between when you were shot and when you became a dung beetle? Did you see the Lord?"

`nothing and no`

"Were other dung beetles reincarnated humans?"

`couldn't tell`

"How did you learn how to be a dung beetle? No, that's not what I want to ask. This is it. Did you know you were a reincarnated human when you were a young dung beetle, or did it just come to you when you were older?"

`older`

"Yeah," Brad interrupted. "He told me it came to him suddenly when he was a grownup dung beetle. It must have been a real jolt when his dung beetle brain was replaced by a human brain. I guess it's what happened."

"The switch is not complete," Judy commented. "He still does some dung beetle things. Wait until you see what he eats and what he does with it before he eats."

"Clarice and I have been talking about this all afternoon," Simon responded. "It really threw me at first. It was so unusual, not like people who've had near-death experiences. I mean, they talk about walking toward the light and feeling joy. Did you see a light when you died?"

`woke up as scarab`

"He likes to be called a scarab, not a dung beetle," Clarice explained.

"Okay, fine," Simon responded. "I guess it might not be the same thing for each person—dying, I mean. Or he can't remember going toward the light. As Clarice keeps telling me, there is so much we don't know. Maybe so much we shouldn't know. What I'll conclude is George is evidence for the idea our soul or our consciousness lives on."

"I guess you're right," Brad concluded. "At least for him it did."

`don't tell anyone`

"Yes, Simon, he doesn't want to become an oddity," Judy explained. "He doesn't want all the attention. As you discovered, he doesn't know any details about how he was reincarnated. He just woke up one day as a dung beetle—excuse me, a scarab. He isn't able to explain it any better than you or I can. He simply wants to be left alone to find out what happened to him. He hasn't thought further."

"In an odd way, he's proof of life after death," Simon pressed. "His story should be shouted from the mountain tops."

Clarice pounced. "Really, Simon. Do people want to learn when they're dead they get to eat shit for a stint while they're a dung beetle?

No offense, George, your current state doesn't seem so wonderful. I say we keep this to ourselves. Simon, you should consider this for more than one afternoon."

"Maybe not everyone becomes a dung beetle."

"There you go," Clarice commented. "You're right. Maybe they don't. So, what we don't know is bigger than what we do. We need to honor his wishes. Keep him secret. Who knows what we'll find out? We only have one little piece of information."

"Clarice is right," Judy added. "I've promised George we wouldn't tell many people about him. The four of us should be enough for the time being."

amen

"Okay, for now. I'll think about it more. It's just so unexpected. I guess you can tell. It's thrown me for a loop."

Chapter Twenty-Five

A HALF-HOUR BEFORE THEY had to leave for the restaurant, Judy fed George. Simon recoiled at the smell of the elephant dung, and he was startled when he witnessed George rolling the poop into a ball before starting to eat. At seven, the five of them left for the restaurant and George's chance to stake out the house on St. Clair. They went to the house first, and George flew out the window. Judy gave him explicit instructions. When they were finished with the restaurant, she told George they would drive beside the house and honk. When he heard them, he was supposed to fly to their car on the next block up St. Clair. They didn't want to stop beside 1287. It wouldn't be a good idea to give the people there the notion they were being surveilled.

After leaving the car, George flew down to a tree from which he could see in the windows at the back of the house. While there was a light on somewhere, he didn't see any movement. Fifteen minutes later, when he was getting thoroughly bored, he heard movement in the tree above him. It was a squirrel jumping from limb to limb. George wasn't happy about what he saw, so he shifted under a leaf. Luckily, the squirrel didn't seem interested in him.

When it was completely dark, he heard a car pull into the driveway. The driveway was on the other side of the house, so all he saw were the headlights of the car. Soon lights came on in the house, and George saw a man and a woman walk into the room behind the deck. They opened the sliding glass door and walked out onto the deck. He had a good look at them. The woman was older than the man, maybe in her fifties. She was an attractive brunette, in what looked like an expensive green dress and a nice sparkly necklace. George saw a wedding ring paired with a big diamond on her left hand. The man, who carried a bottle of wine, was probably in his early thirties. He was dressed a little more casually than the woman. He wore a dark blue sport coat and a cream-colored shirt open at the neck. His hair was blonde and looked a little shaggy. George didn't see a wedding ring on him.

The man put down the wine and went into the house for a minute. He returned with two wine glasses and a corkscrew. After he opened the bottle, he poured two glasses and took one to the woman. George thought about moving closer to hear what they were talking about, but he didn't. He was nervous about moving.

As he watched and the couple drank their wine, the woman, who at first had appeared a little stiff, seemed to loosen up. George thought the guy knew what he was doing. He wasn't rushing her. While it was clear she was interested, he didn't push it. During their second glass of wine, he put his arm around the woman, and she settled into him. It wasn't long before the two of them were kissing. After a few deep kisses, they went into the house, and George lost track of them.

With nothing to watch, the night-time noises started to intrude on his consciousness. There were crickets somewhere and a deep-throated frog. Also, occasionally he heard movement in the leaf cover beneath him. It might be squirrels or snakes or he didn't know what else. He wasn't happy just sitting, so he decided to fly around the house to discover what he could see in the windows. The shades on the sliding glass doors onto the deck were open. Maybe some others would be too. He didn't have any luck on the side of the house, away from the street. As he turned toward the street, he saw another car pull into the driveway, so he flew to the roof.

George thought the car was strange. First, it was a Humvee, which seemed out of place. Second, it had turned off its lights and engine before coasting down the driveway. He wondered if whoever it was didn't want the two in the house to know about the Humvee's arrival. A guy dressed in a camouflage outfit got out and headed up the driveway. George didn't know what was going on, so he followed the guy, staying about fifty feet behind him. At the top of the driveway the guy turned right along St. Clair. He walked slowly past the house and turned right again at what was probably the edge of the lot associated with the house.

George positioned himself in a tree to keep track of the guy. It looked like the guy was a guard or something. His head was on a swivel most of the time as he walked. He appeared to be checking out the house and its surroundings. He lost the guy when he went behind the house. George didn't suspect it was a big deal. It wasn't. About five minutes later, the guy appeared again, walking the perimeter along St. Clair. This time he didn't complete his circuit of the house. Instead, he sat down behind the house under a tree close to where George had originally positioned himself.

George decided to fly closer and get a good look at the guy. The whole thing was mysterious. He had a stint as a guard when he was a detective. It was nothing like this. His guard duty had involved a large party. The agency hired some temps, and a whole team of them were scattered around the grounds of a big estate. Nothing happened. It was boring duty. He remembered spending most of his time checking out the girls at the party. This guy had a different assignment.

Two short flights took George to a tree branch about twelve feet behind the guard or whatever he was. The guy was old, maybe in his fifties, and had a gray Fu Manchu mustache. He wore some sort of straps on his camouflage outfit, and George was startled when he saw the straps were there to hold a holster with a pistol in it. The holster was on the guy's chest where the pistol was easy to access.

George couldn't figure out why the guy was there. *What is it about this house that requires this type of security? This isn't a dangerous neighborhood* Twenty minutes later, the guy stood up and did another circuit of the house. He went counterclockwise this time. As the guy was finishing his lap, George saw movement in the house. The man inside came out to retrieve the wine bottle and the two glasses. The guard, who'd also sensed the movement, stepped behind a tree when the man came out.

Five minutes later, the first car left the driveway. He wondered what the guard was going to do next. He didn't have to wait long. The guy walked out to St. Clair and headed toward the house. His walk was different. He wasn't on patrol now. He was hiking back to his vehicle. Sure enough, the guy walked down the driveway, and George heard the Humvee leaving.

George sure wished he had a way of telling time. With nothing to look at, the noises seemed to get louder. He didn't like not being able to see well. The streetlight didn't provide any help where he was. At the same time, his nose was sending him all kinds of unsettling messages. He had to do something, so he flew to the deck. He didn't really learn anything. Just as he was about to see if there was any way to enter the house, he heard a honk. It was Judy and the group. He flew to the car and Simon let him in.

At the apartment, Brad, Judy, Simon, and Clarice were clamoring for a report, so Judy sat behind the computer and George flew off her shoulder to the keyboard.

"What did you see?" Brad asked.

`three people`

"Keep going."

`a man a woman and a guard`

"What were they doing?" Judy asked.

`man putting moves on woman`

"I get it," Brad said. "The guy was trying to get the woman to sleep with him. Right?"

George went to the Y key.

"Did he succeed?"

He returned to the Y key.

Simon asked, "What did they look like?"

"Simon, it isn't easy for him to give long descriptions," Clarice said.

"Let him try."

`woman older than man`

Simon continued. "Did they live there?"

`no came and went in car`

"I see," Brad said "They only used the house for their tryst. Is that what it looked like to you?"

George went to the Y key.

"Strange," Clarice remarked. "I'm getting the impression this house is not a normal family house. I wonder what's going on."

"Tell us about the guard," Brad said.

`drives humvee wears camo`

"This is getting interesting," Simon commented.

"How did you know he was a guard?" Judy asked.

`walked perimeter carried pistol`

"Sounds like a guard to me," Brad concluded. "Did he leave when the other people did?"

`right after`

"The whole set up is weird, if you ask me," Clarice added. "It sounds like the guy has a love nest where he takes women, and he wants to be sure he's not discovered. It's all I can figure."

The others nodded and silence descended. Finally, Judy spoke up. "Did the woman have a wedding band?"

George flew to the Y key.

"What about the man?"

He flew to the N key.

"It's what I expected," Clarice said triumphantly. "This dude is one of those guys who preys on married women. I wouldn't be surprised if he takes pictures of them and then blackmails them. George told us he was younger. The whole thing stinks if you ask me."

"While it certainly fits what he is telling us, it might be something else," Brad said. "Maybe the woman is willing, and it's her house. Maybe she's rich, so she has security. There's no way we can be certain it's the man's love nest."

Judy jumped in. "Brad's right, we don't have enough information to know anything for sure. Also, we don't know how this fits in with George's murder. I wonder if any of his friends or enemies know about this house. This whole thing is confusing. Wait—we haven't asked the big question. George, did this bring up any new memories?"

He went to the N key.

Brad broke the silence following this information. "George, you're going to have to check out this house some more. We don't know if your previous experience with it was in the daytime or at night. And we all believe something fishy is going on. I mean, it's weird to have a guard. I say we should drop you off there tomorrow afternoon."

With everyone staring at George, Judy asked, "What about it?"

George was surprised by Brad's suggestion. He wasn't sure he wanted to experience all those weird smells and noises again. *It was at night. Daytime would be better.*

ok try again

"Good, I have a group therapy session tomorrow in the afternoon. Judy's going with me, so we can drop you off and pick you up a few hours later. We don't have much to go on, and we shouldn't ignore the fact you thought there was something familiar about the house."

"Brad, do you mind if I ask about the therapy?" Simon asked.

The four humans spent the remainder of the evening discussing Brad's PTSD and his thoughts about the group therapy. He didn't think it was likely the therapy would work because the traumas triggering the PTSD were likely to be different for each individual. Then again, the therapists had to know the experiences were different. Simon, Clarice, and Judy were a sympathetic audience, and George thought the discussion was probably helpful for Brad.

Chapter Twenty-Six

THE NEXT MORNING, THEY ALL collected around the table for breakfast. Munching on some toast, Judy turned to Clarice. "I can't help myself. I know I shouldn't be so direct. Still, I have to ask. Are you and Simon an item again?"

"Most likely. He took the news about George better than I thought he would. His inflexibility was the biggest thing getting in the way of us being together. Fortunately, he showed me he can change."

Judy could tell George wanted to type, so she obliged.

`glad to be of service`

"I'm not sure you deserve any credit," Clarice responded. "It wasn't anything you did. It was who you are—a person reincarnated as a dung beetle. It really threw Simon for a while. Then he came through the way I wanted him to. We had some really good talks yesterday afternoon."

"Does it mean you're going to stop seeing Jay?"

"I don't know. I'm going to let Jay stay where he is for now. He's at his football training camp, so I have a chance to get solid with Simon before I have to develop a strategy to deal with him."

Brad spoke up then. "It's called not burning your bridges."

"Yes. I might need to make a hasty retreat."

"I hope you don't have to," Judy said. "Simon is better for you than Jay. I know Jay's hot. The walls in this apartment aren't terribly thick. I've heard Jay and you more than once. It's all you two have. You and Simon have a deeper connection."

"You and Brad should remember what you just said about the walls, Hon."

Judy and Brad exchanged a look and then all three of them started to laugh.

George wished he was able to laugh, too. Unfortunately, he didn't know how dung beetles laughed. He liked being with these people. At the same time, he knew he wasn't really a part of the group in the same way. He decided these kinds of thoughts weren't good for him, so he asked a question. Judy typed for him.

`today's plan`

Brad caught on. "He wants to know what we're doing today. Here's my thought. Judy and I have to go to my first session at the VA at four this afternoon, so George, like we said last night, we're going to drop you off at the house before then. That's all I know so far."

George had been wondering about the notion of spending more time looking at the deck and the hot tub. All things considered, he thought it would be a waste of time. Still, he didn't want to argue the point. Brad was definite, and he knew Judy wasn't about to countermand Brad's wishes.

Clarice got up. "I'm going to shower and get dressed for work. You three go ahead and plan your day."

George was happy to see Jangles follow Clarice into her room. The cat hadn't been aggressive in a couple of days. Still, he knew he had to be on guard anytime the cat was around.

"Brad, you've left something out," Judy commented. "You still have a very small civilian wardrobe. We should go shopping before your VA appointment. We'll drop George off earlier. He can spend more time at the house."

"I guess you're right. I do need civilian clothes, but can't you pick them out for me?"

"No, Honey, you have to go with me. I can't try things on. And you might not like what I'd pick out. You can do it."

"Okay, don't take me to any really crowded stores. Crowds still bother me."

Judy stood up and kissed Brad. "I forget. I'm so sorry. I'll be careful to help you avoid crowds. Just tell me if you're getting nervous or whatever. We can adjust."

"It comes and goes. The nervousness, I mean. I was okay at the restaurant last night. I'm feeling a little edgy today. Maybe it's the VA appointment. I don't know."

George indicated he wanted to type, so Judy sat down.

`take my food`

"He's right," Judy responded. "If we let him off at the house before we go shopping and don't pick him up until we're finished with the VA appointment, he won't have had anything to eat for quite a while. I guess we can bring some food for him to eat when we pick him up."

"We can drive home with the windows open. I'd hate to have the smell trapped in the car."

`smells good`

"Let's agree to disagree," Judy remarked as she left the table. "I'm going to go shower. I hope Clarice hasn't used up all the hot water."

Brad rose and did one of his little tours around the apartment, checking all the windows and even going to see if the door was locked.

George had noticed he was a little jumpier this morning, and he'd heard him last night too. He'd been up several times. Maybe this therapy wasn't a good idea. The very thought of it seemed to make Brad's PTSD symptoms a little worse.

An hour after lunch, they took off. Judy had given George a large helping of dung, and he'd eaten as much of it as he wanted. He was happy to see Judy had remembered to bring his evening meal. He liked riding on the dashboard and looking at the city as they drove. Brad suggested they should let him off in front of 1287's next-door neighbor, not directly across from the house. Brad slowed, and George flew out the window.

He flew to the tree he'd used last night and inspected the house. Nothing was happening. The house looked to be completely empty. He settled onto a comfortable spot on the tree. He was covered by a bunch of leaves, so he didn't have to worry about any squirrels seeing him. It was hot, and he was sleepy from his big lunch. He dozed and then caught himself. Eventually he gave up and took a nap.

A strange sound awakened George. When he was fully alert, he saw a guy in a white coat on the deck. He must have heard the sliding glass door opening. The guy looked at the backyard, and then turned and yelled something toward the house. George didn't understand what the guy was saying. It was in Spanish. The guy returned to the house, and George saw him and another guy moving around in the room off the deck. After about ten minutes during which he couldn't really see what the people were doing, he decided to fly around the house. When he reached the driveway, he saw a white van parked there. He flew a little lower and read the sign on the side of the van—Andrea's Catering and Party Planning. Whoever lived in the house was going to have a party sometime later.

George continued his circuit of the house. Most of the windows were curtained. The exception was a window off the kitchen. He landed on the window ledge and peeked in. As he'd thought he would, he saw the catering crew. They were setting up party platters for a fairly small gathering. He saw a Champagne bottle on ice. There were two workers, and they were doing their last cleanup. While he watched, the workers left the kitchen. A few minutes later, he heard their van leaving the driveway.

He flew to his spot in the tree. He thought he would see some action soon. He was wrong. Nothing happened, even though he stayed alert this time. There was going to be a party, and he hoped it happened before Brad and Judy came to get him.

Meanwhile, Brad and Judy parked at the VA hospital. Brad had a room number where he was supposed to report. The receptionist at the front door gave them directions. Brad and Judy were able to follow the directions with only one wrong turn. When they were straightened out, Judy saw Brad pause at the sign over the entrance to the suite of offices—Psychiatric Ward. Judy squeezed his hand, and they entered. There was a nurse's station in front of the office corridor. Brad went up to the nurse and checked in. She took his information and looked at his credentials. She gave him a stack of forms on a clipboard and asked him to fill them out. Finally, she told him Doctor Morrison would be with him in a few minutes.

Brad sat down beside Judy and started filling out the forms. Most of it was routine stuff Brad had filled out several times in the Army. He was annoyed. Several of the forms asked the same questions. He thought, *the Army loves its paperwork, so I shouldn't be surprised the VA is no different.*

Judy saw him starting to tense up. "Do you want me to fill out the next one, Honey? I know most of the answers."

"Thanks. Yes. I'm getting tired of filling out the same information on each form."

Judy finished the last two forms and only had to ask Brad about two things. She had him sign the forms, and he took them up to the nurse.

"Here you go. Don't lose them. I don't want to fill them out again."

The nurse smiled and didn't respond. Brad walked toward Judy, but he didn't sit down beside her. He did one of his walks around the waiting room, looking out all the windows. While Judy thought she had some notion of what Brad was going through, maybe she didn't. She hoped Brad would calm down before they were called to see the doctor.

Brad made a couple of circuits of the waiting room, and then he came back and sat beside Judy. She reached out and grabbed his hand. "Are you all right, Honey? I know this must be stressful."

"I'm not feeling great. Just hold my hand. It helps."

Three minutes later, the nurse called, "Mr. Curry."

Brad and Judy rose and followed the nurse who led them down a corridor to Dr. Morrison's office. Judy's first impression was, *this guy's too young to be a doctor. He looked like a college kid.* He was skinny and had longish brown hair. He didn't look military at all. When she made it a little closer, Judy saw he wasn't as young as he first appeared. In any event, he wasn't much older than she was.

As they entered, the doctor came out from behind his desk with an outstretched hand. Shaking Brad's hand, he said, "I'm James Morrison, Brad." Extending his hand to Judy, he continued, "And who is this? I expected Brad to be alone."

"I'm Judy Clayton, Brad's girlfriend. I want to help him with his therapy. It's okay if I'm here, I hope."

"Yes, it's fine. In fact, we encourage our patients to have a support person. Brad is lucky you're willing to come. You won't be able to accompany him everywhere. For example, we don't allow nonparticipants into the group sessions, but you can observe them."

Dr. Morrison went behind his desk and gestured to the chairs, so Brad and Judy sat down. The doctor opened a folder. "You're a little bit of an unusual case, Brad. We don't see many active-duty people. I see here you have a couple of weeks before you'll be discharged."

"Yeah, I'm here using up my leave. I'm going back for three days or something. The doctor I talked to before I left Afghanistan suggested I get a jump on therapy. He arranged for me to come here."

"You're right. Dr. Lenderman. I don't know him. The way I see it, he's done both of us a favor. It's much better to start treatment as soon as we can. PTSD is a difficult diagnosis. Addressing it early and aggressively can be very beneficial."

Judy reached and squeezed Brad's hand. She felt him relax a little. It was difficult for her to see him so tense.

Doctor Morrison patiently explained PTSD and its many manifestations. When he went over the possible symptoms, Judy was surprised Brad admitted to having occasional flashbacks, as well as unease in crowds, and the inability to sleep because of his need to patrol the apartment.

Morrison wasn't judgmental and seemed like a good listener. As they reviewed Brad's symptoms, Judy thought it was odd the doctor didn't appear to want to delve into Brad's experiences in Afghanistan, the ones that might have triggered the PTSD. As Morrison eventually explained, those discussions happened in group sessions. Brad was scheduled for his first group session later in the afternoon.

As things were winding down, Judy, who had been almost entirely silent during the meeting, spoke up. "Doctor Morrison, I'm a freelance writer. My pieces have appeared in several national magazines. Would it be all right if I wrote a story about Brad's PTSD treatment? PTSD is not well understood by the general public. I'd like to shine a light on the condition and its treatment. I wouldn't use any names or give any information identifying anyone in treatment."

The doctor paused and thought for a while. "I don't know, Judy. The VA wants to control any publicity. They have silly rules, but they're rules, nevertheless. If it were up to me, I'd be happy to have you write a story. I'll have to check. In any event, I expect my bosses would want to review your story before it went to press."

"I can live with your restrictions," Judy replied. "I'll take some notes today. If you find out I can't write the story, I'll tear them up."

"Good. My clock tells me your group is about to start, Brad. Let's go. I'll introduce you to everyone. And Judy, I'll show you where you can observe the group session. There's a one-way mirror in the room."

Meanwhile, George was getting restless. No one had shown up for the party, although the catering people had left quite a time ago. Once again, he was frustrated by his inability to know what time it was. He guessed the food had been sitting out for forty-five minutes or an hour. *The caterers should have put the stuff in the refrigerator.*

George decided to fly and see if anything was going on at the neighbor's house. It seemed a shame to be able to fly around and peek into people's windows without taking advantage of the possibility. As he was about to leave, he heard a car come down 1287's driveway. It was quickly followed by two other cars. Itching to do something, he flew around the house to look at the cars. Two of them were nice new sporty cars, a Porsche and a Lexus, and the third was the Humvee he'd seen before. He flew back to his perch with the view of the deck.

He counted five people walking around inside the house in the kitchen and the room beside the kitchen, a great room or a family room or something. He was startled when the guard guy with the mustache from last night came out. He'd changed clothes. Today he was wearing a tuxedo, not his camo outfit. He carried a little table out, set it up, and then flipped some switches on the hot tub before returning to the house. George figured the guard had morphed into a waiter. He set up the catered food complete with the Champagne. When he was finished, four other people came out, and the guy stood off to one side, ready to help if needed.

George didn't recognize any of the people attending the party. It was two couples. One of the women was a large blonde. She wasn't unattractive, but he thought she would have looked better without so much makeup. She was probably in her late forties, if his guess was right. The other woman had black hair and was much thinner, perilously skinny. She was roughly the same age as the other woman and had on a bright red dress with a short skirt. The men reminded him of the guy last night. They were younger than the women and dressed a little more casually. He remembered to look for wedding bands. There were none on the men or the thinner woman. Only the blonde woman had one.

George watched as the guard/waiter opened the Champagne and poured glasses for everyone. The people looked like they were having a good time drinking and eating. After a while he determined they were two couples, matched by size. The taller, thinner woman went with the taller, thinner guy, and the wider woman went with the wider guy. Everyone seemed to be enjoying themselves. He was a little jealous.

Each time they finished one of the plates of food, the guard/waiter swooped in and removed the plate. He also filled Champagne flutes when needed. Otherwise, he didn't interfere. When he was off to the side, he seemed to be scanning the yard. He hadn't abandoned all his guard instincts. When they'd finished the food, both of the women went into the house. The guard/waiter guy went to the hot tub and removed the cover. Next, he dipped his fingers in the water to check the temperature and turned some dials.

A few minutes later, the women came out of the house. They had changed into bathing suits—bikinis—and had towels with them. They climbed into the hot tub and started it bubbling. George heard one of them yell, "Come on you guys. Go get changed."

The two men hustled into the house, and the guard/waiter guy stood there, watching without seeming to be staring at the women, whose bathing suits were quite revealing.

In short order, the men came out in bathing suits with towels of their own. They hopped into the hot tub beside their respective women and gave them kisses. After a few minutes, one of the couples splashed one of the others. While George didn't notice who started it, fairly quickly everyone was splashing. As he watched, something clicked in his head. He had witnessed one of these splash fights before, and it was where he'd seen the tattoo on Greg's wife's arm.

George thought hard, and it started to come back to him. He'd been following the wife of one of his clients. Some guy had picked her up, and he trailed them to this house. It was early evening, so he'd settled into what he thought was a good hiding place behind one of the trees not far from where he was now. He was ground level, not up in a tree. By the time he'd sneaked into position, the people he'd been following, and another couple, were in the hot tub. Now he knew the other woman was probably Greg's wife. He remembered taking pictures of the splash party in the hot tub.

George figured he must be close to where he was when he was murdered. He'd been hoping he finally remember something, and the splash party in the hot tub brought it back. He was thrilled. At the same time, he was a little chagrined by his response to Brad's suggestion about going to the house today. Now he recognized it had been an accidental stroke of genius.

He sat back and watched the action in the hot tub. When the splashing stopped, he noticed the larger woman's bikini top had been removed somehow. Her breasts weren't exposed very often, because her boyfriend or whatever had his hands on them. Pretty soon both couples were out of the hot tub and toweling off. They went into the house, and he lost track of them. As he sat there, George realized he was getting hungry. He hoped Judy and Brad would appear soon.

At the VA, Judy felt a bit guilty looking at Brads' group session. Brad didn't say much. Some of the other guys opened up a lot. Judy heard harrowing stories about the traumas these guys relived through flashbacks. She also heard stories about people diving under tables when they heard a loud noise. And some of the guys were like Brad on his bad days. They always had to be on the edge of the room. She took notes furiously, wondering if Brad wasn't participating because he knew she was watching.

When the group session ended, they made their way out of the VA hospital. Brad didn't seem to want to talk, so Judy kept quiet. Halfway through the drive, she couldn't stand the silence. "I wonder if George has discovered something?"

"Hard to know, and we won't find out until we get him home. It's a little frustrating."

"True. When I was first interacting with him, I thought it was nice to be the one who controlled the communication. I was able to shut him up any time I wanted to. In this situation, it's maddening."

"I agree."

"Wait a minute. Once before I extracted some answers without having a computer. I had him jump once for yes and twice for no. He can give answers to some questions."

"Sounds like a great idea, Honey."

When he heard the horn, George flew to the meeting place quickly. Before Judy was able to instruct him on her yes and no idea, he flew past her and landed on the paper bag containing his meal.

"He's hungry," Brad said. "I'll open the windows and pull over here so you can get the container open for him."

When Brad stopped the car, Judy leaned over the seat, and George moved so she could extract the Tupperware from the bag and open it. When he saw the dung, he dove in. Judy turned around and fastened her seat belt. "We aren't going to get any information out of him for a while."

Chapter Twenty-Seven

WHEN BRAD PARKED AT THE apartment building, Judy suggested, "Why don't you stay in the box, George? I'd rather carry the box than you. I bet your mouth and feet are covered."

Judy helped George clean his face and feet. He didn't understand why she was being so fastidious. *It must be a human thing I don't remember.*

When he was clean, he went with Brad and Judy to the computer, and Judy moved into position to type. "Did you learn anything?" she asked.

`remembered just before killed`

"Wow, fantastic!" Brad exclaimed. "Some of your memory came back. Does it mean you were killed at 1287 St. Clair?"

`probably`

"What were you doing there?"

`following client's wife`

"Do you remember the client's name?" Brad said.

George went to the N key.

"It doesn't matter, Brad. We need to figure out what goes on at the house. Remember we thought it was some guy's love nest. Is it true?"

```
not one guy
```

Brad and Judy exchanged a puzzled look. "Do you mean there was a different guy this afternoon?" Judy asked.

```
2 different guys
```

"And two different women?" He went to the Y key. "What were they doing?"

```
party champagne hot tub
```

"Two different guys were romancing two different women with a party where they had Champagne and used the hot tub," Brad said. "I'm starting to get the picture. How'd it bring back your memory? Did you witness a similar event the night you were killed?"

He went to the Y key.

"Wow, Brad, you get on George's wave-length really fast."

"It made sense. Look, he has more to say."

```
guard guy there too
```

"The guy you saw last night who acted like he was security for the house? He was patrolling today?"

```
not patrolling waiter
```

"You saw the same guy, the one who dressed in camo last night, acting as a waiter for the little party today. Is that what you're saying?"

George went to the Y key.

Brad and Judy exchanged another puzzled look. Judy spoke up. "This whole thing is very strange. It looks like guard/waiter guy might be the key. And he might be the one who killed George."

"I see it," Brad concluded. "On the night George followed his client's wife to the house, the guy might have been in guard mode, and he might have seen George. As a private detective, George would have been taking pictures. With his attention on the deck, the guard might have been able to sneak up and shoot him."

"Sounds plausible," Judy commented. "Is that what you think happened?"

```
best guess
```

"We can't go to the police with a guess," Brad said. "We have to have hard evidence. Can anyone figure out how to get some good evidence?"

Silence followed Brad's question. Finally, George indicated he wanted to type.

```
blood
```

Brad perked up. "Good idea. If you can figure out where you were shot, there might be evidence of blood. Even though the police report said your car was cleaned out, the guy's wouldn't have cleaned up blood in the woods. He may have scuffed some leaves on top of it. It still could be there."

"You really think so, Brad? It's been quite a while. More leaves have fallen, and there's been lots of rain and some snow. Even if we found evidence of blood, we'd have to prove it was George's. It won't be easy. Suppose we did both of those things, a big suppose, we'd only have found the scene of the crime, not the murderer."

"If we did pin down the scene, this guy is the security for the house. If we go to the police with what we know, he'd be a suspect. They'd investigate him. Maybe they'd be able to match ballistic evidence to his gun. People have been convicted on flimsier evidence. Let's look for traces of blood."

"I don't know. I guess we don't have anything else. Still, how are we going to look for it? I don't want you traipsing all over the woods looking for blood. I mean, we're thinking the security guard is someone who kills people. I don't want him killing you."

`I can look`

"Great. The good troop volunteers before the officer gives him an assignment. You're just the beetle for the job. You have an idea where to look, and you have a good nose. I'll prick my finger and give you a chance to smell human blood. It's our best chance to move the investigation where it needs to go."

Judy looked skeptical. "Is almost two-year-old blood from a forest floor going to smell like fresh blood? I doubt it."

"Good point. Nevertheless, it's worth trying, and he is willing to look. Maybe we shouldn't spend too much time with it. It's a long shot, so we should be thinking of other ways to gather evidence."

"I say we should try to find out who the guard/waiter guy is," Judy said.

"Great idea. How?"

"Good question. I'll work on it. Right now, I'm going to fix our dinner. George has already eaten, and I'm getting hungry."

Before Judy had a chance to stand, George wanted to type.

`fashion show`

Judy laughed. "Brad, he wants you to model your new clothes."

"Not on your life, buddy. You'll have to pick the new ones out when I wear them. Let Judy fix dinner now."

George scanned the room for Jangles. He'd been remiss not looking for the cat when they first arrived. He'd been too excited about telling Brad and Judy what he'd remembered. He finally spotted the cat asleep in a corner. It was a good thing cats slept a lot. As he sat there, he wondered whether searching for blood on the forest floor would be productive. He suspected there wasn't much chance. Even if he found traces of blood, there was another problem. *How was he going to get a sample? He'd have to lead Brad or Judy to the place to get the sample. It would be risky.*

When Clarice came home, Brad and Judy gave her a short description of their visit to the VA hospital. She was particularly interested in what the doctor had told Judy about the possibility of her doing a story. "I hope you can write a story. The country needs to hear more about the sacrifices people make."

"The problem's been buried for a long time," Judy responded. "Some of the guys in Brad's group are dealing with things they'd experienced in Vietnam. At least they're getting help now. There were a whole lot of men who returned from World War II or Korea, who never received the help they needed."

"No doubt. Have you had a chance to read up on PTSD?"

"Some. I still have to do a lot of research to write a good story."

He was losing patience, so George flew to the keyboard, and Judy sat down to type for him. "George made a big discovery today, and it looks like he wants to tell you about it."

"Oh George, not everything is about you, you know," Clarice remarked as she came to sit where she could see the computer screen.

`discovered where`

"Yes," Judy said. "Some of his memory came back, and he remembered what he was doing right before he was shot. He had followed the wife of a client to the house on St. Clair we've been looking at. Anyway, there's a guard there, and we suspect he shot George while he was getting pictures of the cheating wife."

"Marvelous. You know who killed you. It must feel wonderful to have made this much progress."

`no proof`

"Yeah," Judy responded. "It has the three of us baffled. Even if we were completely positive this is the guy, and we're not, how will we be able to prove it? George and Brad think we should search for blood in the woods behind the house."

"Wouldn't any blood be gone by now? I mean, it's been a long time."

"That's what I told them. I'm going to see if I can find out anything about the guy who we think shot him. It looks like he works for whoever owns the house. The first evening he was there, he worked as a security guard. This afternoon, he worked as a waiter for a party two guys had with two women. It's weird, it wasn't the same men or the same women as the other time, and the guy was a security guard one time and a waiter the next."

Clarice spoke after a short pause. "This guy drives the Humvee, right?"

Judy nodded, so George didn't have to go to the Y key.

"Find his license plate number. When we have it, I can get my brother to run the plate. He's done it for me a couple of times to help with stories. I'm not sure he's supposed to do things like that, so I haven't asked often."

`no problem`

"How surprising," Clarice said, laughing. "George has volunteered to get the license plate number. The guy's been there both times he's staked out the house, so I guess it should be easy."

"Great, once we have his name, I can start researching him," Judy commented. "I'd say this is a red-letter day in our quest to find out who killed George. Most of the time so far, we have been spinning our wheels. I mean, we looked at the people he's suggested, and pretty much eliminated all of them. I guess we didn't completely eliminate his old girlfriend Monica and her current boyfriend, but they don't seem likely."

Brad joined the conversation. "It looks like the murder didn't have anything to do with George in particular. This guard would have tried to kill anyone who was snooping around the St. Clair house. Based on what we've seen going on, I'd say it's odd. Normal houses don't host events like the ones George witnessed the last two days."

"So, your idea is the house is some kind of hangout for a bunch of young guys who want to romance older women?" Clarice asked.

"It's what we've seen so far. That's all I'm saying."

"You're right," Judy said. "It's creepy. And maybe we've seen it another time. George, was the guy with your client's wife younger than her?"

He went to the Y key.

"There you go!" Brad almost yelled. "Good, Judy! I'd forgotten about his trip to the house when he was shot. There's one more thing I want to ask. When you were shot, were the people still on the deck?"

George thought for a minute. *Where were the people?* They'd been in the hot tub. Then he remembered taking a picture of the client's wife getting out of the hot tub and pulling the guy into the house. *I must have been killed soon after that picture.*

`people going into house`

"Makes more sense," Brad said. "The guy had to use a silencer when he shot you. Even then, if the people were on the deck, they might have heard something. Unless the guy caught you right before you fell, your body would have made some noise. If they were going into the house, they wouldn't have heard a thing. I bet the guy would have been able to drag your body out of sight without anyone being the wiser."

George thought what Brad said was probably right about two things: the silencer, and about his not knowing his killer. None of the suspects he'd suggested had panned out. The guy who killed him probably didn't know him from Adam. It was a bit of a blow to his ego in some strange way. He'd always just assumed he'd know the person who killed him. George couldn't figure why it bothered him. Unfortunately, it did.

Chapter Twenty-Eight

THE NEXT MORNING BRAD AND Judy dropped George at the house early. They promised they'd honk when they came by an hour later. He complained he didn't carry a watch. They couldn't find any way to deal with the problem, so the discussion didn't go anywhere.

Before they dropped George off, Brad pricked his finger and gave him a chance to smell his blood. George had to admit it had a distinctive smell, so maybe he'd be able to locate some blood. He flew around the house. There were no cars in the driveway, and he didn't see anyone in the kitchen or through the sliding glass doors leading onto the deck. He headed out to the wooded section behind the deck to the tree he'd been in yesterday afternoon. From his perch there, he tried to determine where he would have been to get the view he'd remembered.

He saw a tree he might have been beside and flew to it. He landed on a low branch close to his human eye level. The more he thought about it, the more he thought he remembered bracing his camera on a branch. *I might be on that branch right now*, he thought. He sniffed and didn't smell anything like Brad's blood. He flew down to the ground and sniffed some more. Everything smelled like mold, dirt, and rotting leaves. He moved some leaves out of the way to get rid of the top layer. Still he didn't smell blood. He flew up and circled the tree at what would have been his head level. If he'd been shot in the head, he'd have bled on the tree as well as the ground. He didn't smell any blood there, either.

He flew to his resting spot, disgusted. He hadn't been there ten minutes, and he'd completely struck out. Nothing was going to happen at the house in the morning. From all he knew, the place was only used in the afternoon and evenings. There was no telling how long the four people stayed yesterday. Their cars were gone. *Come to think of it, the cars left the first night.* His evidence suggested no one slept in the house. If he didn't find any blood and didn't see anyone in the house, this trip would be a complete waste of time.

He decided to inspect more of the grounds. The guard guy was big, so maybe he carried him out of the yard. More likely he dragged him. If so, his blood might be in other places. While he realized it was a long shot, he decided to do a sweep of the yard.

He started on the St. Clair edge of the yard and flew slowly close to the ground, trying to sniff. When he reached the edge of the property, he turned around and flew back about five feet from his last sweep. On his fifth or sixth trip, he'd lost track, he smelled something he thought was human blood. He stopped and dropped down to get a closer smell. He was right—there was a trace of dried blood on two of the leaves. He decided to fly a circle around the leaves, and he found more blood. Another circle around the second blood spot yielded more blood. The three traces of blood lined up. He guessed he'd discovered a trail left by someone dragging a bleeding body through the woods.

George followed the trail to a tree. At its base, the smell of blood was very strong. He was mystified. He was quite certain this wasn't the tree he was hiding behind when he was taking his pictures. Still, his memory might be hazy. He wasn't absolutely sure, and there was blood here, no question about it.

George couldn't figure how they were going to get a sample of the blood. He made sure he knew how the bits of blood he found lined up. He flew down the path to where it came out onto St. Clair. He tried to memorize the trees, so he'd know where to enter when he was leading Brad or Judy to the best source of a blood sample. He figured they would come there early tomorrow morning. There would be no one around, and they'd be in and out in a hurry.

He wondered how much time had gone by. It hadn't been as much as a half hour. What was he going to do with his extra time? He didn't want to just sit in 1287's yard. Then he remembered yesterday. He had been about to investigate the neighbors when his ride showed up. Now he had plenty of time. He'd go see what he could find out.

He flew to the house adjacent to the far edge of the lot. It was a brick ranch-style house like many in Cleveland. It appeared to be much older than the 1287 house. George landed on the windowsill of what turned out to be the kitchen window and saw an older couple eating breakfast at a kitchen table. He wondered if they had any idea of the goings on at their next-door neighbor's house. He looked back at 1287. Because of all the trees, he could barely see the house.

George felt a little creepy looking at the couple, so he decided to investigate their backyard. They had a little patch of grass, and then a big, well-tended garden. It fit the couple in the kitchen. They were probably both retired, with lots of time to spend in the garden.

Beyond the garden, he was surprised to find an alley. He flew out to inspect it. The alley was unusual. It dead ended just past these people's lot. The 1287 house had a bigger lot. He looked down the alley and saw a line of those great big garbage cans behind the houses. The garbage truck would have to back down the alley after dumping all the cans. It was a strange arrangement.

Flying toward 1287, it struck him. Whoever was going to get the blood sample didn't have to access the woods from St. Clair. They could park somewhere and go down the alley. It would be much safer. There was no way for him to mark a trail. As he flew, he tried to memorize the way from the alley to the tree with the blood. Just as he reached his intended destination, he saw something diving out of the tree. In a panic, he veered away from whatever it was. He wasn't quick enough, and the squirrel, *it is a squirrel*, reached out and struck him.

George wasn't able to control his fall, so he landed hard on his back. As he righted himself, he felt a sharp pain on his left side. The squirrel landed a few feet away, so he knew he had to get airborne quickly, no matter how much he was injured. He flew toward the house and landed awkwardly on the deck railing. Looking back, he didn't see the squirrel following him. *Now, what was wrong? Why do I hurt, and why couldn't I make a normal landing?*

He saw himself in the reflection in the sliding glass door. The image was too small, so he flew closer. When he hovered close to the glass, he saw his hindmost left leg had been severed by the squirrel. He returned to the deck railing, being careful to land right side first. From what he'd seen, it had been a fairly clean break. There was some kind of fluid, blood, he supposed, oozing out of his hindmost left hip. It wasn't flowing fast, and the pain was subsiding.

He didn't know much about dung beetle physiology. *Can I walk normally on five legs?* He remembered seeing a video of a dog with only three legs, and the dog seemed to get around easily. While he wasn't quite standing as well as he was used to, he didn't feel too awkward. He didn't remember learning to walk as a dung beetle any more than he remembered learning to walk as a human. *Maybe I've been lucky to lose only one leg to the stupid squirrel. In any event, there's nothing I can do about it now. The best thing to do is to keep a sharp eye out and protect my left side.*

To be sure the Humvee hadn't shown up, he flew around the house. The driveway was clear. He knew it was too much to hope for, so he didn't feel too disappointed as he returned to his perch. After another twenty minutes or so, he heard the horn. He flew to the rendezvous place and into the car with Brad and Judy.

Judy asked, "Any luck?"

George hopped once on her hand. Judy didn't seem to notice how his hop was different.

"Brad, did you see? He gave me the yes signal. He must have found some blood. Is that what happened?"

He hopped once again.

"I guess I'll have to eat my words," Judy said. "I thought finding any traces of George's blood was an incredible long shot, maybe even impossible."

"Now we'll have to figure out how to get a sample of the blood," Brad commented. "There's no way he'll be able to do it."

"You're right. I hadn't thought about it. I'm going for perfection here. George, did you get the license number?"

He hopped two times. All this hopping wasn't easy on him. He was starting to see how he relied on all six of his legs.

"Too much to ask for. I suppose the Humvee wasn't there."

He hopped once.

When they arrived at the apartment, they gathered around the computer, and Brad took charge. "Tell us about the blood."

`I lost a leg`

"Oh my God!" Judy exclaimed. "What happened?"

`squirrel`

"I can see it," Brad said as he bent down and looked closely at George. "You don't have the back leg on the left side. Does it hurt?"

`not anymore`

"Oh George, we're so sorry. I can't think of what we can do for you.

It wouldn't be sensible to take you to the vet. Do you want an aspirin to chew on?"

He didn't respond.

"I guess it was a silly question. Okay, if there's nothing we can do for your leg, tell us about the blood."

lots of it not where I thought it would be

"I see," Brad responded. "If there's lots of blood, it should be easy to get a sample. I guess I'm going to have to go into the woods with you. Maybe tomorrow early."

I'll lead you

"I'll need your help for sure."

"I can drop you two off beside the house and come and pick you up in ten minutes or so," Judy said. "You should be able to obtain a good sample in ten minutes."

not beside house

"What? Why not drop us off beside the house?" Brad asked. "If there's no one there, it should be easy to get in and out without anyone knowing anything about it."

alley behind neighbor better

"I don't know what you're talking about. There isn't an alley anywhere near 1287."

"Brad, let's look at Google maps. It would probably be easier than trying to figure out what George is saying. Here, I can find 1287 St. Clair Road and zoom in. We can get a detailed look at the neighborhood. It might show the alley if there is one."

George flew to Judy's shoulder as she opened the internet, and Brad went on one of his little tours of the apartment. When Judy had the

Google maps view of 1287 St. Clair on the screen, she zoomed in. The picture had been taken in the winter, so there were no leaves on the trees.

"Look, you can see the deck." Judy commented.

Brad came and looked at the computer screen. "Can you show us about where the blood is?" Brad asked.

George hovered beside the screen in the area where he'd found the blood.

"Okay, now where is the alley you were talking about."

He moved up and to the left, hovering off the screen.

"Oh," Judy said. "I have to shift the view to the left and up some. I see it. An alley dead ends at 1287's lot. It stops when it passes the neighbor's house."

"I see what he was talking about," Brad added. "He's right. Using the alley is much better than using the street. We can park the car at the end of the alley and walk to 1287. Even if there's someone in 1287, they probably wouldn't see us if we came in quietly. The house is quite a way from the place where he indicated the blood is. Early tomorrow morning should work very well."

"While I admit the blood idea is working out much better than I'd anticipated, I'd still like to get the license plate," Judy remarked. "We'd have a name. I say we should take George out to the house tonight. Every other night the guy's Humvee has come."

"What do you say? Up for another night?"

`not a long one`

"Fair enough, we'll keep it short," Brad said.

At lunch time, Judy put George in his cage and told him she'd be right back with a spoon of dung. When faced with the dung, he realized what he needed his lost leg for. He had used his back legs to shape the dung into a ball. It was going to be very difficult without his back left leg. He tried to use his left middle leg, but the results were unsatisfactory.

He'd never been good at making the balls, but this effort was particularly lopsided. He ate the dung anyway.

Early in the evening, Brad drove George to the beginning of the alley and parked. "We can park here tomorrow morning. Using the alley depends on whether we run into a dog. A barking dog can be a disaster for our operation. That's why I'm going to walk down there tonight. You go ahead and see if the Humvee is there. If it is, get the number and fly back here. I'll wait about ten minutes after my practice walk. If you don't come, I'll meet you here in an hour."

George flew off down the alley, and Brad started to walk slowly toward 1287. There were only four houses he needed to walk behind. He made it past two of them, but he had to beat a hasty retreat when a dog in the backyard of the third house started barking like crazy. He was disappointed. Still, it was good he'd done this scouting mission. The dog would have roused the whole neighborhood in the morning.

At the car, Brad waited fifteen minutes, and George didn't show.

George had flown up the alley and paused. He heard the dog Brad had spooked. *Too bad*, he thought. *Brad is sharp. It was a good idea to do this dry run. I better fly around the house to look for the Humvee.*

It wasn't there. He wasn't surprised. The first night, the night the Humvee guy acted like a guard, he didn't show up until the young guy and the older woman in the green dress had been there for some time. There was plenty of time for the guy to show, so George settled in his watching spot and waited. Though he was hidden behind some leaves, he found himself incredibly nervous. His run in with the squirrel still bothered him. As night fell, all kinds of noises seemed to get louder. Perhaps he shouldn't have agreed to come tonight.

A half an hour later, George gave up. It looked like nothing was going to happen at 1287 tonight. He remembered similar experiences when he was a private detective. Clients sometimes gave wrong information.

One wife was sure her husband was cheating with some woman, and he watched the woman's house for a solid week and followed her everywhere she went. In the end, he never saw the guy. He knew the Humvee guy would show one of these nights, so he wasn't too discouraged, just bored and a little on edge.

Giving the scene of his encounter with the squirrel a wide berth, he went down the alley to the place Brad had parked earlier. He sat on a fence and waited there. Eventually the car showed up. Judy had come along, and she opened the window for him to fly in.

"Any luck?" she asked.

He hopped on her hand twice.

Chapter Twenty-Nine

LATER THEY REPORTED TO CLARICE. She made a big fuss about George's missing leg. He was a little embarrassed. It turned out he was able to walk fine on five legs. Beside the misshapen dung balls, the only difficulty was takeoffs. Apparently, his back legs had a lot to do with launching into the air. He was learning to compensate, so he didn't think it was going to be a lasting problem.

When the discussion turned to the blood, Clarice was skeptical. "You're not going to find any of George's blood. It's too long ago and too much rain and snow. His blood is going to be long gone."

"I thought so too, Clarice," Judy responded. "Brad pricked his finger and let him smell it. Dung beetles have a good sense of smell, and he's sure he found blood."

`scarab`

"Give it up, George," Clarice interjected. "We've all seen you eat. You're a dung beetle."

"Clarice is right," Brad said. "Give the scarab business up."

"I agree," Judy added. "Look at it this way. We all consider you a dung beetle, and we're still working our butts off trying to help find out who killed you. You don't need to be a scarab."

Clarice spoke up next. "Now we have that issue out of the way, how are you going to get the blood analyzed? And how are you going to try to match it with George's DNA?"

"Good question. Brad, you and George came up with the blood business. How are you going to get it analyzed?"

"Private labs will do DNA analysis with any sample of tissue," Brad said. "I'm sure we can find some place to do the analysis for us. And Judy, you remember what my major was?"

"Chemistry."

"Right, so I can do some simple tests, like typing the blood. I'm sure I can get the chemicals. Before we spend any money on DNA tests, we should at least have a good feeling we have some of George's blood. It might be somebody else, you know."

`not where I thought it should be`

"Yeah," Judy said. "I remember you saying so. The blood might not even be his. The whole business is getting frustrating."

"I agree," Clarice added. "Judy's right. Getting the guy's license plate would be more helpful. I don't have high hopes for this blood business."

Early the next morning, Judy dropped Brad and George off beside 1287 St. Clair. Judy watched them go as they crossed the street into the woods behind the house. She pulled over and paused to set the timer on her phone for nine and a half minutes. She decided ten minutes would be more than enough time for Brad to get the sample. All she had to do was find a place to turn around and cool her heels. On her return, she'd be on the right side of the street for the pickup.

Brad tried to be quiet while he followed the beetle to the right tree. George stayed close to Brad so the squirrel wouldn't get any funny ideas.

When they made it to the base of the tree, Brad bent down. "This sure looks like blood to me."

Brad started putting some leaves covered with dried blood into a plastic bag. "We have plenty of time. I should have told Judy five minutes, not ten."

Just then they heard someone shout. "What are you doing in my yard!"

They looked up. George recognized the guard.

"Let's get out of here!" Brad turned around, heading for the alley.

We're going to wake up the dog, George thought as he followed.

Sure enough, the dog started barking as Brad ran by with George flying behind him. At the end of the alley, Brad turned right. After they had passed three houses, he went into a vacant lot and sat behind a tree.

"He's not going to try to follow us. Still, I'd recommend staying here for a while. We need to be safe. I'd better tell Judy where we are."

Brad took out his cell phone and texted Judy, telling her to wait twenty minutes and then pick them up at the end of the alley.

George wanted to have Brad tell Judy to look for the Humvee's license in 1287's driveway. Unfortunately, there was no way.

Just as Brad was finishing his text, the Humvee turned onto the street and poked its nose into the alley they'd just come out of. It paused after going in a little way, so George flew up close to get the license plate. DVES 5. Also, he flew by the front of the car to verify the driver was the same guy he seen before. It was. He repeated DVES 5 to himself as he flew to Brad. A few minutes later, the Humvee backed out of the alley and headed toward 1287.

The guard, Cleat Blanton, wondered what was going on. First, there was a guy in the backyard who'd run down the alley when he'd yelled at him. Though the guy wasn't in the alley now, he couldn't be far away. All the cars he saw were the ones he expected. As he was about to leave, some kind of bug buzzed around his vehicle looking for all the world as if it was checking him out. Blanton thought it might be one of those mechanical bugs with a miniature camera. *Something weird is going on.*

He decided to get into the alley and wait for the guy to show. He didn't want to just drive up the alley. He had gear to retrieve. Also, the guy was probably watching, so he backed out of the alley and hightailed it to the house. At the house, he grabbed his camera and pistol and ran through the woods to the alley. In the alley, he stopped before he agitated the dog, balanced his camera on one of the trash cans, and calmed himself. He had a long lens on the camera, so he had a good view of the street. He waited. This was nothing new for Cleat. He'd been a sniper in the Army.

Ten minutes after he was in position, he started snapping pictures of a car that stopped. A guy came out of the vacant lot near the entrance to the alley and got in the car. At the same time a little fuzzy thing, maybe what he thought was the mechanical bug, flew into the car too. Blanton wasn't sure he would have enough mega pixels to get any resolution on the bug thing. As the car drove away, he snapped a good picture of its license plate.

On the ride home, Brad told Judy what had happened. "And as a bonus, George was able to get the Humvee's license plate number."

"I'm glad the guy didn't find you. All things considered, I'd say this morning has been a success. You have your blood sample and the license plate number. Perfect."

George wondered how perfect it was. Clearly, they'd annoyed the guard guy more than a little. The guy had yelled at them, and they'd clearly left. It seemed a bit unusual for him to chase them in his Humvee. *What did he think he was going to do?* George couldn't figure the guy out.

Cleat headed toward the section of the backyard where he'd first seen the guy. He wondered what the guy was doing. When he reached the

woods, he did a thorough search. He found the trail the guy made when he ran into the alley and followed it to a tree. The leaves at the base of the tree had been disturbed. Cleat took a close look and became very concerned. He saw traces of dried blood on some of the leaves at the base of the tree. *Holy shit! I might be in big trouble.*

At the apartment, they went right to the computer. "What was the license number, George?" Judy asked.

DVES 5

"Great, it's a vanity plate," Brad remarked. "It will be easy for Clarice's brother to track it down. Why don't you text it to her? She'll be able to call him on her lunch break or something."

"I'm on it," Judy said, extracting her phone.

With her text to Clarice completed, she continued. "I'm going to Google DVES and see if I get anything."

"Why bother?" Brad asked.

"The Humvee might be part of a company fleet. You know number five of the DVES company vehicles. It's not a sure thing. I might not find anything, but it can't hurt to look."

"I figured it was someone's initials. I guess I'm being dumb. Who has four initials?"

Judy yelled excitedly. "I found it. Dorothy Vaughn Escort Service—DVES, and they have a Cleveland address on the same side of town as 1287 St. Clair."

Brad interrupted his tour of the apartment to come see what Judy had up on the screen. The Dorothy Vaughn website was extensive. The escort service provided male escorts for women who wanted an attractive young man to accompany them to various functions. They had pictures of couples. All the women looked very pleased with themselves.

Brad almost jumped as he said, "Look, there's DVES one! It's a limousine. Is the guard the guy holding the door?"

George went to the Y key.

"Wow, this guy is a jack of all trades—a guard, a waiter, and a chauffeur. Judy, check to see if they have a listing of staff. We might be able to find the guy's name."

"There isn't anything labeled staff. The only thing I can see is a listing of the escorts who work for them."

"Go ahead and look for him. He might be an escort too. Somehow, I doubt it. Still, you never know."

Judy took out her phone. "I'm going to text Clarice to tell her not to bother her brother. We don't need him."

Finished with her cell phone, Judy switched to the computer and looked at the listing of the escorts. The first photo was obviously a glamour shot. The guy was in a tuxedo and had a great smile. While Judy wasn't going to tell Brad, the guy looked spectacular. Judy read the short bio. It made the guy sound like he was clearly one of Cleveland's most eligible young men. The second escort had a very similar picture and bio. When she switched to the third guy, George flew down from her shoulder onto the keyboard. Judy switched to Word.

`guy from first night`

"Brad, he recognizes one of the guys."

Brad came and looked at the picture. "Are you sure?"

George jumped on the Y key.

"I guess I'll say what we're all thinking," Brad said. "1287 is the party house for DVES's escorts and clients, and there's a lot more than escorting going on."

"I expect you're right," Judy responded. "George's involvement the night he was killed makes sense, too. He was following the wife of one of his clients. She must have lined up one of the escorts for a little party at the house. It's why he was in the backyard trying to get pictures."

"You've got it," Brad commented. "And the security guy, the one we tangled with this morning, is probably the guy who shot George just like we thought."

"There you go. You wanted to come to Cleveland to find out who killed you, and we've done it. This is the guy. I'd bet money on it."

`how do we prove it`

"Great question," Brad said. "I doubt your testimony would be acceptable in court. That's where the blood comes in. We have to get the police involved. I'm going to do some preliminary testing this afternoon, and then we'll have to find some place to do the DNA. When we have more information, we can figure out what to do. We're making progress, but we still have a ways to go."

"I'm going to keep looking through these escorts." Judy nodded at the computer screen. "Like you said, there's some chance the guy from this morning is an escort as well as all his other jobs."

"Before you start, Honey, would you look up medical supply stores? They should carry blood testing kits. I want to get one to see what we found this morning."

Judy obtained the information Brad needed. After a quick lunch, Brad took off to procure his chemicals. Judy cleaned up George and returned to the listing of escorts. When she'd checked out four more escorts, she remarked, "I don't see how anyone makes a decision. All these airbrushed pictures make these guys look great, and the bios are almost indistinguishable. Everyone sounds super. I didn't know there were this many wonderful unmarried guys in Cleveland."

`don't believe everything you read`

Judy laughed. "Yes indeed. Particularly in this case."

She continued looking. Ten minutes later, she exclaimed, "Oh my God, it's Jay! Clarice will be… I don't know how Clarice will react."

She pointed to the screen. "It's her football-player boyfriend. The name here is a fake. It says this guy is Rex Cleary, and it's not. I know him. It's Jay Gregory. The bio is partly true. He was a college football player. They don't mention he's a pro now. Clarice will go crazy."

Judy finished the escort listing. "The guy we're looking for isn't here. I wonder if Jay knows his name."

`clarice can ask`

"Good idea. We'll see what she says when she gets home tonight."

Chapter Thirty

WHEN CLEAT RETURNED FROM CHECKING the woods, he fired up his computer and downloaded the photos. He didn't have any trouble zooming in on the license plate on the car. It gave him a place to start. Unfortunately, he didn't have a good angle on the driver. If he had to guess, he'd say it was a red-headed woman. He had a better view of the guy who'd been in 1287's backyard. As he feared, he'd struck out with the mechanical bug thing. When he zoomed in close enough to get a look at it, all he had was fuzz. Still, he had a distinct memory of the thing following the guy into the car. *What the hell was it?*

Cleat called the company's source on the police force, Will Ferguson, one of his old Army buddies. The person who answered told Cleat Will was off today. *No problem,* Cleat thought. *I'll call his personal cell.* The phone rang five times with no response, so he left a message.

Cleat was frustrated, so he finished checking the house. The new cleaning people weren't always as thorough as some of the clients liked. It was part of Cleat's job to be sure the place was spotless. The special clients paid top dollar, so they deserved top-flight service. One of the bathroom mirrors still had smudges. Cleat cleaned the mirror. He'd have to remember to tell the cleaning people about it. Satisfied with everything, he locked up.

On the way to the office, Cleat wondered how much he should tell Dorothy. She'd laugh at his idea the people had a mechanical bug. He wouldn't mention it. Still, she had to know someone was snooping around, and maybe they'd found traces of blood. She'd probably yell at him for not cleaning up. They had plenty of history, so she'd yelled at him often. He'd be able to take it. He wasn't looking forward to the meeting.

At the office he parked the Humvee beside the other DVES vehicles. They had six reserved spots behind the office. Inside, the receptionist/secretary, Jill, told him Dorothy was busy, so he sat down in the waiting room. He didn't really like working for his ex-wife, but the smartest thing he did in the divorce was hang on to twenty percent of the business. Working here let him keep an eye on what was going on. About fifteen minutes later, a young man walked out of Dorothy's office. Cleat overheard him tell Jill, "Mrs. Vaughn told me to give you this paperwork."

Must be a newby, Cleat thought as he stood up. *The guy looked like all the rest of them. Too young and too pretty*. Cleat tired of them really fast. *Most of them are so conceited. They don't have an ounce of real-world experience among them.*

"Buzz me in, will you Jill," Cleat asked when the guy left.

Dorothy Vaughn was at her office door, so, before Jill reacted, she yelled, "Come in, Cleat."

"Watching his rear end as he's leaving?" Cleat couldn't help himself.

"Yes, as a matter of fact I was," Dorothy said with a smile. "He's going to be a good one."

Cleat marveled at the way she'd kept up her appearance. He knew she was pushing sixty, but she could pass for forty-five on a good day, and most of her days were good. She was tall, which helped. She'd had her boobs done. While not real big, they stood right up. Cleat didn't suspect her breasts represented her only plastic surgery. Still, it was the one he noticed most. She dressed well and always had on high heels. Cleat knew she always tested the guys out before she enlisted them for special duty. As far as he knew, the guys didn't mind the test.

Cleat sat down. "We might have some trouble brewing. I was at 1287 checking on the cleaning crew, and I saw a guy in the backyard. I yelled at him, and he ran off, down the alley. When I got in the Humvee and went to the end of the alley, he wasn't anywhere to be seen. I went to the house and picked up my camera. The long and short of it is, I took pictures of him and the car coming to pick him up."

"Doesn't seem like a big deal, Cleat. There must be more to it. What is it?"

"Yeah, I got back to the yard and found out where he'd been. Some leaves had been disturbed. The bad thing is there were traces of blood on the leaves at the base of the tree the guy was looking at."

"Where the last shooting occurred?"

"Yes, and I'm baffled. Will, my contact at the police department, told me the shooting is already in the cold case file. The police gave up trying to find out who was involved. I was astounded when I saw the blood. I thought falling leaves, snow, and rain would have eliminated any traces. I don't go and clean up after myself in the woods."

"Somehow I thought you did. I thought you were proud of how much you cleaned up."

"I am and I do. The case is a cold case because I cleaned out the victim's car so well. That's where I stashed the body. And I do go into the woods to be sure no one can detect where I've dragged the body. I don't go around looking for traces of blood."

"Have you found out who these people are?"

"I have a message into Will. He's off today, and he hasn't returned my call yet. When he does, I'll have him trace the license plate. I should know who owns the car soon, at least by tomorrow."

"This guy in the backyard wasn't an undercover policeman, was he?"

"I doubt it. It's not the way they operate. They'd come in with warrants and crime techs. When they search for evidence, they're looking for stuff they can present in court. No, this guy was an amateur of some kind. While it's not the police, I still don't like it."

"What should we do? Should I look to close down 1287? I'd hate to do it. It's possible if we have to. It shouldn't be difficult. It's real hard to trace our ownership of the house. It's all done with offshore accounts and what all. Just to be cautious, I'll have my real estate guy start looking for another place. Even if we don't have to move operations, it's good to have a backup. We don't want to have to interrupt the special dates. It's where most of the money is in this business."

"I agree. It's good to have a backup. Still, I don't believe there's a reason to do anything in a big hurry. Let me figure out who these people are, and what they're up to. I'll also have Will keep his ears open around the police department."

"Cleat, thanks for coming to me right away. You know I like to keep track of what's going on. Report to me when you learn anything."

"Will do, Boss," Cleat responded as he rose and walked out of Dorothy's office. The conversation had gone better than it might have. He didn't get bawled out at all. Cleat thought maybe it was because Dorothy was so pleased with the new recruit. It put her in a good mood.

Brad returned from the medical supply place with a couple of kits and some bottles. He went right to work without giving Judy much of a greeting. Judy was looking at a website on PTSD and taking notes, so it didn't bother her.

George flew to watch Brad as he cleared off a place on the kitchen counter. Next, he grabbed the plastic bag with the blood samples. He took out a leaf with what looked like a big patch of dried blood on it. Brad then dissolved the dried blood in some fluid he had in one of the bottles. After he mixed the dried blood in the fluid, he took a card out of one of the kits. With a dropper he put water in the center of each of four circles on the card. Next, using four different sticks of some kind, he put a drop of blood on each of the water circles. Brad turned the card to be sure each drop of blood covered the surface of its circle. Finally, he went to the computer, motioning for George to follow.

"What's your blood type?"

`a plus`

George had always been proud of being A positive. An A+ was the best grade. Even if it wasn't the best blood type, it still made him proud. In fact, it was a very common blood type. He was just being silly.

Brad stood up and compared his results with a card in the kit. "It's not your blood, George. This blood is O positive."

Judy came over. "I'm not surprised. He didn't think it was the right tree. My best guess is that what happened to George happened to someone else, too, probably after George was killed. There was no sign of blood by the right tree. It must have all washed away. This blood was deposited more recently, so there hasn't been time for the blood to disappear."

"I can't fault your reasoning."

"What does it tell us?"

"It tells us the guard guy probably murdered at least two people, George and this guy with O positive blood."

"We don't have any evidence about George, do we?" asked Judy.

"No, I guess we don't. We only have his memory, and like I said before, no judge is going to accept his testimony."

"Who is the guy with the O positive blood?"

"Good question. Do you still have the cold case reports?"

"Yes."

"As soon as I clean up all this blood analysis stuff, I'm going to look at them. Maybe I can find Mr. O positive."

"I'll get them. It's funny. I almost threw them out. I thought George's case was the only one we'd be interested in. I rifled through them searching for his name. I didn't look at any of the others in any detail."

With Brad looking through the police reports and Judy studying up on PTSD, George found the whole proceeding quite boring. There was nothing for him to do. He'd found the blood evidence very disappointing. He realized everything wasn't about him. Still, he was disappointed. This wasn't the first time. When they'd started the search for his murderer, he'd been convinced he would know the person who did it. Finding it was probably the guard made it look like he was just a guy who'd been doing the wrong thing in the wrong place. He didn't know the guy, and now he learned he probably wasn't even the only one the guy'd killed. While he was mad at himself for wanting to feel special, he guessed he did.

Cleat received the return call from his police contact, Will, late in the afternoon. Cleat gave him the license plate information, and Will told him to meet at the station in three quarters of an hour. He promised Cleat he'd find out who'd registered the car and have a copy of his or her driver's license.

When Cleat made it to the station, Will was waiting out front, holding an envelope. Cleat didn't even have to get out of the Humvee.

"It's all in here, Buddy."

Cleat briefly looked in the envelope. "You do good work."

Will sidled up close and whispered, "Keep the monthly checks coming."

Cleat laughed. "Will do."

Three hours later, Brad announced he'd thought he knew who Mr. O positive was. He called Judy and George. "I tried to find similarities between what the police found with George and one of these other cases. There weren't many. The locations and where the bodies were found were all different. I chose this guy, Ronald Anderson, because of the way his car was cleaned out. He was found in his car, just like George, and the car had absolutely no clues in it, again just like George. No fingerprints or anything. It had been cleaned out completely."

"What did Anderson do for a living?" Judy asked.

"He worked for an insurance company. He was a lot older than George and married. When the police asked his wife what she was doing on the night he died, she didn't appear to have a very good story. My guess is he followed her to the St. Clair house, and the guard saw him."

"You're guessing, aren't you?"

"Yes, I am. I've looked at all the cold cases newer than George's, and it's the only one with any similarities. The super clean car is a real good clue. Also, Ronald Anderson died of the same kind of head shot as George. I forgot to mention that."

"Okay, so we have a good idea whose blood we have. Is it enough to go to the police with?"

"Good question. Not yet. If it turns out the blood matches, it would give the police the location where Ronald Anderson was shot. Though the guard guy's a prime suspect, we need more. If Clarice can find the guy's name from Jay, we can make more progress. Right now, I'm hungry."

"I'll fix dinner in a minute."

Two hours later, when Clarice walked into the apartment, Judy rushed up to her.

Clarice put up her hands. "Hold on girl. Let me get settled."

Backing off, Judy said, "We need you. We're real close to solving George's murder."

"Why do you need me?"

"Here's the deal. We found the license plate on the Humvee. It's DVES 5. DVES stands for Dorothy Vaughn Escort Service."

Walking Clarice to the computer, Judy continued, "Come look at their website. It'll show why we need you."

On the way to the computer, Clarice nodded to Brad, who was headed to the computer too. Judy showed the flashy website to Clarice and then started scrolling through the escort pages.

"Slow down, Girl, some of these guys are really hot."

"You can look at them later, Clarice. There's one in particular I want to show you. Here he is, Rex Cleary. You know him."

"Oh my God! It's Jay!"

Clarice stared at Judy and Brad in silence. Then she looked at the computer screen and read the bio for Rex Cleary. "Some of this is right for Jay. It's short, so it leaves out a lot."

Brad broke in at this point. "We would like you to call Jay. We're pretty sure the guard guy who drives the Humvee shot George, and someone else too. Unfortunately, we don't know his name. If Jay worked for DVES, there's a good chance he knows other people who work there. Judy, find the limo picture the guy's in. It might help Clarice to know what he looks like."

While Judy was searching for the limousine picture, Clarice asked, "How do you know he killed another guy?"

"We found blood in the woods behind the house today. It wasn't Georges. Wrong blood type. We suspect it belongs to a guy named Ronald Anderson. Brad found him in the cold case files your brother gave us."

"Whoa, you guys have been busy."

"Here he is," Judy said. "The chauffeur. We want you to ask about him."

"I see. Sure, I'll call Jay. I don't know if I can get through, his football training camp keeps him real busy with meetings in the evening."

George indicated he wanted to type.

`thanks clarice`

"Don't mention it. Always willing to help a friend. I'll text him to find out when would be a good time for me to call."

Ten minutes later, Clarice came back from changing clothes. "Jay returned my text. He has a few minutes free at eight, and he'll call me."

"Thank you so much, Clarice," Judy said.

George paced around, rolling his dung into a ball in his cage. He found it difficult to do with only one back foot, but he managed. He was still unsettled about the notion of being killed by a complete stranger. Also, he had to admit he didn't like knowing he'd let the guy sneak up behind him. Maybe he was being too hard on himself. The two women involved in the splash party were very good looking. It was only natural for them to grab his attention. Still, he should have been more vigilant. He couldn't help being very dissatisfied with himself.

At five after eight, Clarice's phone rang. Brad and Judy jumped. Clarice gave them a look and let the phone ring a couple of times before answering. She went into her bedroom with her phone.

Twenty minutes later, she emerged. "I didn't find anything out. Jay knew who I was talking about, but he didn't know the guy's name. According to Jay, the guy's assigned to help the escorts who worked for clients who want special services. It's the phrase Jay used—special services. When I asked if he was saying those escorts were gigolos, he hemmed and hawed. He just told me he didn't do anything like that for Dorothy Vaughn. He only went to the theater, a couple of weddings, and several dinners. No special services, and he didn't know anything about any houses on St. Clair."

"Thanks for asking," Judy said. "Did you tell him about Simon?"

"No. Actually, we talked a lot about him. He has a minor injury, and he's afraid of what the team will do if the injury doesn't clear up. He gets most of his playing time on special teams, so he's not one of the players who are really critical to the team. He's afraid they'll cut him. I spent lots of time trying to make him feel better. I'm not sure I had any success."

CHAPTER THIRTY-ONE

BRAD WOKE UP MORE SUDDENLY than normal at 2:15 in the morning. He'd felt a compulsion to get up and secure the apartment before. Tonight was different. He tried not to rouse Judy and checked the kitchen window first. Nothing was out of place. In the living room, he went to the sliding glass door to the balcony. He moved the curtain aside and looked out on the parking lot.

He shifted the curtain back in a hurry. A Humvee had stopped behind Judy's car. *The noise of the Humvee must have been what woke me.* He couldn't see the license plate on the Humvee, but he had a terrible feeling it would be DVES 5. He had to get closer to see what the Humvee was up to, and he had to wake George. He'd have him tail the Humvee when it left.

Brad hurried to George's cage and shook it to rouse him. When George walked out on his hand, he whispered, "Come with me, there's something funny going on."

George inspected Brad. He looked weird. He had on boxer shorts, t-shirt, and slippers. He was startled when Brad headed toward the front door in this getup. He had no idea what the heck was going on.

When they reached the hallway outside the apartment, Brad spoke as he ran down the stairs. "There's a Humvee out in the parking lot, and it looks like it's pulled up behind Judy's car. If it's DVES 5, I want you to find out where it goes after it leaves."

With George riding on his shoulder, Brad slipped out of the apartment building and ran around toward the parking-lot side. They both peeked around the corner toward the parked cars. The Humvee was the one Brad thought it might be, and the guard guy was just getting up from under Judy's car. As they watched, he walked toward his vehicle.

Brad said, "Follow him, and see where he goes. I'll meet you at the end of the alley."

George flew off, and easily caught up to the Humvee, which, to keep the noise down, was driving slowly. He landed on the top and searched for a secure place—one good enough for him when the Humvee picked up speed. Luckily, the coach work on Humvees wasn't as precise as it was on many cars. He found a narrow channel along the back hatch to secure the three legs on his right side. It wasn't ideal, because he had trouble facing forward. Still, he was sure he wouldn't be blown off.

Cleat was satisfied with his efforts. He had no trouble finding where the girl, Judith Clayton, lived. He was sure she was the one in his photos. The driver's license listed her as having red hair. He knew he was taking a chance rigging the bomb under her car—not a big one, though. In the middle of the night, he was almost certain no one saw him. The explosion would be a big story on the news. It wasn't every day a car was blown up in a parking lot. If he was lucky, he'd waste both the woman, Judith, and the guy, whoever he was. Even if he didn't get the guy, he'd be able to find out who he was. Will would be good for the information. *It was a good night's work.*

When Brad went inside to put on some clothes, Judy woke up because of the extra noise. "What's wrong, Honey?"

"Our friend who drives the Humvee was visiting our parking lot."

"What?" Judy asked, bolting out of bed.

"He's gone. George is riding on his car to find out where he lives. I'm going to see if I can figure out what he did to your car." He grabbed the flashlight from the shelf on Judy's side of the bed.

"I'm coming with you. Wait a minute. I'll throw on some clothes."

"Okay, let's be quiet. We don't want to wake Clarice."

Sneaking out of the apartment, Brad and Judy walked slowly toward her car, and Brad shined the flashlight at it.

"Everything looks normal to me," Judy said as they walked around the car.

"Let's look underneath." Brad knelt and shined the light under the front of the car.

"Oh my God, what the Hell!" Judy exclaimed.

"My guess is it's some kind of explosive device. I'm not sure. I'll have to have better light. My guess is it's rigged to go off when the car starts."

Judy stood up with a horrified look on her face. Brad jumped up and put his arms around her. "It's going to be all right, Honey. We know it's there. We can deal with it. What I don't know is how he found out who we were."

Judy shuddered. "I'm just thinking what would have happened if you hadn't seen the Humvee. You saved our lives."

George worked hard to hold on as the driver of the Humvee took turns way too fast. Brief glimpses told him they were headed toward the party house. Then he remembered hearing Judy say the Dorothy Vaughn office was close to the St. Clair house. Just when he was getting really uncomfortable, the guy turned into an office park and backed into a parking place beside several other vehicles with DVES license plates.

He's dropping off the company car and taking his own vehicle, George thought. *I'd better get ready to find a place to hang on.*

He flew toward the front of the Humvee and saw the guard guy get on a Harley with lots of chrome. The engine revved up, and the guy tore out of the parking lot. All George could do was look at the license number as the motorcycle sped away. LIR-350. He was pretty sure. LIR-350. He'd have to memorize it.

As he flew toward the St Clair house, George thought he deserved a B-minus or C-plus for his performance. While he'd hung on long enough to know where the guy went, he'd failed on his mission to find out where the guy lived. It only took him ten minutes to reach the house and another two to get to the end of the alley. As he settled down on a patch of grass, he wondered how long it would take Brad to come get him. He was afraid he was in for a long wait.

Brad and Judy were unable to get back to sleep. After about twenty minutes of trying, they gave up and fixed breakfast. The smells and the noise woke Clarice. She came out of her room wiping her eyes. "What the hell are you guys doing? Do you know what time it is?"

"Yeah, four-thirty," Brad remarked with a smile.

"Judy, this isn't like you at all. I've never seen you up before six. What's going on?"

Judy and Brad filled Clarice in on what Brad had seen and what they'd found on Judy's car.

"Holy cow," Clarice said. "How did this guy find out who you are?"

"I'm stumped," Judy concluded. "Brad guesses he must have seen me pick up Brad and George when they grabbed the blood samples. It's the only possibility."

"I guess so. How are you going to get George? You can't use your car."

"I know," Brad said. "I was thinking of asking to borrow your car for a quick trip."

"So now I understand why you guys started cooking the bacon. You wanted to get me up and ask to use my car. Very clever."

"Don't give us too much credit, Clarice. We were trying to be quiet. I didn't even consider the smells. Sorry."

"Me too," Brad added. "Now that you're up, can I borrow the car?"

"Yes, you may," replied Clarice with a smirk.

"Don't give him a hard time about his grammar, Clarice. Consider what time it is."

"Oh, may I borrow your car?"

"Sure, I'll get the keys."

George roused each time a car came down the street perpendicular to the alley. When they didn't stop, he closed his eyes again. He was startled when a car he didn't recognize stopped beside the alley. Brad got out, so George flew and landed on his outstretched hand.

Brad let him fly to the dashboard and started the car. "This is Clarice's car. Judy's can't be used for a while. The guy put a bomb under it. Most likely, it's rigged to go off when someone starts the car."

George wondered why he hadn't recognized Clarice's car. Then he remembered. He'd been in the pendant when he'd gone to church with Clarice. The view wasn't very good. Once he'd figured out the car, he moved to the more startling news. The guard guy had booby-trapped Judy's car. *How had he known about Judy? We are lucky to have Brad doing his little patrols of the apartment. This whole thing is getting serious.*

At the apartment, Brad brought George right to the computer. "Were you able to follow the guy home?"

`no went to dorothy vaughns`

"Right, he was using a company car, I guess. Did he get into his own car after he parked the Humvee?"

`hog`

Brad laughed, and Judy and Clarice gave each other a quizzical look.

Brad explained, "He's telling us the guy exchanged the Humvee for a motorcycle."

`harley`

"I guess there wasn't anywhere to hide on the motorcycle."

`no chance`

"So, we've reached another dead end," Judy lamented.

`license lir-350`

"Good work, you have the motorcycle's license plate," Brad said. "Clarice, can you get your brother to run the plate?"

"Sure thing. I won't tell him why I need it. Like I said earlier, he's done it to help me with stories before. It should be no problem. He won't be up for another couple of hours. I'm going to see if I can get another hour or two of sleep myself."

"Sounds like a good idea," Judy said, yawning. "I'll give George a little snack, and then I'm going to give sleep another try. Brad, why don't you come with me? There's nothing you can do until you have some tools, right?"

"Yeah, I'm sure I'll need wire cutters at the very least. I'm probably too wound up to go to sleep."

"Come try anyway."

Two hours later, Brad left Judy and Clarice sleeping and headed out to the parking lot. In the expanding daylight, he saw his initial guess had been right. The explosive, two blocks of C-4 wrapped together, was wired to the starter. It would be easy to disarm the device with wire cutters. Next, he started walking to the Home Depot, which was a couple of miles away. He'd done a lot of hiking in the Army, and he enjoyed it. He would be back to take care of the car in a little over an hour.

While he walked, Brad wondered what to do. This guy, whoever he was, played hardball. Two blocks of C-4 were enough to blow Judy's car sky-high, killing her and maybe some innocent bystanders. He'd have to be sure to retrieve the explosive, which was attached to the car with duct tape, without disturbing any fingerprints. He thought finding fingerprints was a long shot. This guy probably used gloves all the time.

As he thought about how to handle things, he realized the big problem. Though George was their best witness, he couldn't be put on the witness stand. Heck, they weren't even able to tell the police about him. No one would believe them, and anyway, he didn't want to be used that way. They had to catch the guard somehow. They didn't have enough to go to the police yet. If he'd had the right camera last night, he'd already have the evidence he needed.

When Brad returned to the car with his new tools, he realized it had been a long time since he'd done a forced march. His knees were telling him he should have slowed down. As he came up beside Judy's car, he saw her coming across the parking lot. "I've been waiting for you," she shouted. "Can I help?"

Brad gave her a big hug when they met beside the car. "Yeah, you can help. It should be easy. Still, it's good to have two sets of eyes. Let me show you what's going on."

Brad showed Judy the two blocks of C-4 and the wire coming from them. "The wire is attached to the starter. I don't have to mess with the starter part yet. At this end, the wire goes into a detonator stuffed into the C-4. If I clip the wire, I can take the C-4 and the detonator off the car. With the detonator removed, the C-4 won't be dangerous at all."

"Is there a chance cutting the wire will set off the C-4?"

"I don't see how. I'm not going to create a spark with these cutters," Brad said as he held up the wire cutters.

"It sounds like you know what you're doing."

"Thanks. This isn't a sophisticated bomb. This is a bomb made by a guy who doesn't think his bomb will ever be found."

"Do you need anything else?"

"Oh, yes I do. I need a paper bag or something to put the C-4 in and a plastic sandwich bag for the detonator. We need to keep them clean so the police can check for fingerprints. I'm going to wear these gloves I bought. Also, I'm going to take pictures of everything before I get started."

Ten minutes later, Brad had the C-4 and the detonators in their bags. Then he opened the hood and found where the wire was connected. He took another picture before disconnecting the wire from the starter.

When Cleat woke up, he turned on the local news. He thought a car blowing up in the parking lot of an apartment complex would be big news. After he watched a half-hour of the news and weather, he guessed the girl, Judith Clayton, hadn't used her car yet. *I shouldn't be so jumpy about the whole thing.* He made himself breakfast and headed to work. On his way there, he decided to take a detour to the apartment complex. He drove his Harley through the parking lot. Clayton's car was still there.

Cleat checked the news on his phone four times every hour. It was giving him fits. By the afternoon, he figured there were two possibilities. Maybe Clayton wasn't going anywhere today. The other possibility, somehow his device hadn't worked, wasn't very likely. The device was so simple. There wasn't much to go wrong. When he'd finished his work schedule, he drove by the apartment again. The car was in the same place, so Clayton must not have gone out today.

Brad saw Cleat on his motorcycle in the morning and snapped several pictures with his phone. Judy and Brad took an Uber to Brad's PTSD therapy at the VA, and George took the sentry duty. He saw the Harley doing a check a half-hour before Brad and Judy returned.

Chapter Thirty-Two

IN THE UBER THEY'D TAKEN from the VA, Judy received a text from Clarice. Her brother had tracked down the motorcycle license plate. The Harley belonged to Cleatus Blanton who lived at 1553 Olaf Street in Mayfield Heights.

When they got to the apartment, they told George what they'd learned from the text, and he reported on the results of his sentry duty.

`came at 4:30 on Harley`

"He must be wondering what happened to his bomb," Brad commented.

"Would he be able to tell it was missing?"

"I doubt it. Did he slow down behind the car, or was it like this morning where he simply drove by?"

`drove by`

"We'd better hide the car somehow," Brad commented. "If I were him, I'd come to check the connections on my bomb tonight. He wouldn't really be able to do it in the daylight. We can't have him finding we've discovered the bomb."

"He's going to know it didn't go off. A bombing would make big-time news."

"I guess you're right. I hope he'll think the bomb malfunctioned somehow. We can park on one of the streets in the neighborhood on the west side of the apartments. I don't believe you need a permit to park there. We want him to wonder what the heck happened."

"What are we going to do for transportation? It wouldn't be a good idea to check out his Mayfield Heights house in my car. He might spot us."

`rent a car`

"He's right," Judy responded. "We'd better reserve a rental car. We can't use my car for a while."

"I only have another week before I have to go to officially get out of the Army. I can rent a car for a week. Let's go to the airport. We can use your car to pick up a rental. There won't be much chance of running into Mr. Blanton."

"Speaking of Mr. Blanton, let me see what I can find out about him on the internet."

`I have an idea`

"Go ahead."

`c-4 under dves 5`

"No way!" Judy responded. "I want to figure out a way for the police to get this guy. It's all I signed on for. I'm not interested in becoming a criminal. Besides, what about collateral damage? No, we want to put Cleatus Blanton in jail, not blow him up."

"Judy's right, George. Planting a bomb on his car, even though it sounds tempting, isn't the way to go. Let's see what we can find out about him. We're closing in on him."

Judy searched for Cleatus Blanton and came up with very little. She found he was a past president of the Cleveland Riders, a motorcycle club, and he was also listed as a member of some veteran's group none of them had ever heard of. Otherwise, he was a complete blank.

"Not much," Judy said after she'd shown the results.

"It looks like we'll have to do some more digging ourselves," Brad commented.

`take me to his house tonight`

"It would be risky using Judy's car tonight. We wouldn't be able to get you very close."

"Let me bring up Google maps," Judy responded. "We can get a look at—where is it?"

"It's on the text from Clarice."

"Oh yeah. Here it is—1553 Olaf Street in Mayfield Heights."

Judy found 1553 on the map and then switched to the overhead view. The house didn't look like anything special. It was in a tract housing neighborhood. All the houses on the block looked like they had close to the same floor plan. Judy switched back to street views. They confirmed what they'd thought. All the houses looked very similar. While some had added rooms, and some had enclosed their garages, they all started out the same.

"When it's dark, it will be safe enough to get you within a couple of blocks, no closer," Brad said.

`no problem`

"And we can't leave you there very long," Judy added. "If he was savvy enough to figure out what car I drive, he certainly had a chance to look at you when you flew right in front of his windshield. You'd better be careful."

will do

After dinner, the three of them rode in Judy's car. A light rain was falling. Despite the rain, before Brad started the car, he made a thorough inspection. When they reached Mayfield Heights, they found a Starbucks in a shopping strip about three blocks from Blanton's house and parked in the back lot where Judy's car wouldn't be visible from the street. The rain had picked up at this point.

"Do you still want to go?" Judy asked.

George responded by flying to her window.

"I'd say he wants to go," Brad commented. "Keep it under an hour."

Judy pushed the button to lower her window and George flew out. Flying in the rain was a little slower, and it was more difficult to know exactly where he was. He found Olaf Street and landed in a tree in front of Blanton's neighbor's house. Blanton's house had several motorcycles parked in its driveway. He wondered if Blanton had a bunch of roommates. There was a light on in one of the windows.

He picked out a place to land on a bush in front of the nearest window and took off. From his perch on the bush, he could only see a window blind. He did hear some talking coming from the room with the light on. Before he had a chance to approach the window, someone opened it, and he heard, "The rain cooled things down. I'm opening the window. Turn off the air, Cleat."

George flew to the corner of the screen on the newly opened window. His guess was the room was a bedroom converted into a den. A six-sided card table dominated the middle of the room, and four guys sat around the table. A moment after he started looking, Cleatus Blanton came in the room. "I turned off the AC. Just for you, Jim."

"Yeah, thanks," said a red-faced gray-haired guy who had an impressive beer belly.

"Shut up and deal the cards," said a completely bald, younger guy.

George decided these must be guys from the motorcycle club. He watched a few hands of poker. They were playing with chips, so, at first, he couldn't to tell how high the stakes were. Then he concluded they couldn't have been too high, because most of the guys were doing as much drinking as they were card playing. The talk around the table was inconsequential and bawdy. Some of the guys thought they were really clever. George disagreed. The only piece of information he picked up was that Blanton lived alone. All the other guys were visitors.

Fifteen minutes later, George realized he was bored, so he flew around to investigate the rest of the house. As far as he could tell, it looked like a normal house. It didn't appear Cleat had any roommates, and there wasn't a feminine touch to be seen through the three windows he investigated. After checking out the house, he watched a little more poker and then flew to Judy's car.

Brad drove into the neighborhood next to the apartment complex and parked in a secluded spot a couple of blocks in. "This should be far enough away. I'd be shocked if the guy comes anywhere near here."

Luckily the rain had stopped completely, so they were able to get to the apartment with no trouble. Brad asked George to report.

`poker with cycle buddies`

"Did you learn anything?"

`call him cleat`

"Does he have a wife, or a roommate?" Judy asked.

He went to the N key.

"It looks like another dead end to me," Brad concluded. "We didn't learn much. Blanton lives alone, and even if George had made it into his house, he wouldn't have learned very much."

`take me to dves`

"Makes sense, Brad. The killings of George and Ronald Anderson were part of Blanton's job. The real helpful information might be at the Dorothy Vaughn place."

"Okay. Yeah, you're right. It's a plan. First thing tomorrow we go to the airport, and I'll pick up a rental car. I can reserve one in a minute. When we have the rental car, George and I can go to Dorothy Vaughn's. With any luck he can find out how things work there."

"And when I return from the airport, I should park where we have the car tonight?" Judy asked.

"Yes. We have to work quickly. This guy Blanton is likely to try something else. I've been wondering if we should move into a hotel for a few days. If he knows about your car, he knows about this apartment."

"I hadn't thought about the possibility. Should we go to the police?"

"Let's see what George can find out. Then maybe we should get the police involved. While I'll keep watch tonight, I'm not worried about Blanton doing anything tonight. I bet the poker players were drinking."

`lots of beer`

"Doesn't surprise me. We're most likely safe for tonight, and we have a plan for tomorrow."

Just after Brad made his pronouncement, Clarice walked in with two men. George recognized Simon but didn't know who the other guy was. He was big, maybe six foot two, and solidly built. Judy seemed to know him because she went to greet him. George didn't hear the name she used. Brad stood up too and hung back while Judy greeted the guy.

Finally, Clarice made the introductions. "Brad, this is Lewis, my brother. Lewis, this is Brad Curry, Judy's boyfriend. I'm going to let Lewis explain why he's here. It's kinda official business, and then maybe it's not."

"You're with the police, aren't you?" Brad shook Lewis's hand.

"Yes. I'm with the vice squad, and when I tracked down the license number Clarice gave me this morning, I recognized the guy. Cleatus Blanton is a person we've been interested in for a long time. We suspect his employer, Dorothy Vaughn Escort Service, is running an illegal sex-for-hire business. Unfortunately, we've never been able to prove it. I need to know why you're interested in Mr. Blanton."

Brad and Judy exchanged a quick look, but neither spoke.

Clarice finally broke the silence. "Look you two, you'd better tell Lewis what's going on. The guy put a bomb under Judy's car last night. He might be coming to this apartment tonight. You need help, and Lewis can provide it."

"Tell him about George too," Simon said. "I'm dying to see his reaction."

"Clarice, you shouldn't have," Judy said.

"She has, Honey," Brad said. "We were going to have to involve the police eventually. It's just a little earlier than we'd planned." Looking at Lewis, Brad continued, "What do you want to know? You'll find some of it hard to believe."

"Why don't you tell me everything? Start at the start."

Judy began the story in Africa, explaining how a bug had introduced himself as George Wilcox who'd been reincarnated as a dung beetle.

Lewis looked very skeptical. "Surely you're kidding."

"Here, sit down at the computer," Judy said. "We'll do the demonstration we used to convince everyone else. This is what you wanted, wasn't it, Simon?"

"Yeah, Lewis, sit in front of the computer. The dung beetle will indicate the keys to hit."

The policeman sat reluctantly.

`clarice your sister`

"Holy shit. Simon, you and Clarice told me I had a surprise in store. It's a crazy trick. How the hell are these guys doing this?"

"It's not a trick, Lewis. Ask him a question."

"Okay. I'll play along. Mr. Bug, how did you run into Cleatus Blanton?"

`guards house on st clair`

Lewis gave a quizzical look, so Brad spoke up. "The house at 1287 St. Clair Road is used by Dorothy Vaughn Escort Services as a party house. George thought it was familiar. He didn't have any memories of the day he was shot. Anyway, he saw Mr. Blanton guarding the house one night when he had it staked out."

`patrols around house`

Lewis pushed himself away from the computer. "It's really a clever trick."

"No, it isn't," Simon said. "George Wilcox was a classmate of mine at Oberlin. The bug knew details about our college experience only he would know."

"Is it okay if I don't believe you, Simon?"

Simon looked a little hurt, so Clarice jumped in. "I have an idea. Lewis, why don't you and George go into my bedroom." Reaching into her purse, she extracted a pen and a pad of paper. "You write a number between one and ten. Let him see it, and then come back here and see if he can type it. All the rest of us will stay here. Only you and George can see the number."

"You're making it sound even more like a magic trick, Sis."

"Go do it," Simon urged.

Lewis took the paper and pen from Clarice. Followed by George, he went into the bedroom reluctantly. In the bedroom, Lewis wrote, "Fly around the room."

George flew around the room. Lewis shook his head, astounded. Finally, Lewis wrote the number eleven and showed it to him.

Lewis and George returned to the others. "I wrote a number. Let's see if this bug can get you to type it, Clarice.

11

"It's just like you Lewis," Clarice commented. "I told you to pick a number between one and ten, so you picked eleven. Show us what you wrote."

Lewis opened the pad. Simon was the first to respond. "See, I told you, the bug is my old college friend, George Wilcox."

"I guess at this point, Judy, you'd better continue with your story."

Judy and Brad, with occasional help from Clarice and George, brought Lewis up to date. They stopped their narration with their plan to have George investigate the Dorothy Vaughn operation tomorrow.

Lewis, who had been silent throughout, finally spoke. "This is fascinating, and there are aspects of what you've told me I can't deal with. Like I told you, I deal with the vice. I'd have to involve homicide to cover the murder. From the vice angle, we've been trying to gather evidence on Dorothy Vaughn's operation for some time now. There's nothing illegal about an escort service. Sex for hire is illegal. You're telling me it looks an awful lot like sex for hire."

"You're right, Bro. At the moment, our only real witness is a dung beetle, and no judge would be willing to admit his testimony," Clarice added.

"I can see the problem."

"Wouldn't the blood sample be helpful?" Brad asked. "It would tie the murder of Ronald Anderson to the property on St. Clair."

"You didn't obtain the blood sample legally. It isn't evidence we can use in court."

"Couldn't it be used to get the homicide detectives involved?" Judy asked.

"Maybe. I'll have to think about it. Right now, I want to focus on the vice angle. I'm halfway interested in your idea of letting the bug investigate Dorothy Vaughn. Three years ago, we raided her offices and didn't find a thing. Somewhere she has to have a list of clients, and the financial records for the illicit part of her operation. All we found was legitimate business records. We were lucky to have her to drop the idea of suing us for police harassment. It was touch and go for a while. I'd love to have a mole inside her operation."

"We're not offering you a mole," Brad remarked, smiling. "Just a bug on the wall."

"A bug on the wall will do."

Simon and Lewis left a half an hour later. Before they left, Lewis called to get an officer to watch their apartment building. Given the drinking he'd been doing, they weren't very worried about Blanton doing anything. Still, it was better to be safe. Brad and Lewis agreed to meet near the Dorothy Vaughn office the next morning, and Lewis spent some time briefing George about what he should be looking for. As he was leaving, Lewis asked Brad to let him take the blood samples. Brad was happy to provide them.

As Lewis and Simon were approaching the door, Judy added one thing. "Lewis, please don't tell anyone about George. He only wants a small group of people to know about him. He's afraid of becoming a circus freak or something."

Lewis nodded. "I can see the problem. I'll keep quiet."

Chapter Thirty-Three

THE NEXT MORNING, THEY HEADED to the airport. Judy drove home to hide the car, and Brad and George took the rental to their rendezvous with Lewis. Lewis had some last-minute instructions. Though George didn't find them very interesting, he listened calmly.

As George flew off, Lewis shook his head. "This whole thing is just plain weird. I mean, when I brief my men, I can tell from the looks in their eyes whether they get it or not. I have no idea if the bug understood anything. "

"He's very sharp. I'm sure he understood his assignment."

George landed on a bush beside the entrance to Dorothy Vaughn's. It was a quarter till nine, and the internet indicated they opened at nine. He did a tour of the building. He remembered the parking lot behind the building from his previous visit. He didn't learn much by looking in the windows, so he returned to the bush.

The first person to arrive, right at nine, was a young girl who opened the door. George flew in and landed on a potted plant in what looked like a lobby. George decided the girl, who was a nice-looking petite brunette, must be the receptionist. She put a big purse in her bottom desk drawer and then took a paper bag into some back room. He guessed it was her lunch.

Nothing happened for the next fifteen minutes. He didn't like being still, but he knew movement might give him away, so he stayed put. He planned to move the next time someone came in the door. Five minutes later, the door opened, and a guy in work clothes came in and started chatting up the receptionist, who George learned was named Jill. When the guy was pointing out something on her computer, he made his exit from the potted plant.

Flying low, he made it to the corridor off to the left of Jill. The nameplate on the first door he encountered announced it as the office of Dorothy Vaughn. The door was ajar, so he went in. The office clearly belonged to the boss. It was big with an impressive desk dominating one end and a conference table with six chairs at the other end. There was also a more intimate seating area with three chairs in the corner across from the desk. He figured Dorothy Vaughn had one-on-ones in the intimate area and larger meetings at the conference table. After looking the room over, he searched for a hiding place and spotted another potted plant. It was off to one side behind the big desk, so he'd have a good look at the room.

Being sure no one was coming, he flew out to look at the rest of the place. There were several closed doors, none of them labeled. He was discouraged. As he was headed back toward Dorothy's office, he heard someone come in the front door.

"Morning Boss," Jill said.

"Hi Jill. I have some letters for you to type in the brown folder. The green folder has invoices to prepare, and this red folder has the entries for the accounting package."

"Wow, you were busy last night."

"Somebody has to keep this ship running."

While the women talked, George flew into Dorothy's office and settled in a comfortable place among the plant's leaves. Dorothy swept into the room wearing a weird coat. She took off the coat and hung it on a coat hook inside the door. When he'd seen a picture of Dorothy Vaughn on the firm's website, he hadn't paid much attention. As she took off the coat, he saw she was quite something. He decided the expression "dressed to the nines" fit her. She had on a deep purple dress with a tight skirt and a plunging neckline. She wore matching high heels and loads of jewelry. One of her most prominent features was two improbably positioned breasts. He was sure they were fake. Looking closer at her neck, he saw some wrinkles suggesting she wasn't as young as she dressed. Still, the entire package was well put together. He decided she would probably appeal to her clients—rich older women who wanted nice-looking young men as escorts.

Dorothy had a ledger with her, which she put in the middle of her desk. Next, she fired up her computer. He realized his perch on the potted plant allowed him to see what she was typing. The first thing was a query for a password. He was thrilled when he saw it: SexyMe62. Dorothy started transferring numbers from the ledger she'd brought onto an Excel spreadsheet. He wasn't able to decipher the headings on the columns or rows, so he couldn't figure out what she was doing.

Twenty minutes after Ms. Vaughn started entering numbers in Excel, an intercom buzzed, and George heard Jill telling Dorothy she had a call, a Mrs. Simms.

"Oh Cathleen, how are you doing," Dorothy said when she picked up her phone.

She listened for a moment, then she said, "Let me check the bookings."

George saw her switch to a different spreadsheet. Then she spoke again. "I'm sorry, Rafe is already booked for two days from now. We might be able to arrange something for another day. It's difficult. He's very popular."

He wondered if the woman was trying to book this guy Rafe for special services. While there was no talk about the house on St. Clair, there was no talk about a function the woman, Cathleen, needed an escort for. It was hard to figure out when he was hearing only half of the call.

Dorothy finished the call, during which she agreed on a day for the woman's date with Rafe. Then she made an entry in the ledger and went back to work. The next couple of hours passed with Dorothy Vaughn seeming very busy. She took two more calls from clients and arranged for escorts for them. After one of the calls, she made another entry in the ledger. She also called a catering company to arrange for a small party at the St. Clair house. He concluded it was the one the guy Rafe was involved in. It was the right day. The caterers were probably the same ones he saw setting up the other day.

At about eleven, Dorothy was interrupted by Jill announcing she had a visitor, Rafe Velasquez. Dorothy took a mirror out of her purse and checked her makeup. Then she stood up from her behind her desk as she asked Jill to send him in.

"Rafe, darling," Dorothy purred as she came up and gave the guy a hug and a rather long kiss before directing him to one of the chairs. "Aren't you the popular one. Not less than twenty minutes ago, I made a reservation for you with Cathleen Simms."

George had to admit this guy Rafe was good looking. Tall, dark, and handsome came to mind. He also gave the impression he was comfortable in his skin. He was casually dressed—khakis and a polo shirt. He took a chair facing Dorothy.

"Great, Cathleen's a big tipper."

"I know. She wanted the day after tomorrow. I had to tell her you were busy. We settled on another day, sometime next week. I'll have Jill send it to your calendar. I haven't had time to get to all the details."

"I wanted to talk about the next date. I've never worked with Chad before. Is he new?"

"No, Chad has been with us for two years. I didn't realize you've never worked with him. He knows the score. You won't be breaking in a newby. And the women are faithful clients. Genevieve Morton is your date. This will be her fourth date. She's told me she wants to try out our entire stable. Obviously, I objected to her language. She just laughed when I made my objection."

"How about Chad's date?"

Dorothy went to her desk and checked some file. "Sybil Gomez, yes I thought so. It's her second time with Chad. It should go very well."

Rafe looked stricken. "Oh my God. I used to date Yolanda Gomez, and her mother was named Sybil. Sybil Gomez can't be a common name. I suspect it's her. It won't be any problem, will it?"

Dorothy went to the chair and sat. "It shouldn't be. Everyone knows the rules. We're all anonymous. Even if you meet somewhere or see each other on the street, you're not supposed to react. Sybil knows the rules."

"Okay, I guess I can pretend I'm meeting her for the first time."

Dorothy smiled. "I know how some mothers are about their daughter's boyfriends. With a guy like you, there was probably some envy involved. I bet Sybil calls soon requesting you."

"Maybe. I guess it would be no problem."

"There isn't anything to worry about for your upcoming date. Nothing is going to go wrong. Cleat will be there to provide security. You've done this several times."

Rafe stood up. "I only want to be sure about everything. Like I said, I don't know Chad. I'll get out of your hair now. I know you're busy."

"No problem. Drop by any time," Dorothy said as she rose and gave Rafe a goodbye kiss.

While George couldn't tell whether Rafe enjoyed the kiss, it looked like Dorothy did. He guessed the boss was permitted to handle the merchandise.

After Rafe's departure, Dorothy settled back to her routine. Twenty minutes later, she was interrupted by Jill announcing the arrival of Cleat.

Upon entering the office, Cleatus Blanton took Rafe's place in the chair without any direction from Dorothy. Dorothy went to her chair. There were no hugs and kisses for Cleat.

Dorothy started the conversation. "Anything going on with the people you found poking around the St. Clair place?"

"No, unfortunately there's nothing to report. I don't know what went wrong. I…"

Dorothy interrupted. "I don't need any details. Anyway, it doesn't matter. I found a new place. It's time to move operations, anyway. You'd already had two encounters with guys watching. This last one makes three. The little party in two days will be the last time we use the St. Clair house. The new place will be ready for next week's dates."

"Wow, you move fast. So, you want me to do my guard routine, nothing more."

"Yes. You know what we want. It's a double date. Be sure the house is ready. It shouldn't be a problem. The guys both have keys, so you won't have to let them in. They don't need a waiter either. They are both very experienced."

"Where's the new place?"

Dorothy stood up and went to her desk. "Here, I'll show you the real estate ad."

Cleat looked over Dorothy's shoulder. George tried as hard without moving to find out the address of the new place but didn't succeed. The house looked very nice. It seemed big. Dorothy and Cleat talked about the details of the new house. While it was clear they knew each other well, George thought their interactions were a little frosty. They weren't friends, just a boss and her employee. There might have been some history between them. In any event, Dorothy had acted very differently with Rafe.

After looking at the new house for about ten minutes, Cleat started to leave. At the door, he turned. "Are you sure you don't want me to follow up with the people I saw snooping around St. Clair?"

Dorothy looked up from the computer. "No, leave them alone. In a few days we'll be out of the house, and there will never be any record Dorothy Vaughn Escort Service ever had anything to do with it."

"Okay Boss," Cleat said as he left.

George stretched a little while Dorothy worked on her computer. Her back was turned to him, so it was safe. A half hour later, Dorothy called Jill on the intercom. "I'm finished here for the day. Forward any calls to my home phone. I'll be there when I've finished lunch and my trip to the gym."

"Fine. There's nothing on your calendar."

Dorothy, who was standing at this point, headed for her coat and commented under her breath. "I know, dummy."

George took a big chance when Dorothy turned her back to put on her coat. He flew and landed on the folds in the coat's hood. Dorothy was unlikely to put the hood up, and he wasn't heavy enough for her to notice. He didn't want to be locked in her office. While it had been open this morning, it might not be open all the time.

Dorothy walked by Jill without even saying goodbye. When Dorothy walked around to the parking lot, George extracted himself from the folds of the hood and flew. Keeping a safe distance, he followed her. Five DVES vehicles were in the lot, and there was a white Jaguar too. he was surprised when Dorothy didn't go directly to the Jag.

When she walked behind DVES 1, the Humvee limousine, George flew so he could see what she was doing. She put her hand on one of the bricks and seemed to push hard. Much to his surprise, four of the other bricks to the right of the one she was pushing slid to one side, revealing a safe in the wall. He flew closer to pick up the combination of the safe. He wasn't able to get a good angle without taking a big chance of Dorothy seeing him. He was in luck, because Dorothy recited the numbers as she spun the dial. "Three, seventeen…" He didn't hear the last number because her voice faded a little. With the safe open, Dorothy put in the ledger she'd been working with and closed the safe door. When she pushed the brick door shut, he heard a click. It must have been coming from the brick she'd used to open things.

Dorothy walked to the Jag and drove off. George didn't think he'd learn anything more at DVES, so he flew toward the park where he'd agreed to meet Brad and Judy. They'd told him they were going to bring a picnic lunch and stay there for the afternoon, so they should be there. It had to be close to lunch time. It was a good thing he wasn't stuck in the offices for the entire day. He would have been famished.

He found Brad and Judy with no trouble.

Chapter Thirty-Four

JUDY AND BRAD WERE HAPPY to see George. "Great," Judy remarked. "It's getting hot out here. I was hoping you'd come soon."

"Did you find any useful information?" Brad asked.

He flew into Judy's hand and jumped once.

"It's his signal for yes. You should call Lewis, Brad. See if he can come to our place this afternoon. We need to debrief George. You have good information for him, don't you?"

Again, he jumped once.

"Let's pack up; one of us can call Lewis on the way," Brad said.

George flew down to the picnic basket.

Judy understood. "We'd better get out his food and let him have lunch on the way home. He's a real chow hound sometimes."

Lewis was waiting for them when they returned to the apartment. "What did he find out?" The excitement was obvious in his voice.

"Hold on, Lewis," Brad said. "We don't know what he found out. Believe me, you want to let us clean him up before you start asking questions. He's just had his lunch, and you know what he's been eating."

"Elephant shit, right?"

"Yep. Judy will clean him, and then we can get to the questioning."

When they were ready, Judy sat down to type for George, and Lewis started. "What did you find out?"

`two sets of books`

"That's what we expected. When we raided them two years ago, all we found were the books for the legitimate operation. It doesn't do us any good to know there are two sets of books unless we have both sets."

`I can show you both`

"Fabulous. How did you get the information?"

`safe with illicit books`

Lewis appeared to be puzzled, so Brad broke in. "He's saying, he knows where the safe is holding the books for the illegal part of the operation."

"We didn't find any safe when we raided them before."

`brick wall behind limo`

"Wonderful. When we go out there again, he should be able to show me where it is?"

He went to the Y key and then wanted Judy to type.

`press on brick to reveal safe`

"I'll have to remember to have the guys bring the equipment to open a safe. There are some drills and other stuff we'll have to bring."

George indicated he had more to say.

`combination three seventeen something`

Lewis looked up from his notebook where he was furiously taking notes. "This is fabulous. With two of the three numbers, it's a piece of cake to open a safe. We won't need special equipment. The records for the legal operation are probably on computers in the regular offices. It can be hard to figure out the passwords, but usually we can get them."

`password SexyMe62`

"Wow, you got her password. Is it to Dorothy Vaughn's computer?"

He went to the Y key.

Lewis rocked back in his chair with a big smile on his face. "I feel greedy asking. Is there more?"

`last st clair party day after tomorrow`

The three humans were confused. Brad finally asked, "Are you saying they are abandoning the house on St. Clair?"

He went to the Y key.

"They may have become nervous," Lewis said. "Putting a bomb under your car suggests they're very serious about keeping the house secret. They must have changed their mind. They can probably sell the house and get another one easily. It's better than having a place people know about."

`cleat will be doing security`

Lewis again rocked in his chair. "I'm sure I have enough at the office for a raid on Dorothy Vaughn's operation. With what George has found out, we'll be successful this time. With both sets of books, we can nail her and shut down the operation."

"It's what you want, isn't it?" Judy asked.

"Yeah, but if that's all we do, this guy Cleat goes free. He'll clear out of town as fast as he can. There's no way we'll be able to touch him, let alone get him on a murder charge."

"It's going to be difficult to bring in the homicide people without giving George away," Brad said.

"No problem. We use confidential sources all the time. I can just tell them I have a confidential source. One I can't divulge. Frankly, I really don't want to divulge my source in this case. I know some guys in homicide who will go along with me."

"All Cleat is doing is patrolling the private property of his employer," Judy said. "No matter how crooked the employer is, we don't have anything on Cleat."

"You're going to have to set Cleat up," Brad added. "You're going to have to entice him to shoot at someone. I guess you might be able to set up a dummy and get him to shoot at it, or maybe someone in a bullet proof outfit."

"I see what you're saying," Lewis responded. "I gave your blood samples to our lab. If it turns out the blood you found matches Ronald Anderson, I probably can arrange something with my homicide friends. It's going to be tricky. At least we have a day and a half to set everything up. I need to go now and get my warrant. Afterwards I'll check with the lab, and, if the blood matches, I'll get with homicide."

"Please text us about the blood," Judy asked.

Lewis rose and headed for the door. "Thanks for all your help. I don't know when I've been so excited. I never knew all I needed was a dung beetle."

"A very special dung beetle," Judy called out as Lewis went out the door.

"I don't know why he's so surprised," Brad added. "We told him George had experience as a detective before he became a dung beetle."

In the middle of the afternoon, Judy received a text from Lewis. The blood sample they gave him matched with the blood the police had collected from the body of Ronald Anderson.

"Great," Judy texted back.

Forty-five minutes later, Lewis texted again. The homicide guys were interested, and they wanted a meeting with Brad tomorrow morning.

Brad and Judy talked it over. They decided George could tell Brad everything he remembered about how Cleat behaved, and if the police asked a question he couldn't answer, he'd text Judy who would relay George's reply. They all agreed this should work, so Judy texted saying Brad would be there, though he might have to text with his confidential source for some details.

After dinner, Brad asked George for a briefing. They enlarged the google maps overhead view of 1287 St. Clair as much as possible, and George described the path Cleatus Blanton took when he did his rounds. He remembered Cleat had done his rounds in one direction on the first trip and the opposite direction on the second trip. Also, he showed Brad the tree he thought he had been behind when he was shot, and they agreed on the location of the tree where Brad obtained the blood sample. The whole thing took about an hour. It was tedious. Brad seemed really nervous, and George thought his questions became repetitive toward the end.

The next morning, Brad met Lewis outside the downtown police headquarters. Lewis took him into a briefing room and introduced him to a Lieutenant Bowers. "Nick Bowers," the guy said. "Call me Nick. The others will be here in a few minutes. Here's what's going to go down. We're going to do simultaneous raids tomorrow night. Lewis and his group from vice are going to hit the Dorothy Vaughn offices at the same time we're going to spring a trap on this guy Cleatus Blanton. How much do you know about Blanton?"

"Not much, really. He works for Dorothy Vaughn and drives one of their Humvees when he's working. As far as we know, his only other vehicle is a Harley. He lives in Mayfield Heights in a modest house—no roommates. He performs several functions for Dorothy Vaughn. Mostly he's a guard, and we know he's going to be a guard tomorrow night."

"It's quite a bit, really. We procured his Army records. He served seven years, combat in Iraq. He never made it past E-3. He was in the infantry. According to the records, he attempted to get in the Military Police. Something caused them to turn him down. It was right before he left the Army. I suspect there's something more serious than the two Article 15s on his record."

Two minutes later, four more policemen showed up. Brad was introduced to all of them. It was too many names for him to remember all at once. When the team was assembled, Nick explained who Brad was and outlined the operation. It was simple. Their information told them the target, Cleatus Blanton, would get there after they were in place. Nick showed them where they were going to be. One of the younger guys, Simpson, Brad thought, was the one in real danger. He was the bait. The idea was to catch Cleat Blanton in the act. Simpson would be in a bullet-proof outfit pretending to be taking pictures of what was happening on the deck. Just before Blanton had a chance to shoot him, Nick would put on a searchlight, and the other three guys would jump up from where they were concealed and grab Blanton. The whole thing would be filmed.

When Cleat was captured, two squad cars would remove the couples in the house and take them to the nearest station. Two members of Lewis's unit would be there to greet them. The people would be told about the raid on Dorothy Vaughn's operation, so there was a chance they'd be willing to talk. The police planned to tell them they'd get off with minor charges if they told what they knew.

Brad filled them in on Cleat's pattern of surveillance and what he knew about the backyard of 1287 St. Clair. A discussion of the proposed hiding places for the three policemen followed. There was no way to hide on the St. Clair side of the street, so they decided to position an undercover car nearby to guard against any potential escape. The car would appear at the point the spotlight went on.

They all agreed to meet tomorrow at four-thirty. Nick and Simpson would go to the neighbor's house and keep an eye on 1287. They'd already called the neighbors and cleared everything with them. When Nick gave the others the okay, they would individually infiltrate the area and get into their respective hiding places. He thought they should be in place by seven. Simpson was going to go out to his place in the woods a little while after he saw the couples arrive. While there were a few questions, Brad didn't have to use his confidential informant.

Brad thanked all the homicide policemen and left with Lewis. Lewis said goodbye at the entrance to the headquarters. "I have to go be sure everything is straight about the warrant I need to raid DVES. Though it should all be in order, it's always good to double check. I'll be by the apartment tomorrow at six to pick up George. I need him to show me how to get into the safe. I'm not sure how I'm going to explain him to my men."

"I'd let him out before things start. He can fly where you want him, and you can find him there. He said it was behind the DVES one limo. You really don't need him—all you need to do is push on all the bricks. Don't tell him I told you, he'll want to come along."

"Good enough. None of my men will have to know anything about it."

Brad drove home and reported to Judy and George.

George wasn't sure what he thought about everything. He felt he should be happier. The police were probably going to capture Cleatus Blanton, and he was almost certainly the guy who'd killed him. It was what he'd wanted. Now it felt anticlimactic. He came back to Cleveland with the idea of finding out who had disliked him enough to kill him. He was sure he'd know the killer. Now it was a stranger. Some poor slob doing his job. It made him feel insignificant, just when he should be feeling fulfilled. It made him a little depressed.

Chapter Thirty-Five

THE NEXT MORNING, JUDY AND Brad didn't tell Clarice anything about the night's planned activities. Lewis had told them not to. He knew she was a reporter. They kept things light by asking how her relationship with Simon was progressing. Clarice wasn't sure, or at least that's what she said. Judy thought Clarice wasn't in a mood to share.

After Clarice left, they tried to stay busy with other things. None of them were able to totally ignore thinking about the upcoming police raids. In the late morning, Judy finally broached the subject. "Brad, I have a question about tonight."

"Shoot."

"That's it precisely. When you explained it to me, you said the searchlight was supposed to come on right before Blanton was going to shoot the guy. How can they accuse him of murder if he doesn't shoot?"

"I thought about the same problem. My guess is pointing the gun in a threatening manner is enough to charge him, and the Ronald Anderson blood will also come into play. I know the police guy, Simpson, will be in a bullet proof outfit, but still the police don't want him shot at."

George was jumping up and down on the computer.

```
sneaking up on guy
```

"Good point," Brad said. "They will have it all on film. It will show Blanton sneaking up on Simpson. And he'll have a silencer on his gun. Any normal person would be yelling at an intruder to get out of his yard. Sneaking up on the guy is clearly suspicious. That, the silencer, and Anderson's blood should be enough to sink Blanton."

"I hope you're right. I don't like the idea of letting Blanton shoot at the poor policemen. Even with bullet-proof vests, I understand people can get a serious bruise."

"It's not any fun. I hope it all works. It's a little maddening not to be involved tonight. I wasn't invited."

Judy stood up from the computer and started to pace. After a few turns around the living room, she spoke up. "I want to go to St. Clair Road tonight. Not when it's happening, mind you, but later. I want to see them arrest Blanton."

"We can do it. In fact, I have an idea of where we can wait. Let's go to Quincy Street, where they found George's body. It's real close to the St. Clair house, and far enough away to avoid being in the way of the police."

"I'm glad you agree. We can head out as soon as Lewis picks him up."

"I guess we'd have to make it back here before Lewis brings George. You can have Lewis text you to tell us when he's going to bring him. I don't know which one of the police actions will take the longest."

George indicated he wanted to type, so Judy came to the computer.

```
lewis has schedule other on cleat
```

"He's right, Judy. Lewis is going to strike at a particular time. The other operation springs its trap when Cleat decides to make his rounds. It isn't scheduled on a clock we know precisely. I think the two police actions are going to be simultaneous, but it's not necessarily true."

With this discussion completed, they settled into what they'd been doing. Brad picked up his book again, and Judy returned to outlining her story on PTSD. George flew to his cage. They'd removed the louvered plastic cap on the chimney thing, and he found he liked coming and going on his own. They all wondered why it took them so long to think of it.

As he sat snuggled up to a small ball of dung, he wondered if Brad had been right. The case against Cleatus Blanton would be a slam dunk if Blanton took a shot at the police guy. If they stopped him before he took the shot, they'd still have a good case. Why not go for the slam dunk? He didn't want the policeman, Simpson, if Brad had the name right, to get hurt. Still, the plan as it stood didn't sit right with him. The whole thing bothered him. He hadn't really had a role in designing the capture of Blanton, and there was nothing to do about it. He'd be at the DVES offices with the vice squad.

They had an early dinner, so they were ready when Lewis rang the doorbell at five to six. George flew and landed on his shoulder.

"He likes to ride on the dashboard," Judy remarked. "Good luck tonight."

"We're hoping we don't have to rely on luck," Lewis replied. "We've done a great deal of preparation, and I've assembled a good team."

"Not to mention an amazing amount of scouting by George."

"Yes, of course. He provided the key information. I'll text you when we're finished."

Brad went to the window to be sure Lewis's car was gone. "There he goes. Let's wait five minutes and then take off."

George found a reasonable place to sit on the dashboard of the police cruiser. He'd never been in a police car before, and he found it interesting. There were all kinds of gadgets, and he wished he could ask Lewis what they were. Lewis drove to a parking lot in front of a beauty salon in a shopping center close to Dorothy Vaughn's office. There were two other police cars there. Four policemen came to Lewis's car and shook hands with him when he got out. Lewis briefed the men about the operation. They all looked as if they were straining to pay attention. *This was probably the third briefing these guys have received*, George thought.

The operation was simple. Lewis was going to go to the parking lot and get the ledger from the safe. The other guys were going to break down the front door, take any files, and get into Vaughn's computer to see what was there. They would then either print her files or decide to take the computer. If they decided to print, they'd brought their own printer. They figured Lewis would be there with the ledger before they had to make the print-or-take decision.

It was clear the police didn't expect to run into anyone at Dorothy Vaughn's. No one had been around the last two nights. Tonight might be different. They knew Blanton had to pick up the Humvee for his guard duty. Because of this problem, Lewis was going to be the first one to go to Dorothy Vaughn's. He would signal them if DVES 5 was still there, and they'd have to hold off until it left.

George overheard everything, and it made perfect sense to him. His only job was to point out the brick to Lewis. Afterwards, he wasn't useful at all. He started to wonder what he wanted to do.

When the briefing was finished, the cops milled around the parking lot telling war stories about other raids. Basically, they were killing time, and they were a little nervous. At ten minutes before eight, Lewis told everyone to get in their cars. He would go first to check on the Humvee.

As Lewis and George drove down the main street on the way to the DVES offices, they saw the DVES 5 Humvee pulling onto the street. Cleat Blanton gave the police car a nice wave as they passed. Lewis radioed the other cars, telling them the Humvee was clear and they should come in two minutes.

Lewis let George out as he parked on the street in front of Dorothy

Vaughn's office. George flew around the building into the parking lot. Behind the limo, he realized he wasn't completely sure which brick Lewis should push. He looked at the bricks closely in the dimming light and saw the seam for the door. Finding the seam narrowed his choice to two bricks. Lewis came up beside him, and George landed on one of the bricks.

Lewis asked, "Okay, I press on this brick. Move over."

He moved and Lewis pressed, but nothing happened.

George went one brick lower. "Try this one. Is that what you're saying?"

George had no way of responding. He was happy to see Lewis press the second brick and even happier when the door slid open, revealing the safe.

"Wonderful!" Lewis exclaimed. As he bent down to inspect the safe, the other two cars arrived. It didn't take Lewis long to open the safe. He removed the ledger with a big grin on his face, and George took off—heading to the St. Clair house.

Flying as fast as possible and knowing just where to go, he reached the St. Clair house before the action. He saw Cleat Blanton pausing on his walk down the St. Clair side of the woods. *He must have spotted the Simpson guy*, George thought. As he flew closer, he was sure he was right. Blanton was taking out the silencer and screwing it on the pistol. With the gun held on his right side, he walked about ten yards the way he'd been going and then very slowly and quietly he started sneaking up on the policeman.

George was able to fly quite close to Blanton. Blanton was concentrating on how he was moving, and George was approaching him from the back and side. The timing of this whole thing was critical. The plan was to wait until Blanton had his gun pointed at Simpson before the searchlight would go on and the guys would spring up and try to tackle Blanton. Taking his eyes off Blanton for a second, he had to admit the three policemen were well concealed.

Meanwhile Blanton was closing in on Simpson. He flew closer. As Blanton was raising his gun, George flew right into his trigger finger, causing the gun to discharge and throwing off Blanton's aim. He saw Simpson diving behind a tree unharmed. The searchlight went on. Making a big mistake, Blanton turned around to see what was going on. The light temporarily blinded him, and before he reacted, two of the previously hidden policemen tackled him. George flew up to a tree branch to see what happened next.

While Judy and Brad didn't hear the gunshot because of the silencer, they saw the searchlight come on. They hopped in their car and raced around the bend to see what was happening. They parked at the cross street just as two police cars pulled into the driveway at 1287. Getting out of the car, Brad and Judy saw the police already had Cleat Blanton in handcuffs. Brad recognized Nick Bowers in front as Blanton was being led toward a waiting police cruiser. Three minutes later, the front door of the house opened and two women, dresses all messed up, came out led by two policewomen. Shortly thereafter, two men followed. The four people were bundled into the waiting police cars and driven off.

"I guess it's finished, Honey," Brad commented. "There's not going to be any more action. They've arrested Blanton and the two couples. It looks like it went off like clockwork."

"I guess we can get in the car and go home," Judy responded.

Before they turned toward the car, Brad saw Nick Bowers headed their way at a fast walk. "Wait, Judy. I want to talk to Bowers, he's the policeman in charge of this operation."

Brad and Judy started to walk toward Nick, so he slowed down. When they met, Brad spoke first. "Looks like it went off like clockwork."

"No, no way! It was almost completely messed up. Blanton took a shot before I turned on the searchlight. He missed, and then like a dummy he looked back into the searchlight. It gave us enough time to grab him.

The funny thing is, it looked like some kind of a bug attacked him right before he shot. It's likely why he missed."

Brad and Judy exchanged a knowing look. "Sounds really weird," Brad said.

"Isn't it better? Him taking the shot, I mean," Judy asked. "It's plain and simple attempted murder now."

"Oh, Nick, this is my girlfriend, Judy Clayton."

"Nice to meet you, Ms. Clayton. I guess you're right. We didn't want him to shoot. Even though Simpson was in protective gear, those shots can be painful."

"It will be interesting to see what those folks in the house have to say, and I guess what Lewis and his crew found too," Brad said.

"Yeah, most days, even in a big city like Cleveland, police work can be boring. Not tonight, for sure. Anyway, thanks for your help, Brad."

"No problem. Happy to help."

When Brad and Judy returned to their car, George was sitting on the hood. Judy grinned at him as he flew up to her shoulder.

"Been busy tonight?" Judy asked.

Chapter Thirty-Six

WHEN THEY MADE IT HOME, Judy received a text from Lewis saying he wasn't able to find George anywhere. She texted back, telling him they had him and asked how the raid had gone. Lewis sent a one-word response: "Fabulous."

Clarice arrived at ten in the evening, and they told her the whole story. She seemed a little annoyed to have been kept in the dark. She wanted TV cameras showing the arrests.

"I promised the police I wouldn't tell anyone," Brad responded.

"And we're telling you now," Judy added. "Your network will still have the story before any of the others."

"Okay," Clarice said as she reached for her phone. "I'm still pissed at you guys. I'm going to make some calls, so we do have it first."

The next morning Clarice left early so she could break the story on the morning news. Brad, Judy, and George gathered around the television to watch. After several commercials, a few inane gossipy stories, and several checks on the weather and traffic, the station finally went to Clarice positioned outside police headquarters. She explained a well-known escort service was being charged with solicitation and prostitution. Then she ran some film of Dorothy Vaughn being taken from a police car around midnight the previous evening. It looked like most of the arrests of notable people. Dorothy was trying to hide her face with little success. The story was going to be a sensation, and Clarice looked pleased. The segment finished up with a short interview with Lewis. Neither of them mentioned they were brother and sister.

"Wow, that was fast," Judy said. "They arrested Dorothy Vaughn last night. I'm surprised."

"Either Lewis found a smoking gun in the material they took from her office, or one of the people they picked up in the St. Clair house spilled the beans quickly."

"It might even have been both."

"I guess the arrest of Cleatus Blanton isn't as newsworthy as what they just showed. I wonder how many of Vaughn's clients are big-time names in the Cleveland area. When it's a bunch of men in a bust of a prostitution ring, often important names come out. I'm not sure how they're going to handle it with women."

Clarice came flying in at ten o'clock to change clothes. They all congratulated her on the morning story. "I can't talk now," she said, running to her room shouting. "Watch the station at three. We're going to do a special report then. You wouldn't believe the names Lewis found on the ledger he took from the Dorothy Vaughn place. It's amazing."

She ran out the door with two dresses under her arm.

They assembled in front of the television again at three. The station had blocked off a ten-minute time slot. Clarice narrated some hastily put together footage with Dorothy Vaughn's glossy webpage, her office, and the St. Clair house. The highlight of the special report was an interview Clarice did with one of the men the police had captured at the house last night. The guy had obviously decided it was best to turn state's evidence. They blacked out his face and disguised his voice. He said part of Dorothy Vaughn's operation was legit—the escort part, not the sex for hire. Toward the end of the interview, when Clarice asked if he would reveal any names, he said the police had told him not to.

"Wow, I wonder how many rich women in Cleveland are quaking in their boots," Judy commented.

"I'd be staking out the airport if I were the police," Brad said. "Lots of the women may well run. This is going to be a big deal."

George flew to the keyboard, and Judy followed.

`guy was chad`

"Oh, did you know the names of the guys who were in the house last night?" Brad asked.

`rafe and chad`

"Rafe Velasquez? Is that who you're talking about?"

He went to the Y key.

"You know him?" Brad asked. "Or do you remember him from looking at the escorts?"

"It wasn't on the web. I was buzzing through the escorts fast, looking for the guy with the mustache, so I missed Rafe. I met him once earlier. We were at a bar, and he was trying to put the moves on Clarice. She wasn't buying it. He was a bit too smooth for her. I have to admit he's very good looking, and I expect he's a big hit with the older set who frequented Vaughn's operation."

The interview with Chad was repeated on the six o'clock news as part of a story Clarice presented. She said the police had complete records, including names and addresses. She mentioned numbers of people the police were pursuing, and while she hinted there were big names involved, she didn't reveal any. She ended by saying this was an evolving story and urged people to stay tuned.

Clarice came home late, still excited about her day. "This story is big. It's been a whirlwind at the station. While I'm still a little peeved at you guys for not telling me earlier, I guess I had an hour head start on the other stations and even the papers."

"Did it help to have Lewis involved?" Judy asked.

"For sure, he made it possible for the interview with the guy."

"Chad?"

"How did you know his name… Oh, I get it. George had all kinds of inside information. Lewis told me he was critical to the whole operation. Also, you'll be happy to know he warned me not to mention his involvement."

"Right," Brad said. "While he's the real hero, he doesn't want anyone to know."

George listened to this exchange and felt really proud. At the same time, he couldn't help wondering what was going to happen next. He'd been single mindedly pursuing his killer, and he'd been lucky enough to enlist Judy, Brad, and Clarice. Now they'd succeeded. His involvement was finished. What came next? He didn't have any idea. Brad and Judy had lives to live. Maybe they'd keep him on as their pet dung beetle. He wasn't sure he'd be able to stand being someone's pet.

The next morning, Brad bought a physical copy of the *Plain Dealer*. Judy had a subscription to the online version, but Brad wanted the real thing today. The paper had a big spread on the Dorothy Vaughn story. They didn't really have any important details about the actual raid of her offices, but they'd done a lot of background research on Ms. Vaughn and her business. Like Clarice's station, it appeared the paper had decided not to mention any of the names of the clients, at least not yet.

After he read the front-page story about the raid, Brad searched the paper for other stories. "Here it is. It's in the police blotter." He read, "The police arrested Cleatus Blanton of Mayfield Heights and are charging him with attempted murder. It mentions Mr. Blanton is an employee of Dorothy Vaughn Escort Services."

"Not much there," Judy commented.

"Yeah, it's short. I wonder if they're asking Cleat to tell them all he knows about Dorothy Vaughn's operation. No doubt he knows more than Chad or anyone else."

Clarice appeared from her room at that point. "I'll ask Lewis."

"You look a bit tired today, Champ," Judy remarked.

"Yesterday was tiring, I guess. I was probably on an adrenalin high all day. Now I'm crashing. I'd better find a way to rally."

"I recommend this as a start." Brad took a cup of coffee to Clarice.

An hour later, Judy said, "I have to go to the zoo today. We're running short on dung. Want to come?"

"No," Brad responded. "I have some errands to run."

While Judy looked a little disappointed, she seemed to recover. "It'll take me about an hour. Is there anything else we need? I'll be going right by a grocery store on my trip."

"No," Brad said. "I was thinking of going out to eat tonight to celebrate."

"Sounds nice. I guess we deserve a celebration."

George had trouble getting out of his funk after Judy and Brad left. Though he was glad Judy was going to the zoo to get him more food, it was difficult for him to hang on to the feeling for long. He had to do more than eat. He guessed maybe it was all dung beetles worried about. Then he thought, *Procreation is probably their other concern*. He didn't figure procreation was in his future. While he thought there was always a little let down when big projects ended, his depression was about more. He didn't like feeling this way, but he couldn't shake it.

Judy returned before Brad. She had the two Tupperware containers filled with fresh dung. "I told them my pet dung beetle preferred the African dung, so they tried. I can't guarantee they succeeded. At least they tried."

`don't like indian`

Judy smiled. "Yeah, I remember. You told us it was too spicy."

where is brad

"I don't know. He was a little closed mouthed about what he had to do this morning. He told me he had errands to run. You don't have any ideas, do you?"

He went to the N key.

"Me neither. I guess he can have his secrets, even if I don't like it."

Brad texted Judy at twelve-thirty, telling her he'd get lunch out.

"His errands must be taking him longer than he thought," Judy said. "We'd better eat our lunch."

George thought the new dung was excellent. He ate a big lunch and decided to take a nap. He was still depressed about having nothing to do. He'd been trying to figure out something. So far, he'd come up empty.

Brad came home in the middle of the afternoon full of apologies for being gone so long. While Judy seemed a little peeved with him, he was in a really good mood. Brad's mood was infectious, and soon Judy was happy too. Brad told her he'd made reservations at an expensive restaurant. He wanted it to be a big celebration.

Brad and Judy's mood rubbed George the wrong way. They were all happy about their upcoming dinner. Judy modeled a couple of dresses for Brad, who told her he liked her in either one or out of either one. *Ugh,* George thought. *They're all happy and I'm so depressed. What am I going to do with the rest of this life?*

Judy and Brad returned from dinner late. Much to George's surprise, Brad woke him and took him to the computer, where Judy sat with her hands on her lap. George thought she'd put them on the keys when it was his time to talk.

Brad spoke first. "We have an announcement."

A silence followed until George finally became impatient and jumped up and down demanding to type. When Judy put her hands on the keyboard, he saw the big diamond on the ring finger of her left hand.

congratulations

"Thank you. I can't believe I was mad at Brad for being gone so long today. Now I feel like an idiot."

"It turns out not all diamond rings are the same. There are lots of choices, so picking one takes some time. And I had another errand to run, and it wasn't quick either."

"George, you should be really interested in his other errand. Do you want to hear about it?"

He took his time getting to the Y key. All this happiness wasn't sitting well with him.

"Okay, you remember when we were at your old employer, the Acton Agency? I've been reviewing the visit. Gregory Acton was trying to recruit me. No offense, but chasing cheating spouses or providing security for private parties didn't seem appealing. Today I went to him with a proposal."

"Yeah, this was your day for proposals," Judy interrupted with a laugh.

"I guess so. Anyway, I would like to investigate some of the cold cases I looked at earlier. The Cleveland police are so undermanned they drop cases really fast. My idea is to approach a victim's family and offer to try to solve the case. I wouldn't ask for much money unless I solved the case. I'd use a connection with Acton to give me credibility. Greg was willing to give it a try. I didn't tell him why I thought I'd be any good at solving the cases. My ace in the hole, the key to the whole proposition, is you, George. Your ability to infiltrate places—to be a bug on the wall—would be invaluable. So, what do you say? Want to be my partner?"

ABOUT THE AUTHOR

Robert Archibald was born in New Jersey and grew up in Oklahoma and Arizona. After receiving a BA from the University of Arizona, he was drafted and served in Viet Nam. He then earned an M.S. and Ph.D in economics from Purdue University.

Bob had a 41-year career at the College of William & Mary. While he had several stints as an administrator, department chair, director of the public policy program, and interim dean of the faculty, Bob was always proud to be promoted back to the faculty.

He lives with his wife of 49 years, Nancy, in Williamsburg, Virginia.

CPSIA information can be obtained
at www.ICGtesting.com
Printed in the USA
BVHW080018120921
616415BV00001B/29

9 781948 979665